The Big Bamboozle

The gorillas came together in the centre of the grassy clearing. They embraced and began stroking each other, then dropped to the ground and thrashed around as they mated.

Suddenly there was a loud *smack!* and Bamboo felt his female companion go limp in his arms and drop away from him. He was pulled forward with her, just as a second shot rang across the clearing. Bamboo felt a wind brush past his body. He did a shoulder roll and tumbled down the slope into the long grass near the trees. The female lay stretched out on her back, unmoving.

"King Kong and *The Planet of the Apes* have an exciting successor."
Don Carlson, CARPNews

Books by Hal Sisson

COOTS, CODGERS & CURMUDGEONS
(with Dwayne W. Rowe)

CAVERNS OF THE CROSS
(published by Arsenal Pulp Press)

THE BIG BAMBOOZLE

The Big Bamboozle

A burlesque novel

Hal Sisson

SALAL PRESS
Victoria, BC

Canadian Cataloguing in Publication Data

Sisson, Hal C., 1921 -
    The big bamboozle

ISBN 1-894012-03-8

    I. Title

PS8587.I79B54 1999   C813'.54   C99-900143-4
PR9199.3.S5363B54 1999

Cover photo courtesy of the Gorilla Foundation
Woodside, Ca
Cover design: George Clement, Sun Electric Arts

Printed and bound in Canada
by Transcontinental Printing Ltd.
Louiseville, Quebec
First printing: April 1999

Salal Press
P.O. Box 36060
Victoria, BC V9A 7J5

Acknowledgements

Special thanks to the Gorilla Foundation and the Toronto Metro Zoo for their inspirational example in protecting endangered species. The author wishes to thank Kevin Connelly and the Gorilla Foundation for their generosity in providing illustrations for the cover. Thanks also to Dr. Gilbert Brodeur, the Peace Players and all gorilla mongers and lovers everywhere.

Dedicated to the great apes,
old-time burlesque comedians
and ecdysiasts, and the tireless
workers in every zoo on
this United Nations
planet of killer humanoids.

And to something else —
all the friends who
made this book possible.

If all the beasts were gone,
Men would die from great
loneliness of spirit.

Chief Seattle, Suquamish Tribe,
from an address to the governor
of Washington Territory, 1855

1

UNDER THE GUN

The two gorillas crouched in the shelter offered by a clump of young hagenia and vernonia trees. Flame-coloured reeds called red-hot pokers sprouted from the tall, quivering grass of the sub-alpine meadow that surrounded them. Above, boundless thin clouds streamed off the crests of distant volcanoes. The latticework of leaves over-head was shot through with tropical African sun-light, obliterating the usual mist that concealed them in times of danger. Nothing broke the silence but the intermittent, muffled *purrit-purrit-purrit* of a bright-breasted roller bird perched among the pointed leaves and brilliant yellow flowers of a nearby hypericum tree.

Strange voices called back and forth across the clearing, gradually closing in from opposite direc-tions. The apes huddled anxiously, wondering what would happen next. The roller bird recalled pressing business elsewhere and flapped away. *Trapped.* The sounds they heard were unfriendly and they looked at each other in growing fear and anger.

"Who is that rotten hairy-faced creature?" the male wanted to know, pointing to the man lying face down in the sunlit grass at the edge of the grove.

His female companion shook her head. "Who knows who these strange creatures are or what they want? We only know they're dangerous. He was carrying this thing," she said, flourishing a tranquilizer pistol.

"I'm red mad!" He grunted audibly, his large nostrils flaring.

"I hit him hard," she declared, striking her own jaw to illustrate.

"This is big trouble, I know it."

"What can this be?" she wondered, looking down at the gun, her finger curling around the trigger. "Strange. What does it do?"

"Do? Do? What does it do?" he mouthed, staring into the barrel of the unfamiliar object in her hand.

Suddenly there was a loud *whoosh* and Bamboo felt searing pain in his throat. He dropped to his knees, his hands clutching his neck. Blood oozed through his fingers and he slumped to the ground. An overpowering lassitude seeped through his body and into his brain, dimming his mind.

The pistol dropped from the female's hand as she recoiled in surprise and fear. What had happened? What was wrong with her friend?

Springing to his side, she tried to lift his dead weight; tried to wake him, but couldn't. The strangers' voices were louder and more excited. She could hear them coming closer, pushing through the grass beyond the patch of jungle growth hiding the gorillas from view.

After many moments of indecision, she uttered a high-pitched scream and dropped onto the knuckles of her hands. She loped away through the shrubs and grass as fast as she could, away from the strangeness and toward the protection and security of her own little band of apes.

2

PLANNING OF THE APES

"At a thousand bucks a plate, it better not be beans on toast. That's all I have to say," Don Jessup grumbled. "Yeah, I know, don't say it: 'It's for a good cause.'"

"Yes it is, dear. Now it's time to get ready." Olive Jessup's muffled reply came from her dressing room. The room was just one luxury feature of the Jessups' newly renovated and oh-so-glamorous sinkhole in fashionable Rosedale.

"Okay. Remind me again. Who's the guest speaker?" her husband called from the bedroom.

"Dr. Pearl Baldwin."

"And she's with the.....?"

"The GO-APE Society. You know, Gorilla Organization and Protective Endowment. They try to save wild gorillas and support those nice people who teach gorillas sign language so they can communicate with humans."

"Hell, she's been at it a long time, hasn't she?

Still working the gorilla pitch, eh?"

"Now, don't put on an act, put on a shirt. You know you're going and you know you support saving endangered wildlife."

"All right, already."

"You're not wearing that shirt, are you?"

"Of course not, I'm just wearing it while I wait for you to get ready. But I'll change if you don't like it. All I really need is my jockstrap and my wallet."

The Jessups, still trading barbs, soon joined the well-groomed herd of Toronto socialites streaming into the charity banquet at the Royal Hotel.

The event, held under the auspices of the GO-APE Society, drew some prominent figures in conservationist circles, including Phil Travers, primatologist, doctor of zoology and administrator of the Ontario Provincial Zoo.

Travers hung on every word of Dr. Baldwin's speech. He found himself agreeing with most of what she had to say.

"Once again, just when the long-term survival of the mountain gorilla seemed achievable, a new threat has materialized. Violent civil war has broken out in Rwanda. You've all heard the horrifying news reports of another ethnic bloodbath, with hundreds of thousands of Hutu and Tutsi people, government officials, aid workers, children, hospital patients and peacekeepers being slaughtered in a repeat of the atrocities of a few years ago.

"Rwanda, one of the poorest and most densely populated countries in the world, has plunged into utter chaos. Foreign aid has been suspended and UN peacekeepers have been thwarted in their attempts to broker a lasting peace, and even prevented from delivering food and medicine to the victims."

Travers held his breath, waiting for Baldwin to get to the heart of the matter—the war's effect on the gorillas. While the human slaughter appalled and disgusted him, the fact was that his professional reputation was closely tied to the fate of the wild gorillas. He leaned forward as Baldwin warmed to her subject.

"There are at most six hundred mountain gorillas left in Rwanda's Volcanoes National Park. They are not willing participants in this human drama; they just want to be left in peace to live their own lives. But those very lives now depend on the actions of the warring humans who surround them.

"Not only are these gentle, intelligent creatures caught inside a war zone, their numbers are being further eroded by poachers."

"That figures," Phil muttered to the Jessups and the other couple sharing the Travers' table. "People are hungry and they'll eat anything and try to sell the skins."

"Rwanda's economy is in tatters," Baldwin continued, "and there are no tourist dollars flowing into the treasury. The park is being overrun by hungry poachers, refugees, soldiers and others seeking food and shelter. The region also harbours over a dozen species of monkeys; no one knows where they've gone, but there are reports they're still alive."

An obsequious waiter soft-pedaled around the room replenishing empty coffee cups, and Travers sipped his refill as he reflected: If I don't do something soon, mountain gorillas could be gone in just a few years.

"The gorillas need safe havens, as do other threatened species. That's why we're working so hard to develop alternate gorilla preserves. The total global population of mountain gorillas lives in three of the most politically unstable nations in Africa: Rwanda, Uganda and Zaire. The vast tropical forest these great apes once inhabited has been reduced to a fraction of its former size, and it's hemmed in by farmland and other human development. Some gorilla conservationists say if we can't save the gorillas in their natural habitat, we can't save them at all. Well, I agree that's the best way, but it's not the only way."

"She can say that again, and I think I know how it can be done," Travers whispered to his wife, Joan. She patted his arm absently, intent on the doctor's words.

"Some gorillas can be saved in zoos. Over the past twenty-five years, many zoos have learned how to breed the western lowland gorilla. I firmly believe the same thing could be done with other gorillas."

"That's exactly what we're working on right now at the zoo," Travers told his dinner companions excitedly. Olive Jessup glanced at him with admiration, while her husband looked annoyed at the interruption.

"In the meantime," Baldwin added, "growing human encroachment on their territory means that eastern lowland gorillas will also face a desperate situation within a decade. Do we wait until they're on the brink of extinction as well, or do we take action while there's still time?"

She paused, then concluded with: "The great apes need sanctuaries right now, and I urge you to contribute generously to our society...before it's too late for these magnificent animals."

And many of those sanctuaries are zoos, Travers thought as he joined in the thunderous ovation that swept Baldwin off the podium.

Travers had some very serious gorilla problems of his own. The male gorillas at the OP Zoo weren't doing their job of impregnating any of the strong-willed matriarchs, who had rejected their sexual advances. Travers knew he had to find another male, but Baldwin's speech strengthened his resolve and galvanized him into action.

That's what I have to do, he thought, galvanize myself into action. We have to get ourselves another male ape for that bunch of frustrated females. Some new blood, some new sperm. And to hell with the arguments I'm getting from the board, that a zoo shouldn't rob the wild to get animals for exhibition. Why kid ourselves? The mountain gorillas in Rwanda are doomed any-

way. Let's get in there and get some before
they're all gone. Phil knew just the outfit for the
job: Fluck Brothers Animal Procurement Ltd.
One of the brothers, Irving, was his new chief of
security at the zoo.

Travers was lost in the details of his plan for
several moments, until Joan tapped him on the
arm and he realized they were among the last to
file out of the banquet hall.

3

SHOT IN THE ACT

Phil Travers often used an ancient African proverb in his lectures to zoology students: "The monkey who is alone does not amuse himself in front of many." Phil knew that as recently as the 1890s, there were tens of thousands of the rarest of all wild animals in tropical Africa—the gorillas—constituting a fair-sized audience by any standard. Not so in the late 1990s.

In the good old days, the great apes wandered around in a lush pollution-free climate with the orangutans, baboons, chimpanzees and the gibbons and various other monkeys that made up the greater and lesser ape population of the day. Little was known about the gorillas' social patterns or intelligence, or their ability to communicate. An obvious ancestral link to humans, the gorilla used to be as mysterious and almost as elusive as the Abominable Snowman or the Sasquatch, arousing the curiosity of romantics and scientists alike.

Travers figured that somewhere in the Virunga mountains of East Africa near the Rift Valley, in one of the last gorilla habitats in the world, there had to be a male gorilla that would solve his breeding problems at the zoo. Phil didn't know how right he was.

THE GORILLA'S NAME WAS BAMBOO. HE'D LEFT his mother's band in adolescence and had been travelling alone for several years. Sometimes he kept company with others of his kind, but he preferred to be a loner, rarely making friends with other gorillas.

In Bamboo's home region, the forests had once merged imperceptibly into savannah, the savannah into steppes and the steppes into the ever-encroaching desert. Now the savannah was fast disappearing and Bamboo had never even been close to the steppes, nor to the desert.

Along the fairly clear demarcation line between the rainforest and what was once the grassy plain, patchwork clumps of trees and small shrubs grew, surrounded by grassland. On one side of the line all was warmth and light, while on the forest side, all was rain-soaked, dark and humid. Predators still roamed there, and the fruit and leaf-eating animals lived mainly in the lofty, densely packed trees that sometimes towered two hundred feet above the forest floor.

Although Bamboo spent most of his time on the shadowy side of his realm, the frontier area offered more room to roam. The region's open forest allowed both predators and prey to move more easily in their continual search for food.

If Bamboo roamed very far afield, he came to places populated by great numbers of baboon-like creatures who bore only a slight resemblance to gorillas. They were of different colours and most of them had very little hair on their faces and bodies. All wore a covering over their loins, while others wore things that not only covered their gender but their whole body. For the most part, they seemed an odious, vicious and rascally species, best to avoid altogether.

Bamboo had spotted the creatures several times recently, and once he'd seen something glide by with some of these strange, large monkey types sitting in it. They'd passed him at speed but he'd been hidden in a thicket. When they stopped nearby, one of the creatures got out and lifted a long stick to his shoulder. There was a loud noise and a zebra at some distance fell on his ass, then rolled over and just lay there. The strange creatures, who were remarkably ugly in Bamboo's opinion, rushed over and took the skin off the zebra and some of the meat, leaving the rest to the vultures floating in slanted circles overhead and the hyenas observing from the ground.

Bamboo stayed to watch the weirdos and listen to them talk. They didn't speak the language of any gorilla Bamboo had ever met—no croons and bark-belch-hootserie-like noises in varying ranges, cadences and intonations. They used sounds he'd never heard before.

Bamboo followed a jungle trail along the edge of the rainforest, moving slowly and carefully, which is how he avoided stepping in the leopard turd in his path. He was proud of the fact that he was more fastidious than baboons; a baboon would likely have picked up the feces and shown his friends just what it was that he hadn't stepped in. Baboons either had a great sense of humour or they were just plain dumb, and Bamboo suspected the latter.

The excrement was still steaming, so the leopard who had fouled the footpath had to be nearby. Although he could probably spot the cat by the merest movement of its head or the twitch of its tail, Bamboo took to the trees immediately just to be on the safe side, and in keeping with his gentle, kindly nature. He liked to live in peace with all other animals. True, leopards didn't often tangle with gorillas out of respect for their physical prowess, but prudence dictated keeping one's distance. Faced suddenly with a leopard on a jungle trail, who knew what moves the leopard might make, and why risk getting your balls clawed for no good reason? So Bamboo kept to the trees, scanning the jungle floor and its surroundings.

It wasn't so much the leopard he was worried about; he felt he could handle the feline if he had to. It was those strange apes with firesticks that really concerned him. You couldn't trust them as far as you could throw a melon.

When the trees thinned into prickly grass and scrubland, he descended and began to lope in a semi-upright position toward an excellent communal watering hole some distance to the south that he knew about from previous forays. There were fig and pear trees there, and just maybe, some young females. That would be good. In fact, he might get lucky. He realized how long he'd been foraging alone.

Occasionally, when the need in his loins dictated, he visited communal groups for sex and social contact. As a loner, he was often cut off from opportunity, but he was far from willing to give up sex. He was getting tired of roaming the jungle alone, eating and exploring by himself, occasionally fighting when he had to and trying to coax strange females into copulation. Maybe it was time to start his own harem, acquire his own territory, his own family group. He knew what he wanted, but he'd be happy with what he could get.

His sexual cravings weren't always easy to satisfy, since gorillas were generally scarce. The females were well organized and stuck together in groups for protection and mutual support, and a young male often had to contend with older silverback males, whose aggressive urges were sparked by sex. They wanted it clearly understood who was the dominant male, and adopted an extremely pugnacious attitude toward interlopers. If Bamboo ran into an old silverback, he just hung around the group for awhile, acting in a friendly and unobtrusive way. Eventually, he might be accepted, particularly by the gregarious females.

As fathers go, Bamboo thought, we aren't much. We leave it all to the females to bring up the young. Females spent several years suckling a baby and teaching it to fend for itself, and only gave birth about every four years. They came into heat when they wanted another baby, and Bamboo knew that when they were in heat, it made for a hair-raising experience.

The older females usually copulated with the silverback who led the group. A system that catered to the greedy, not the needy, thought Bamboo.

But if the young ones liked a stranger, they soon let him know. Bamboo couldn't entirely rule out the more attached females either, because as soon as they stopped carrying a baby on their back, they were available again. Once their pregnancy was well along, though, they lost much of their interest in sex and went back to rearing their young.

In Bamboo's view, it took two to tangle, but he had no intention of tangling with most of the silverbacks he'd met. He recalled one big brute: no neck, no waist, looked like a tree stump with hair, until he started to move toward you. Then you saw the massive legs and long, powerful arms that knuckled the ground. His huge, rubbery nostrils flared as he checked you out, his deep-set, beady black eyes fixing you with a cold stare. *Ugh!* And talk about no sense of humour!

Don't let him catch you screwing one of his harem, Bamboo thought. It's enough to scare the living crap out of a good-looking itinerant like me. My plan has always been to creep in, copulate and crawl out; meander in, mount and melt into the bush; sneak in, slip in and slip out. I don't fancy having a silverback's fangs in my throat. Let them strut and thump their chests all they want. I can do the same, but it's tiring and dangerous, and not the best way to get satisfaction.

Bamboo wasn't a fighter, but he hadn't been a lover for some time, either. He felt something had to happen soon.

He peered through the foliage at a small watering hole. It wasn't the one he remembered, but it showed few signs of overuse. A larger and better pool farther upstream probably drew most of the traffic, since many creatures preferred safety in numbers to privacy. A trickle of water fell from the rocks a few feet above the pool. Not being the rainy season, the gully on either end of the pool was mostly dry sand and rock.

Bamboo's eyes, ears and nose detected no movement nearby. He stepped out of the trees and walked to a rock at the north end of the pool. He tasted the water and it was good. He studied his reflection in the calm water: tall, well set up, a dark reddish crest of hair on the top of his head, coarse black hair sparsely covering his black leathery skin, and thicker, more grizzled silver hair along his thighs, neck and shoulders. Saggital crest and pronounced canine teeth, not too beetled a brow, and a nose of more than average prominence.

He hated to admit it, but some apes didn't seem to like his looks, ridiculing him for his big nose and, compared to theirs, his thin coat of hair. He figured both features were adequate to the job he required of them. His sense of smell was as good as anyone's and the only time he missed having heavier fur was on rainy nights in the colder jungles of the highest cloud-covered mountain heights. Then he simply fashioned a comfortable, springy, oval-shaped nest by bending and interlacing bamboo fronds with narrowleaf ferns and long wispy strands of lichens.

He didn't hear her footsteps until she emerged from the underbrush on the other side of the pool. Nor did she see him sitting motionless, blending into the rock, until she caught his reflection in the water. They were both slightly startled but kept their places. After all, they were of the same species. Her wide, haunting eyes met his and held. Then his gaze unabashedly settled on her face and body. Bamboo stood up. So did she, moving around the pool to the right and then walking back into the jungle. He moved to the left and disappeared into the foliage as well, then set off in the same direction as the female.

A few minutes later, she crossed a sunny forest glade with a clump of trees in its centre. The clearing was bordered by grass, flowers, bushes and a tall, spindly hypericum tree. She stopped in

the open. Over her shoulder she could glimpse
Bamboo standing at the edge of the mountain
meadow. Their eyes met again and she turned
suddenly away and bent over as if searching the
earth for berries or something else to eat.

It was an invitation and a refusal at the same
time. Bamboo squinted into the sun, wearing a
lop-sided grin. He noticed that her buttocks were
highly visible—a big turn-on. With a rush,
Bamboo came up behind her, spun her around
and they locked in a face-to-face embrace. Their
bodies thrashed and rolled around on the slope of
the hill, as his male organ became a throbbing
part of her. In their lust they searched madly for
something, anything, to bite, unable to stop their
frenetic thrashing until, satisfied, both gorillas
shifted their bulky bodies and lay exhausted in
the crushed grass.

For a while they remained still and silent. Then
they got up and retraced the route to the watering
hole, both now calm and knuckle-walking without looking at each other. They sipped water from
the pool and wet their arms and faces. Then, still
not speaking, she went off in one direction and
Bamboo in another.

Their coupling hadn't been entirely a private
affair. Seated on a low branch on a nearby knoll,
his back against the trunk, a tough and tanned
adventurer in a tropical helmet had his binoculars
trained on Bamboo and the female as they mated.

"A peeping Tom on monkeys! That's what I've

come to. Oh, well, one for the money, two for the show; I better get ready, these apes gotta go," Frank Fluck murmured to himself. The money that Phil Travers and the Ontario Provincial Zoo were paying was too good for Fluck Brothers Animal Procurement Ltd. to pass up.

Frank was a contract animal hunter who roved the jungles of the world to bring 'em back alive to the zoos, menageries and circuses of whichever country required his services. Frank knew he was the handsome member of the Fluck duo. He felt he cut a fine figure, with his Errol Flynn moustache and goatee, gleaming knee boots, immaculate jodhpurs and the great rhinoceros whip hanging from his belt. He replaced his binoculars in their case and smiled as he climbed into the land rover.

Further down the mountainside, the young female was searching for turtle eggs in the dry summer stream bed that cut across the foothills. A few succulent leaves and some roots would complete the egg salad. Tough fruits grew on trees at the edge of the forest—these would be dessert.

Bamboo was hungry as well. Grasping a stick, he rooted out tubers with practiced skill, eating his fill and prudently storing the balance, along with a few ripe melons, in a small hole in the bank of the rock-lined stream bed. Wandering further afield, he climbed through dense vegetation up the slope on which the massive, moss-clad hagenia trees grew. Here he harvested the narrowleaf fern that hung down from the moss pads.

For the rest of his prodigious supper he ate a gen-
erous helping of his favourite—a parasitic plant
with red blossoms related to the mistletoe.

With the African dusk fast approaching,
Bamboo swung up into the vernonia trees, chose
a comfortable crotch and built a nest, weaving the
tough thick branches and padding them with soft-
textured leaves. The task finished, he settled
down to sleep through the night.

The dawn broke, the sun rose and so did
Bamboo, once more acutely aware of an urgency
in his groin. When the sun got warmer, he made
his way back toward the glade. He waited there
most of the morning, then he detected a faint,
sweetish, slightly choking smell. The young female
was approaching the glade from the opposite side
of the meadow, carrying turtle eggs and fruit in her
hands. They looked at each other, slowly, calmly
and naturally, as if they had known each other for
a long time. Placing the food on the ground, she
lay on her stomach beside him in the thick grass.
Bamboo lay on his back gazing up at the sky. Both
made low purring noises in their throats.

Frank Fluck, who was about a hundred and
fifty feet downwind of the animals, had heard that
gorillas court and make love much like humans,
and he figured that was one reason humans
seemed so taken with the animals. No such senti-
mentality for Fluck, who had a job to do.

Fluck's finger was knotted around the stock of a
rifle loaded with a dart containing succinyl

choline, a curare derivative that would almost instantly paralyze the gorillas' muscles, provided the dart penetrated their skin without striking any bones. The apes would never know what hit them.

But today is not the day, thought Frank. Now that he knew where they were going to be, he could organize the others. He watched the gorillas' courting ritual through the shrubbery that concealed him. Their posturing and gestures clearly signalled their intent to mate. They were communicating in some kind of language; he could hear a wide spectrum of grunts, croons, a wraagh-like sound in various ranges, chuckles, purring, *naoom, naoom, naoom*, and once or twice a couple of hoots. No way of knowing how wide the scope or how broad or varied the meaning, but Fluck knew they were carrying on a conversation of some sort. And indulging in lovemaking in the same way as Americans, native Africans or Europeans. Well, maybe not the French, but it was only a matter of degree!

Bamboo rolled onto her back, pinning her stomach to the ground with his weight, and entered her from behind. Frank watched until they finished; this time he noted that they left the mountain meadow together. That meant they would probably stay together for a while.

Adolescent females usually travelled with small bands of other apes. Bamboo's companion was no exception, as she was all but bonded with another young ape, and shared food and sex with him. If a

female didn't have a mate, she left the group to
find one. Not that anyone would worry too much
if she were gone for several hours or even a night;
but the band shared and operated as a family unit,
and fidelity and loyalty made good sense.

So her situation with Bamboo was unusual. She
could switch bands, but he didn't belong to a
band—he was a loner of no fixed abode. If he was
looking to establish his own harem, she'd be
number one. There were only a few simple rules,
and besides, she liked Bamboo.

They went back to the dry sandy gully, where
overhanging brush formed a protective covering
and provided shade. They fed on tubers, melons
and various blossoms, pods, leaves and berries
they'd gathered. She began to give off nervous,
non-verbal body gestures as the day wore on.
Bamboo asked her what was wrong.

She indicated that she was worried about getting back to her band and her mate, who might be
expecting her return. Bamboo pulled her down
onto the warm sand and asked her why.

"They'll miss me and ask questions," she said.

Bamboo tried to reassure her. "You're free to go
anytime," he said. "We don't have any bonds. But
it will be dark soon, so stay till the morning. I'll go
to the same meadow every day. You come if you
want to, or stay with the band and argue with them."

She didn't think she should come back after
tonight, but he didn't believe her. They lay in
each other's arms as the black equatorial night

descended with its usual suddenness. Bamboo enjoyed the extra warmth her body provided.

When she awoke in the morning she scooped a shallow hole in the gravel of the gully and watched the water seep in. Cupping her hands, she drank. She looked over her shoulder at Bamboo, still sleeping on the bed of leaves and grass. Then she took off at a trot for the place where she expected to find her family group.

He waited patiently in the meadow every day, because he knew she'd come. Three days later he saw her approaching across the open ground in the afternoon sun.

Frank Fluck hadn't pulled the trigger yet, although he'd had Bamboo fixed in the cross-hairs of his rifle several times. His group was waiting for the female to show up, as two apes were better than one. His men were positioned, everything was set. The gorillas came together in the centre of the grassy clearing. They embraced, both knowing what they wanted, and began stroking each other, then dropped to the ground and began thrashing around again as they mated.

Suddenly there was a loud *smack!* and Bamboo felt his female companion go limp in his arms and drop away from him. As she fell, he was pulled forward with her just as a second shot, like an echo of the first, rang across the clearing. He felt a wind brush past his body. He did a shoulder roll and kept tumbling down the slope into the long grass near the trees. The female lay stretched out on her back, unmoving.

"Son of a bitch! Did we get 'em both, Youbou?" yelled Fluck, climbing quickly down from the big tree he'd been hiding in.

"Maybe yes, maybe no, boss," replied the Rwandan rifleman, "but I think maybe only the female."

"Dammit! He's in that clump of tall grass near the vernonia. I bloody well hope he's unconscious, because if he isn't, he's going to be just a tad riled up."

"I would be, too," Youbou remarked.

"We're going to have to go in there and get him."

"What do you mean 'we,' white man?" asked Youbou, smiling at Fluck. "I'm not going into any long grass after a wounded gorilla."

"I promised the zoo some gorillas and they want a male or we don't get paid. If you're too chicken, I'll go down there myself with my tranquilizer pistol and get him up close if he's still conscious. Who's on the other side of the clearing?"

"Joe McCloskey. Scraggly and the other boys are spread around, but we couldn't put anybody upwind."

"Well, McCloskey won't let him get out the other way without a fight. Joe hates gorillas."

"Yeah? Why is that, boss?" asked Youbou.

"How the hell should I know? Maybe his wife ran off with his pet gorilla."

"Yes, I know, and he sure misses that monkey!"

They both laughed.

"Enough with the jokes, we got a job to do. Circle around the clearing and tell McCloskey I'm going in from this side. He should come up slowly from the other side so we can flush the ape. If he's not immobilized already, we'll hit him again. Now get going."

Bamboo had been watching closely from the tall grass at the edge of the clump of trees. He saw a near-ape come out of the forest, moving slowly forward with a strange object in his hand. The beast wore a funny round thing on his head and a patch of hair on his face, something that Bamboo had never seen, even on these odd-looking creatures. His body was covered with a dirty white something that didn't look like his own skin, and his feet and legs were brown and smooth and gleamed in the sunlight. The creature approached slowly and warily, staring at the clump of vegetation where Bamboo was hiding. When he came to the fallen female, he dropped to his knees beside her. The object in his hand was thrust forward.

Sensing his presence, Bamboo's friend lay very still while he inspected her. She was just coming out of the concussive shock caused by the impact of the dart, which had glanced off her skull. The female saw the strange creature as in a fog.

Satisfied that the female was out cold, and not realizing that she'd only been stunned, Fluck turned his full attention to the stand of foliage.

The female, though wounded, was young and strong, and as the hunter turned, she swung her arm and caught him a savage blow across the temple. He went down instantly, falling face first into the grass, where he lay unconscious. The tranquilizer pistol fell from his grasp.

Bamboo called to her in sharp bark-like noises, grunts and hand gestures, urging her into better cover. Not really knowing why, she grabbed up the object from the ground and ran into the concealment of the grove of trees where Bamboo waited. They crouched close together, their eyes searching the surroundings. They heard strange voices coming ever closer and wondered what would happen next.

4

THE OLD FART

Dwart Farquhart hadn't always travelled alone, but he'd been a bachelor for many long years. He'd left his native prairies early in life and after many peregrinations, had ended up in downtown Toronto.

He was trying to slip back into a dream, but he knew he was waking up. Not good, because then he'd have to get out of bed, and things were pleasant just as they were. The dream was fading fast, but he'd trained himself to remember dreams by lying very still, letting no other thoughts intrude and letting the images flow through his brain.

The night before, he'd gone to an Alfred Hitchcock revival film *Vertigo*, with Jimmie Stewart and Kim Novak, and his dream seemed to be weaving in and out of the movie's plot. He hadn't seen *Vertigo* in over twenty-five years, but it was a dandy. God, that Kim Novak was a fox. Absolutely beautiful! Barbara Bel Geddes may have been a far better actress, but for sheer looks, well! The sex in the film wasn't steamy, no graphic nudity like 1990s movies, but it didn't matter. It was like his dream—no steam there, either, just an appreciation of the clean beauty of the woman lingering in his mind, and the feeling that he was in love.

The feeling passed, and Dwart was wide awake, which meant he had to get up and start slogging his way through the welfare-warfare state of the late twentieth century. *What the hey!* He'd been through the catharsis of over-concern regarding the world's problems, followed by the inevitable complacency, and was trying to adopt a quiet acceptance of life's realities. He wasn't quite there yet.

Dwart A. Farquhart was known to his few friends as Farky or Four-Quarts, and to his few fans as The Old Fart. The A stood for Aloysius. His parents must have really hated him to hang such a moniker on him.

"I would've sworn there were no lustful thoughts about Kim in that dream," he muttered, "but son of a gun, it's hard-on city. Better get up and take a leak, 'cause an erection's like Einstein's Theory of Relativity: the more you think about it, the harder it gets."

This one was raising the sheet with its head, glancing to the north and leering to the south, hoping for its favorite hiding place to dunk the dragon. No such luck. The Old Fart wished he had a manservant, like Dudley Moore in the movies, so Jeeves could enter the bedroom and ask, "Shall I call the Madam, sir? Or shall I get the baggy tweeds so you can smuggle this one into town?"

But he didn't have a pot to piss in nor a window to throw it out of, let alone a butler, so Dwart sat up and swung his legs over the edge of the bed, letting them hang over the cold floor of the bed-sitting room, or whatever the damned landlady called the dump.

He didn't stand right away. He'd read somewhere that leaping from a horizontal to an upright position, especially first thing in the morning, was hard on the constitution. It made sense, so he'd developed the habit of sitting for several seconds before he went about his day.

In the old days, when he used to travel around a lot, the habit gave him a chance to recall the name of the town or hotel he was in. Then he'd walk over to the window, and if it was shaded by blinds, he'd say, "If it weren't for Venetian blinds, it'd be curtains for all of us!" Or if drapes did cover the window, he'd throw them open, look out and remark, "What the hey! I always wanted to play Butte, Montana—but not very much!"

Dwart didn't know why such quirks stuck with him. Maybe the ritual imposed a vestige of order on his existence, or maybe it just brought him luck.

Living alone could be a precarious business, but it had its compensations. But did he really want to live alone? No, he thought, not if he could find someone who, despite his compendium of faults, really liked him. Some people were fond of him and to hell with those who weren't. He could take other people's company or leave it, but lately he seemed to be erring on the side of leaving it alone.

Despite his vocation in burlesque stand-up comedy, emceeing at clubs, banquets and roasts, Dwart had never had a social life of any consequence. He'd always been a stage removed from people, knowing how to make them laugh but not how to include them in his personal life.

Dwart knew he'd had an impractical approach to life from a young age. Just after finishing high school, he'd announced to his parents that he wanted to follow in the footsteps of Mr. Jones, his Latin teacher. His father had patiently asked, "How do you beg for a dime on a street corner in Latin?"

Parents used to insist that their children learn some musical instrument with which to torture themselves and the neighbours, and for some reason, Dwart chose the violin. He'd struggled long enough to be asked to play third violinist with the Moose Jaw Philharmonic. It was easy, even boring, but his musical career soon ended as badly as he played. His father was always too busy to attend the performances, so when he finally enquired as to his son's progress, Dwart felt safe in saying he had a small solo in an upcoming concert. His father seemed pleased at the soundness of his investment in Dwart's musical education.

Twenty minutes into the concert, Dwart spotted

dear old Dad entering the hall. Holy Schmidt! What to do? The orchestra only let him play parts so easy he couldn't possibly foul up. A solo was ridiculously out of the question. Dwart began to sweat profusely. Halfway through the performance, stress combined with panic, and Dwart leaped to his feet during a quiet portion of Handel's Water Music, and plucked a series of notes—a *plink*, a *plank*, a *plink, plank, plunk*.

Nothing really fazed the Moose Jaw Philharmonic. Through mud, blood, sweat or tears, they hammered out each symphony for the Moosejavian culture vultures, sounding all the while as though they were castrating cats. So the other orchestra members hid their astonishment at Dwart's impromptu solo and simply continued to play.

Dwart's father rose and stomped from the hall in a state of high dudgeon, remarking to his cronies later on, "Five thousand bucks for music lessons and all that son of a bitch can do is go *plink, plank, plunk*!"

Dwart's life had taken some unusual turns during his seventy-five years, from running amok for a mucking company to a stint as a cabin boy on a Greek Vaseline tanker. Any income he'd ever earned he'd promptly spent, and now he was close to broke and living in a seedy neighbourhood off Bloor Street. He was falling into decay, just like the houses around him. He could barely pay the rent.

He needed something, an ally, a cause, someone or something about which he could give a good goddamn before bucket-kicking time.

His swinging legs searched the floor for his carpet slippers, then he shuffled across the uncarpeted floor to the bathroom. Ruminating on how he could make a fresh start, Dwart decided to start with A and work through the alphabet, like the lawyer who said of his habitual offender client: "My guy only holds up things beginning with an *A*...a gas station, a liquor store, a grocery..."

As he washed his face, Dwart thought, I'm an atheist, I've got ability, I'm accommodating, aren't I? But not acquisitive. Damn near an alcoholic, but missed. Would I climb over ten naked women to get a bottle of whiskey? Maybe, but it would take a while. Certainly adulterous when I got the chance—*but how affectionate were you, Dwart?* Also, I'm an asshole if I continue this rambling.

As he looked at himself in the mirror, Dwart wondered idly why certain parts of the body aged faster than others. Why was his ass smoother and firmer than his face, neck or hands? *It's because your ass is protected from the elements by your pants, unless you're a flasher.*

That was another problem with living alone: no one to talk to.

"Damn it, Irene! I wouldn't have to talk to myself if you were here," he groused out loud as he lathered his face. He'd been in love back then. He was an R.C.A.F. officer in Britain in 1942, and happy banter had been a large part of his short marriage to a pretty twenty-one-year-old W.A.F. It was the first time he'd had both the inclination and the wherewithal to marry. He'd thought nothing could destroy a feeling he could only describe as love, but the German Luftwaffe had done the job. Their bombs destroyed her beautiful body, leaving it under tons of rubble in a bed and breakfast on the Strand. Dwart escaped only because he'd popped out to the pub for cigarettes, although he hadn't felt lucky then, and still didn't.

He figured life was like comedy—your timing had to be right. With Irene, the timing was off. If she'd lived, he might have been saved the time and money he'd been cleaned out of at the equine and gonorrhea racetracks of the world as he tried to forget her.

Now he was just an aging stand-up comic and stand-in emcee at third-rate nightclubs. His net income didn't match his gross habits, and his idea of luxury was getting two towels at the Drummond Street YMCA.

Dwart snapped out of his reverie and finished shaving. Choosing carefully from his well-worn wardrobe, he dressed for his daily appearance in the great metropolis of Toronto. Old grey cords and a still-presentable shirt and green sweater. On the way out he picked up a cream-coloured Aquascutum raincoat and a hat.

He decided to head for the $1.99 breakfast at the Metropolitan and try to figure out what to do with the rest of his day.

Cutting through the park, Dwart expected to
see one of the myriad of signs the bureaucrats
erected to make sure people didn't enjoy themselves in the park. They'd banned skateboards,
radios, musical instruments and anything else that
might give people pleasure. It was as if they were
saying, "This is a recreational area, so piss off."

The first sign he saw was Do Not Interfere With
The Trees. What kind of a pervert do they take
me for? he wondered.

Bill Bumphrey, the friend he usually met in the
park, didn't seem to be around. Bill was getting up
in years and was still playing with a full deck,
albeit not brilliantly. A senior citizen, a senior
fucking citizen. Dwart hated that derogatory term.
He wished he didn't have to take the damned
patronizing discount at the movies, where they
always asked, "Are you an adult or a senior citizen,
sir?" as if he couldn't possibly be both.

Thoughts swirled in his head. *I need something
new to do. I haven't had enough sex lately. Can horizontal refreshment be so hard to find these days? Sex is like
riding a bicycle. Once you learn how, you never forget.
But when you get older, you can lose your bike.* Maybe
he'd use that line at the club on Saturday night.

He needed a new routine for the Pink Pussycat,
where the regular comic was sick. All Dwart had
to do was warm up the audience, introduce the
strippers and entertain with some stand-up
between acts. Not a great living, but better than
playing the old folks' homes.

He was hungry by the time he reached the Metropolitan. He slid onto a stool at the lunch counter, surrounded by the clatter of dishes and the smell of fresh coffee and bacon. He picked up a copy of the Weekly World News and found an article headlined *Eating eggs will make you smarter.*

The article said a research team investigating the mysteries of the human brain had found that eating eggs could reverse senility and boost brain function. If that's true, thought Dwart, politicians should eat at least six eggs a day.

Reading further, he discovered that an ingredient called an active lipid, extracted from the yolk, overcame the buildup of cholesterol deposits that damaged the brain's ability to store and retrieve information.

"So to hell with the whites," Dwart muttered as the waitress appeared and in a time-honoured ritual, proceeded to spread germs around the counter with a damp rag.

"What'll ya have?" she asked. A vision in white she wasn't.

"Scrambled eggs but no bacon. But since bacon comes with the $1.99 special, can I get extra eggs instead for the same price?"

"I dunno, I'll have to ask the chef de maison."

"What I'd really like," Dwart added, favouring her with his most charming grin, "is to inspect the eggs before the cook scrambles them."

"You don't want much, do you?" she chirped. "Okay, I guess it takes all kinds."

Dwart could see her conferring with the cook through the serving counter window, then she came back with two brown and two white eggs.

Dwart rejected the brown ones, explaining that his mother told him brown eggs came from chickens who didn't wipe their bums.

The waitress paused, then burst out laughing. "Okay, mister, I like you. I'll get the cook to scramble four white eggs for you, all right?"

"Great, but could you get him to trade in the whites—use them in meringues or something—and scramble the yolks of eight eggs? This article says the yolks are good for your brain."

She promised to try. Dwart thanked her and quipped, "Your good looks are only exceeded by the magnitude of your, ah..." he tried not to stare at her ample breasts... "intelligence."

The tabloid newspaper featured a front-page picture of a man whose face and body were covered in long hair. His wild eyes stared out at the reader over a caption that read, *Actual photos! Wolf people are a new super race!* According to the article, Chinese scientists were claiming that genes from earlier hominids were resurfacing in the so-called wolf people, whose physical attributes included superior strength and an ability to produce furry offspring even when paired with normal humans.

As he finished his breakfast, Dwart picked up the metropolitan daily, which featured an ad inviting one and all to visit the Ontario Provincial Zoo. The same page carried a zoo story about a female gorilla named Amanda who couldn't seem to get pregnant.

Should get one of the wolf people from China for the job, thought Dwart. That'd start a race of super somethings. He slipped the paper under his arm and went to the cash register, where the waitress presented him with the $1.99 tab.

"So where are you off to now?" she asked.

"I figured I'd accept this invitation to visit the zoo," he replied, showing her the newspaper ad. Dwart plunked down a toonie and told her to keep the change. Which made her burst out laughing again.

5

POST-COITAL DEPRESSION

"The government isn't going to like this, boss."

"What government?" Frank Fluck shouted to make himself heard above the whirling roar of the propeller blades. "Rwanda is ungovernable, Youbou. You know that better than anyone. All these countries are just powderkegs getting ready to blow. So we just get in and out as fast as possible, with a little bit of luck and some big bribes."

"Take me with you, boss?"

"Sure, eventually. But I need you here for a while, to get some more gorillas before they all go for the chop. Which they will, no matter what some people like to hope. Unless, of course, they can survive in those green plastic shacks down there." Fluck pointed to the monstrously large refugee camp far beneath the aging Italian Augusta A109 cargo helicopter, which was chopping its way through the intermittent clouds toward Nairobi.

"I got news on a young male from a vet near

Kibumbo," said Youbou. Maybe three years old."

"Yeah? What's the score on him?"

"Got a real bad foot. Stepped in a poacher's bushbuck snare. The wire cut real deep into his foot when he tried to get free. All his toes got crushed together and it cut off his circulation for a long time. Could die of infection, but maybe the vet can save him."

"Good, keep checking into it. And keep looking. We can sell all we can get. I sure hope this sucker here makes it." Frank jerked his head in the direction of Bamboo, lying behind them on the floor, two animal handlers nervously watching his inert, drugged body.

"We thought you and the ape were goners when we found you both unconscious back there in the grass. How did that happen, anyway?" asked Youbou.

"Damned if I know," replied Frank, "a dart isn't going to do that much damage to his throat at the range we shot at them with the rifles. I don't remember firing from up close with the tranquilizer pistol. But that female that got away sure gave me one helluva whack up the side of my head. Things are still kinda fuzzy."

"When's this one going to come to?"

"He'll be out for a few more hours, so we got time to load him on the transport plane. Then I'll give him more tranquilizer before he starts moving."

"You did a good job bandaging his neck."

"Hope so. But he's going to need a good doctor in

Canada. I'll contact them pronto. They can fix him up at the zoo in Toronto, they've got experts there."

BAMBOO TRIED DESPERATELY TO FIGURE OUT what was happening to him. His mind seemed to fade in and out of swirling mists, much thicker than the fog of the equatorial Virunga Mountains. Then he felt a sharp pain in his thigh, as if something out of that fog was sticking into him, but the pain was nothing like the one in his throat. He had no way of understanding, but he could hear voices coming through the mist.

"That last injection of tranquilizer should keep him quiet for a while," said Fluck to the handlers on the Nairobi airstrip. "Now get him strapped onto that stretcher and into the cage."

"I don't want to be around when he wakes up. He ain't gonna be too pleased!" said one handler.

"Who would be?" said Youbou. "That was the worst case of coitus interruptus I ever saw."

"He's just suffering from post-coital depression," McCloskey remarked.

"And I think I'm suffering from a concussion," said Frank to Youbou. "Should see a doc myself. I wish we'd nabbed the bitch, though. I'd like to give her a worse headache than she gave me."

But Frank knew Travers would be pleased. The male's throat could be fixed, at least he hoped so. If it had been a bullet instead of a dart wound, the animal would be dead.

"Must have been really close range, boss.

Gotta hand it to you for getting that close to a big male gorilla," said Youbou, "but that's what did the damage to his throat."

"We're sure earning our dough this time, guys. They wanted a grown male and we've got them a dandy."

McCloskey spoke up again. "From now on, I'm going to do what we usually do, shoot the mothers and grab their young. You can bet on that."

"Come on, let's get the cage into the plane. And throw a tarp over it. Might keep him calmer if he does wake up. Remember, nobody gets paid unless he gets delivered alive."

The strange foreign sounds and voices faded from Bamboo's mind. The mists thickened into fog and the fog became pitch black. He was in a double bind—he was in a chemical stupor and incarcerated inside a mesh cage. Bamboo didn't know that he'd been doped with a chemical cocktail designed specifically to knock out an animal of his species, weight and size for transport purposes; and he'd never been enclosed before. Much later, the black started to turn grey, and he started to feel a strange vibration as he lay huddled in the dark interior of the aircraft flying him to Toronto.

People in the business of capturing animals were careful to administer the right dosage of tranquilizer. Too much and they could harm the animal; too little and the beast might wake up too soon, and even creatures who were usually harmless would come to in a confused state and become dangerous.

Bamboo wasn't a fighter by nature and certainly no killer. He could put on quite a menacing display, like any gorilla spotting an intruder. He'd learned how from his father. It started with a spine-chiller of a roar that shattered the silence of the forest. Then he'd rise up on his hind legs and swell out his chest. His adrenaline flowing, the hair on his arms and shoulders and the crest of his forehead would stand straight up, making him look enormous. He'd jut out his jaw and start pummeling his chest with open palms, the hollow thuds sounding like war drums. He'd roar his defiance again, drop on all fours and charge! He'd pull up branches, small trees, leaves and grass in his way, hurling them into the sky toward the enemy. That was the way to do it. It was also the way to get shot.

A man with a rifle couldn't distinguish a gorilla's defensive actions from those of a gorilla that wanted to engage in mortal combat. When Bamboo charged, he always hoped his adversary would turn and run before he ever got near. He'd pull up short and start slapping the ground in front of the interloper. That usually got results without provoking an actual fight, where he might have to bite someone's ugly ass. Sheer bluff on his part. But he didn't realize that a man with a rifle will pull the trigger long before a gorilla finishes his fearsome display.

In the vibrating contraption Bamboo found himself in, there was no adversary to be seen and no room to charge even if he'd been able to. A loud, all-encompassing sound came from no particular direction. Alone and afraid, all he could do was lie there and wait and watch. There was some food in the cage, musanga leaves and bamboo stalks, but he wasn't hungry. A bucket wired to the side of the cage contained water.

In their own environment, apes obtained sufficient liquid from the plants that formed the bulk of their diet. But Bamboo was thirsty now, and the water he drank eased the pain in his throat, even though he found it hard to swallow. He wondered what was wrong with his throat, where he was and when he would see his home or another friendly gorilla face again. His surroundings had scared the shit out of him, judging from the amount of it lying on the cage floor.

Bamboo might as well have been in Hotel Limbo for all he saw on his trip from Nairobi to Toronto.

6

THE OPERATION

Phil Travers steered his daily course through the premises of the Ontario Provincial Zoo with a quick, rangy stride, and finished the tour at his corner office on the top floor of the administration building. Despite the job that demanded his attendance at too many meetings, or tied him up at his desk, Travers still spent as much time outdoors as he could manage.

His angular, weather-beaten face bore a year-round tan accentuated by the grey of his well-trimmed moustache and Vandyke beard. His robust condition made him look younger than his nearly sixty years. Only those over six feet tall could get a good look at his bald spot. His dark blue blazer and well-pressed beige trousers gave him a precise, even nautical look.

He navigated his way to his desk, whose position between two corner windows allowed him a view to starboard of the entrance area, with the

Animal Domain on the port side. He liked to think of his office as the bridge and the entire zoo as the vessel he commanded.

Not to be outdone by Montreal's Expo '67, Toronto had conceived the zoo in the days when the city could afford such mega-projects. Designed to display the earth's ecosystems in one of the world's most progressive zoological parks, the zoo had cost only forty million to build, at least half a billion in nineties dollars. The OP Zoo was the city's atonement for the previous eighty years of housing animals in the zoo's horrendously crowded predecessor downtown.

An even line of sharpened pencils lay along one side of the large square of thick glass that topped the surface of Travers' burnished oak desk. He never used a pencil for more than a few minutes before setting it aside and picking up another one. When they were all dull, he sharpened the lot in the electric pencil sharpener next to the picture of his wife and kids on the corner of his desk. Not a devotee of the computer, Phil figured he thought better while doodling or writing by hand. Whatever he wrote could always go on a word processor later if necessary.

He hit the *Play* button on his answering machine. Travers had worked hard to get the corner office, and he expected an equal effort from his employees. He'd done a stint in the Canadian navy, then attended the University of British Columbia, where he'd indulged his main interest, zoology. Making a living in that field wasn't easy, so he embarked on a Harvard business administration program. The combination of the two disciplines secured him steady employment with a series of zoos, and his rapid climb culminated in his well-deserved reputation as an expert, business-oriented administrator of the OP Zoo.

Travers tried to see zoo life from the animals' perspective. He felt that the earth was a far poorer place without sabre-toothed tigers and carrier pigeons, and he was particularly concerned that gorillas might follow them into oblivion. Being a practical man, Travers knew that the violence and complete apathy that were so much a part of human nature did not bode well for endangered species. Many of his acquaintances weren't bothered in the least by the number of disappearing species, joking that if they wanted to see dinosaurs or gorillas, they'd rent *Jurassic Park* or *King Kong*.

Travers had the training and stick-to-it-iveness to realize this attitude just constituted one more hurdle humanity had to overcome, and that his job was to recognize these problems and try to solve them.

And right now he had a particularly pressing problem.

He stared at the phone for a full minute, then resolutely picked it up and dialled Dr. Gil Brodeur, the Sam Spade of private veterinary surgeons in Toronto. Brodeur answered on the fifth ring, in his usual breezy manner.

"Brodeur here."

"This is Phil Travers. You there, Gil?"

"Yeah, I'm still here. The question is, where are you? You still there?"

"Where else?"

"Well, I haven't heard from you lately. What's new and startling in the care and feeding of animals in captivity?"

"If you'd come out more often I'd be glad to show you, Gil."

"Been very busy. You too, I suppose. We really should see more of each other."

"How about right away?"

"I knew this was about something. You're never one for small talk. So what do you really want to talk about? You want something, I'll bet."

"Yes, I do." Travers paused. "I want you to do an operation on a gorilla, preferably this afternoon, or just as soon as possible."

"You want me to do what?!" Brodeur's voice went up an octave.

Travers smiled at the vet's reaction. "We're flying one in from East Africa today."

"On a gorilla!" Now there was a pause on Gil's end. "You're serious? You're not putting me on?"

"No."

Another pause. "How big?

"How big is the operation?"

"No, I don't care if he needs a circumcision or brain surgery! How big is the gorilla?"

"Oh, well, he's not really a big one, a bit skinny for a male, actually—about three hundred pounds, I think, likely over five feet tall."

"So am I and I doubt if I weigh over one-fifty."

"I haven't had a chance to find out, exactly. He's on his way here from the airport now."

"Is he taking a cab or the limo? What's the matter with him, Phil? Why am I asking that? I know you're putting me on."

"No, I'm not. He's got a sore throat."

"Very funny. You don't operate on a sore throat!"

"You do on this one. You'll have to take a look first, of course. He got a tranquilizer dart in the throat from close range a couple of days ago and we have to get it fixed up right away. We don't know the extent of the injury. You're going to have to find that out when we put him out, decide right away what has to be done and then do it."

"Is that all? Well, whoopee." No reply from Travers. Gil paused, then said, "Look, Phil, are you sure you're phoning the right guy? It's almost like operating on a human, so why don't you get yourself a regular surgeon? I've done some odd jobs for you, but operating on a gorilla?"

"You can do it, Gil; we need a veterinary surgeon and you're the best. We can call in anyone you want for consultation. We had two top neurosurgeons do some brain surgery recently on a female ape named Tabitha."

"Get them again, Phil, it won't hurt my feelings. Or maybe you should bring in those hotshots from Loma Linda Hospital."

"Not a chance. My hunch is you're the guy. Furthermore, this pays good money. Now, are you going to do the job for me?"

Brodeur didn't answer for a full thirty seconds. "Give me a couple of hours to bone up on gorilla anatomy, what there is of it, anyway."

"Great! I knew I could count on you. I'll have the operating room all set up and ready to go."

"Have you still got the same anesthetist on call out there? He's the best with animals I ever saw."

"Yes, and we'll have two of our in-house veterinarians riding shotgun."

"Why, Phil? Why don't you let them do the operation? Because maybe they won't like it if I step in. Of course, maybe they've already refused and you need another sucker. If anything goes wrong, you've got to have a flak-catcher who isn't on the zoo staff. Am I right?"

"I didn't say that," replied Travers, "but it's a good point. What else will you need?"

"A lot of luck, and maybe an esophagus transplant, I don't know yet. I don't know how much damage I'm going to find. Once we get in there it may take as much imagination as medical expertise."

"Right, and you might need some new tissue, real or synthetic."

"We won't have time to go looking for whatever it might be, so it has to be there. Where are you going to get some spare windpipe? Are there any other gorillas out there who want to donate?"

"Organ donors, the morgue, autopsies or

maybe an auto crash victim. Maybe a sick monkey. I'm thinking."

"When should I be there?"

"Seven tonight. You know, I'm sorry this has to be done, and it may be the worst job you've ever been offered, Gil. I know you can do it or I wouldn't ask."

"No, it's not the worst I was ever offered, but it's the worst one I ever took."

"Then you'll take it on for sure?"

"Yes."

"I appreciate this, Gil. It's important."

"We have to save our fellow apes. I'll switch appointments and start studying up on this. Good-bye."

Travers hung up and started making some heavy phone calls. By using horse sense and imagination to con a wild animal into co-operating in its own treatment and recovery, Travers had managed to solve many problems a green vet had given up on. Now he needed a surgeon, and Brodeur was one of the best. Travers was determined to spare no effort or expense to ensure Brodeur had everything he needed for the operation.

After hanging up at his end, Brodeur asked his secretary to re-arrange his schedule.

Short in stature but long on ability, Brodeur was a garrulous francophone who made friends easily, and his natty wardrobe, dark, curly hair and good looks made him popular with women. Brodeur played hard, but he worked and studied hard as well, and that had put him near the top of his profession.

Brodeur respected Travers' years of experience and his assurance and expertise with handling animals. Travers wouldn't have called on him unless he really needed help, and Gil's innate empathy for animals made the administrator's request impossible for him to refuse.

Gil spent the afternoon in the library, reading up on human, ape and particularly gorilla throats. Medical knowledge on wild animals was woefully scant compared to what had been compiled on humans and pets. Too bad, thought Gil, because before we get too much of a chance to study rare species they may well become extinct.

He found a quote from authors Gribbon and Cherfa: *The human vocal tract is unlike that of any other primate in several ways, and these differences are intimately bound up with our ability to speak. We have a short muzzle and a sharp bend to the tube in our throats, and a nose that can be blocked off at will, all features that enable us to make the complex sounds we call speech. Apes do not have the same structure, so it is hardly surprising that they cannot speak. But does that mean that they can't use language? Perhaps not.*

The vet came across several references to the guttural pouch, described in one reference book as resembling a Scottish bagpipe without the pipes, just the air bladder. It extended from the back of the throat to the sternum, and the great apes made deep guttural sounds by banging on their chest with their hands, much like a bongo drum. The amount of air trapped in the pouch in their chest determined the resonance and tone of the sound produced. The upper opening in an ape's throat was just a gaping hole with no constrictive muscle to regulate its size or shape.

Brodeur had done a post-mortem on an ape once, so he was familiar with the pouch, but his knowledge was limited and there wasn't much more information to be had at the library. I've been hired to fix his throat, so I'll bloody well fix it once I see what's wrong with it, he said to himself. He headed home to have supper and a nap before leaving for the zoo.

PHIL TRAVERS WAS PROUD OF HIS ZOO; IN 1982, it was the only Canadian facility to be mentioned in the New York Times survey of the world's best zoos. Travers oversaw a skilled veterinary staff and operating team, the finest diagnostic equipment and X-ray machines, the works in animal medicine. At the health unit, the vets also performed the hundreds of autopsies that were required each year. Despite a host of preventative measures and the very best diet that could be devised, the thousands of mammals, reptiles, amphibians, birds and fish met with accidents and other problems that resulted from living in surroundings that could only attempt to recreate their natural environment.

Travers' staff knew he didn't believe that a zoo's primary function was to collect animals for the amusement and entertainment of the public.

Rather, it was to be a refuge for the gene pools of endangered species, the final guardian of the living species of the earth. At his public speaking engagements, Travers would declare that the earth was fast running out of room for many species. All zoo animals should be encouraged to reproduce in captivity. If they did, it would prove that they'd become sufficiently comfortable with their surroundings to survive and possibly re-stock the wild.

The zoo's great apes were a particular concern for Travers, and he was determined to find a suitable mate for Tabitha and Amanda, two female gorillas that needed servicing.

His telephone calls finished, Travers turned to his mail. Some staff joker had sent him a copy of a tabloid article that carried the headline *Ape gives birth to human baby: Doctors use chimp as surrogate mom.*

The article, with a Moscow dateline, said a human embryo had been fertilized in a test tube, then implanted in a chimpanzee's uterus at a secret laboratory in Russia. Nine months later, after an amazingly uncomplicated, full-term pregnancy, the chimp had given birth to a seven-pound, fourteen-ounce baby girl, normal in every respect. A full report of the incredible experiment had been smuggled out of Russia by one of the scientists who participated in the implantation of the human embryo. He was divulging this information, he said, because he was afraid the next step called for a chimpanzee's own ova to be fertilized with human sperm. Religious leaders were reported to be scandalized by the possible result— an unholy monster, half man, half ape.

The sender had scrawled across the bottom of the article: *You could reverse this process, Phil, and get Toronto mothers implanted with gorilla embryos. That'd solve your problem.*

Sounds a lot like B.S. to me, thought Phil; but then again, chimpanzees, gorillas and humans did carry their young for about the same length of time. Many women in the world were unable to carry a child to term, and there were a lot of chimpanzees around. So if it worked with a human, why not try human mothers as incubators or surrogate mothers for gorilla babies? It would certainly eliminate any trauma over whether or not to put the baby up for adoption.

It would have to be a last resort, Travers decided as he filed the article in the wastebasket. He was determined to get the young females bred, but in the regular way. *Which is why I'm paying through the nose to get this new stud out of the wild and into captivity.*

Realizing the ape could arrive any minute, Travers trotted over to the health care building, entering the veterinary offices through the back corridor. Doctor Jeremy Paddon was sipping his morning coffee.

"What about this new ape, Doc?" inquired Phil, stepping through the office door. "How bad is the injury?"

"He's here. And from what we've observed, at as close a range as we can get, it's bad enough."

"I've called Brodeur."

"I figured you'd call somebody. Look Phil, we do the best we can, we have the best equipment and our track record is pretty good, wouldn't you say?"

"No one's saying it isn't," Travers replied. He detected a defensive note in Paddon's voice. "You deal with ninety-eight percent of the animal problems we have, but this is a special case."

"But why Brodeur?"

"A lot of reasons, really. Call it a hunch if you like. Also, he's not on staff, and it's hard to replace you guys."

"You wouldn't be looking for a fall guy if something goes wrong, would you, Phil?"

"Of course not! And why should you care if I was? What's the matter, Jeremy?"

"I'm pissed off!"

"Okay Doc, but you haven't thought this through. Just remember, you'd be a lot more pissed off if that gorilla came out of the anesthesia during the operation you were performing, before you expected him to."

Paddon thought that one over as he took a another sip. "You're right, Phil. Better him than me. Brodeur must be nuts, or else the danger pay's really good."

"It is. Tonight at seven, and bring a friend," Phil said as he left the office.

The *National Independent* had been giving the OP

Zoo a bad time over Amanda, publicizing the fact
that right here in Toronto the Good there was a two-
hundred-pound female gorilla with an assertive disposition who refused to be bred. Nobody fooled
around with her unless she okayed it.

Canada's daily newspaper also reported:
*Veterinary brows at the OP Zoo are furrowed over
Amanda's failure to produce. Unwilling to grant her
any choice in the matter, zoo officials, with a couple of
gynecologists standing by, conducted a medical examination and studied the possible social consequences of
Amanda's bossy nature on her infertility.*

*What right do zoo officials have to come charging in
with their anesthetic gas, chemical cocktails and laparo-
scopes, poking about with their patronizing How-come-
a-nice-girl-like-you-isn't-pregnant attitude? If Mr.
Right hasn't come swinging out of the somewhat limited
selection of males at the zoo, is that any of their business?*

The cute approach, thought Phil. Damn right it
was the Zoo's business, not the media's, and
maybe I've just come up with Mr. Right.

When Doc Brodeur black-bagged it down to
the zoo just before seven o'clock that evening, the
administrator's desperate hopes arrived with him.
Neither of them knew whether Gil would be making easy money or not. The price was right, but it
had to be, to allow for bad publicity if the ape
died. Gil was reassured when he saw that the
administrator had taken the precaution of obtain-
ing a section of windpipe. It was packed in a ster-
ilized cooler. Travers didn't say where he got it.

Unless he was subjected to extreme torture or sodium pentothal, he wasn't about to admit that after ten years he'd finally called his drunken cousin, Gregg, the morgue attendant, to say hi and to trade a case of aged Canadian Club whiskey for the windpipe.

Travers, Brodeur, Paddon another zoo vet named Shirley James, the anesthetist and a human thoracic specialist held a conference. Two strong guards were also present, along with Irving Fluck, the other head honcho of the Fluck Animal Procurement Company.

Travers and the medical team agreed that they had to spare Bamboo the trauma of several doses of anesthesia. His throat would be examined and if Gil decided surgery was required, it would be performed immediately.

They ruled out the use of a tranquilizer gun, which might contain chemicals that were incompatible with the gas anesthetic that Brodeur had decided would be the safest in this case.

Isoflurane was a fast-acting gas, eliminated within fifteen minutes after delivery to the lungs was discontinued. Introducing the gas was the only problem—it had to be started with an intravenous injection of an ultra-short-acting barbiturate like sodium pentothal. To hit a vein in the arm of a person co-operating with a nurse was one thing; the same procedure in a reluctant mini-monster was quite another.

Bamboo's groggy condition in the canvas-cov-

ered cage made it possible. Irving Fluck and the
bully-boy guards snared his hand as he reached for
food through the open space between the bars of
the cage. They clamped down firmly on his arm
with a special apparatus, while Bamboo went
through all kinds of contortions in an effort to
escape. They managed to hold it in place for a couple of seconds, long enough for Gil to hit the vein.
Four seconds later, Bamboo's eyes rolled back in
his sockets and he rolled over onto his back. No
one seemed to notice that Irving gave his arm an
added sharp twist as he was passing out. Bamboo,
however, got one good look at Irving, and he
noticed, and he felt the pain. The last thing he
remembered was the cruel smile on Fluck's face.

The cage was immediately opened and the
anesthetist inserted an endotracheal tube in
Bamboo's throat, right down to the end of his trachea at the entrance to his chest. The vaporizer
was hooked up and within another six seconds,
Bamboo was breathing a mixture of Isoflurane
and oxygen, which settled him quickly into a very
deep sleep. The anesthetist attached a moni-
torscope to Bamboo's arms, chest and legs, and
the constant reading on an electrocardiograph
reassured everyone that all was well.

Next, Paddon braced a sturdy modified horse
speculum between Bamboo's teeth to make sure
that an inadvertent closure of his mouth wouldn't
cost someone a few fingers. Dr. James started an
I.V. drip with lactated ringers and five percent

dextrose, in anticipation of a possibly long procedure, to guard against the risk of shock. She added antibiotics and steroids, along with multi-vitamins to assist in the patient's subsequent recovery and to assure good liver and kidney function. A urinary catheter was inserted and the animal's urine output was monitored as an added safety measure.

Paddon shaved the gorilla's neck and swabbed sterilizer from his mouth to his sternum, then laid a drape over his entire body. The exposed operating field was eight inches long, with the throat wound exactly on the mid-line. All was ready for Brodeur to do a thorough cleaning of the penetrating wound made by the dart. He noted that all the major muscles and nerves in the area had been missed, but the metal fishhook-shaped tip of the dart had penetrated the gorilla's thyroid cartilage, just above the Adam's apple. A portion of his vocal fold had been lacerated, along with some muscle tissue on that side. The piece of dart had imbedded in his left laryngeal ventricle.

Paddon and James figured it would be enough to close the hole in the larynx using the surrounding soft tissue and remove the broken tip of the dart, but Gil and the throat specialist worried that the soft tissue alone wouldn't be able to contain the great pressure exerted on the vocal fold when Bamboo pounded his chest. Gil decided to split the muscles on either side of the larynx and use them as reinforcing bands around the defect in the thyroid cartilage.

The difference between the new and the original thyroid cartilage was that the new one was surrounded by still fully innervated muscle bands. In future, when Bamboo tightened his neck muscles, the vocal fold opening might quiver slightly, but Gil and the specialist felt this wouldn't bother him too much.

Failure to use live muscle tissue would have inevitably resulted in atrophy of the area, and possible failure of the thyroid cartilage, which could prove fatal.

The surgeons debated using some of the windpipe provided by Travers. It would constitute a transplant, no matter how minor.

Gil felt a stirring of pity for Bamboo, a poor abused animal who'd never done anything to warrant his misfortune, except to be born as a species very possibly destined for extinction. So he decided to repair the defects in Bamboo's vocal fold and his vocalis and ventricularis muscles. The repair would return the structures that formed the vocal cord almost to pre-trauma condition, except for some increased tension around the laryngeal ventricle.

Brodeur closed the incision with a continuous, intra-dermal suture that remained open until the very end of the stitching process. Then a gentle pull on the absorbable suture material closed the whole thing like a zipper, with only one tiny stitch sticking out at the bottom of the suture line. To protect the site of the operation, the vets attached a padded plastic Elizabethan collar around Bamboo's neck.

"Voilà!" said Brodeur, stepping back from the operating table. The entire procedure had taken only two hours, and as Brodeur later confided to a colleague over Camparis, "It went as smooth as a baboon's behind."

7

HOTEL LIMBO

After the operation, Bamboo found himself plagued by inanimate objects. He was back in his cage. He awoke to find that when he looked to either side, there was something odd about the view; then he realized he was looking through a sort of clear thickness that stretched around his head. His first reaction was to place his hands on the thing, which was fastened around the base of his neck and extended upward like a funnel. Bamboo had no idea what was under the funnel; all he knew was that he and his throat felt better than at any time since his injury and capture.

He made several gingerly attempts to remove the thing, but ceased his efforts each time when the pain in his throat returned. Instinctively he realized that he'd best leave well enough alone, particularly as his throat no longer bothered him continually. The collar must have something to do with that, plus whatever else the white-eyes had done to him. Strange that one group of his captors would hurt his throat and another group fix it up.

Bamboo felt his best bet was to go back to sleep and wait to see what things would be like the next time he awoke.

A few hours later, he couldn't immediately tell that anything had changed. Again he tugged at the plastic funnel. Once more it hurt his throat, so again he wisely decided to leave it alone. Never having heard of convalescing, he didn't know that was what he was officially doing; he was just relatively happy to be free of pain.

One thing had changed—he wasn't alone. In another cage immediately adjacent to his own, a female gorilla sat in the far corner staring intently at him, with a quizzical expression in her black eyes. When she saw that he was awake and aware of her presence, she got up and began to pace around her own enclosure.

She was the largest and most overpowering specimen of female gorilla Bamboo had ever seen. She had an elegant severity of beauty that he found most distracting. Male gorillas were usually twice the size of females, but this one was almost as large and tall as Bamboo. Blue-black hair from head to toe, and a really classic flat face. None of those ugly protrusions in the middle common to all of his captors. A full, fleshy mouth, close-set, beetle-black eyes. Bamboo was surprised. He certainly hadn't expected to see another great ape, let alone a female. She looked strong, capable and severe, and now she began vocalizing with some soft purring noises, then with a three-note bark of varying range and intensity.

"Who are you?" she asked, although to a human listener it would have sounded like *naoom, naoom*—a deep, prolonged rumble that gradually descended into a croon and ended in a hum. Bamboo listened intently, as she spoke in a heavy accent he'd never encountered before.

Tentatively, he tried to use his injured throat in reply. The speech came out, but it didn't sound like his old voice and he had great trouble controlling it. Startled, he stopped and tried again, very carefully this time, with a series of short, rough, guttural sounds like pig grunts. The usual vocalizing didn't seem to be coming out right and he had to resort to what amounted to a sort of pidgin gorilla. "Where I?"

She must have misunderstood, because she replied, "You are with them, the same as I am with them."

"Who them, who you?" he asked in a low wailing sound.

"I am Amanda. Them are the white-eyes, some kind of ape with not much hair. Most of them won't hurt you, and they feed us as best they can. But something was done to you; I never saw anything like that before," she noted, pointing to Bamboo's collar. You better just rest, you're not going anywhere."

Bamboo considered this advice carefully—his

attempts at gorilla speech hadn't proved successful, just strange and irritating. What had they done to his throat? Puzzled, he complied with Amanda's suggestion. As he lay back to rest, he thought about the strange places he'd been in the past few days, places he'd much rather not have been or seen. When would the confusion stop? How had it all happened? And why? Thinking gave him a headache and he drifted back to sleep on the straw mattress, filled with quiet apprehension.

DWART STARTED UP THE MAIN DRAG TOWARD THE subway station, passing a few watering holes on the way. The New East had become just like the Old West—a bar on every block. I could use a drink to fortify myself for the long ride out to the zoo, he thought. Two draft beers and a tomato juice would do, as long as the bar didn't have one of those goddamn tight-assed bluegrass singers from Elephant's Breath, Alabama, who appropriately called their product Folkin' Western or Folkin' Country music. He'd had enough of them when they were playing gigs where he was emceeing. He recalled how he'd introduced them:

Have we got an act for you here tonight, folks! Yeah, we've got a treat for you that'll knock your hat right back into the creek, if you know what I'm talkin' about. We got us a group called Jack Bandana and his Afghanistan Banana Stand Band, who just had them a big smashit!...That's right, lady, I said smash hit. You gotta learn to separate your words...You remember their

*major release, Onto Toronto Pronto, Tonto...You know,
I wish I could get a major release. At my age, every
release is a major one...The boys in this band are all
from the Southern High Institute of Technology. Yessir!
Good old S.H.I.T...*

Rock bands were even worse—tens of thousands of dollars worth of amplifying equipment
and back-up, synthesized, syncopated shit. Your
only sane option was to leave.

There was a quiet bar handily adjacent to the
main saloon in the emporium he entered, where
the noise level seemed acceptable, although the
whole place was a dive that American spring-
board artist Greg Louganis wouldn't have considered. The drinks were cheaper than in a carpet
joint, so Dwart ordered his beer and juice and
paid two dollars and seventy-five cents. He mixed
the three glasses, creating a Calgary Red-Eye. Not
a bad drink, really, although one of his buddies
had once called it a slime job.

Sipping the mixture, he thought about economic problems, the nation's and his own. *I got
caught in the war, I missed out on the sexual revolution,
and what with the national debt and inflation I bet
they'll cancel the old-age pension. Now that's what I
call a run of bad luck. But when the black widow government spider gets hungry, she'll eat more flies. After
all, she owns the web and we're all caught in it. Not too
many gigs around anymore; I've literally got to find
something else to make me some dough.*

Dwart finished his Red-Eye, walked out onto

sunny Yonge Street, and waited at the bus stop for one that would take him out to the zoo.

He spotted her a hundred yards away, walking toward him. Something in the way she strutted along gave off a nearly imperceptible signal. Her high-heeled black shoes on her long and beautifully formed legs struck the pavement with authority. Conservative yet sexy English tweed skirt above exquisite knees, plain black waist-length jacket and matching black cloche, which hid her hair and ears and gave her a twenties flapper effect. As she came closer he noted alabaster skin and jet-black eyebrows.

For God's sake, you lecherous old bastard, he thought, she's no more than twenty-five! But Dwart still turned and watched her trim behind fade in the other direction.

On the bus, he thought about feminine pulchritude in general. He'd seen some very beautiful young women stripping over the years, but it wasn't the same. Something should be left to the imagination. *Do the strippers know that? I wish I could have talked to her for a few minutes. It's getting lonely out here.*

TRAVERS SAT IN HIS OFFICE EATING A FLUID Drive: an ounce and a half of red wine mixed with a bottle of Guinness and poured over a bowl of Kellogg's Bran Flakes. One serving was a good physic—you joined the regulars. Two or three helpings and you were likely to get diarrhea of the mouth and constipation of the brain.

He and his navy buddies had invented the fluid portion of the drink while stationed in Londonderry in Northern Ireland. If you were "other ranks," it was often difficult to come by hard liquor in any quantity or quality. The pubs saved it for their favourite customers and the officers soaked up the rest. Beer, ale and bitters were often a weak, green mess with a sort of scummy look, but the Guinness Stout, single, double or triple-X, was always top hole. God bless St. James Gate Brewery on the River Liffey. Thanks to the brewery, more recycled Guinness than water flowed from Dublin to the Irish Sea. In the search for relief from sobriety, mixing cheap wine with Guinness cut the burnt-cork taste of the stout, and the whole concoction slid down the old gullet as smooth and soft as a government job. The combination had a good kick to it, but the side effects ranged from mild flatulence to the green-apple two-step.

The addition of bran flakes was Travers' idea. And a good one too, he thought, as he finished licking the bowl and the spoon and began to ponder how he could give his new ape, Bamboo, every possible chance at healthy survival after the operation he'd just been through. That is a beautiful ape, he mused, even though beauty in man or beast is in the eye of the beholder. If you want to see ugly, take a look at some humans. Which is what I'm going to have to do now. He grimaced as he picked up the phone to dial Irving Fluck.

Irving, the North American and ugly end of the Fluck Brothers act, wasn't exactly a friend. He was

an animal specialist, under occasional contract to
the zoo. The board had hired Fluck to check on
the efficiency of the zoo's security system and turn
in a report. Irving had been given an office in the
administration building, and in order to do his
study he had the run of the premises.

The official security staff weren't Irving Fluck
fans, as he'd proven to be a real shit-disturber, insist-
ing that all doors be locked, all channels of access
and egress blocked and all efforts made to keep the
animals inside the zoo. Some said he'd keep the
public outside if he could, figuring they only caused
problems and were a pain in the ass. The regular
guards would be only too happy to see his contract
and review finished so he could leave them in peace
and go back to minding his own business.

Fluck's answering machine said he'd be back
about eleven.

"I know where that joker is," Phil said to the
empty office. He took the elevator down to the
cafeteria, grabbed a coffee and dropped into a
chair at Fluck's table.

"I want to make sure that new ape in the infirmary is kept calm while he gets acclimatized
around here. He needs rest and quiet."

"What do you want me to do," asked Irving
irritably, "hold his hand? He's in good company—
that big black female gorilla, you know, the good
looker, Amanda? She's in there with him."

"Dammit," Phil burst out, "I said I didn't want
him excited."

"Hold it, they're not in the same cage! And it might even reassure him to see there are other gorillas around."

Phil paused before replying. "Actually, that's a very good idea. Sorry I yelled at you."

"That's okay. Anyway, your vets want her to get excited, don't they? They had her in that section of the building already, with some of those gynos doing another medical exam."

"Right. They can't seem to find anything wrong with her physically. She should be able to conceive."

"Okay, so you gotta get someone interested in the bitch, or vicey versey. So we left her in there in the other big cage, so they can sort of feel each other out, if not up!"

"So you think Amanda's good-looking, do you, Irving?" asked Phil, a slight smile flitting over his face.

"Whaddaya mean by a crack like that?" piped Irving, then chuckled. "Well, for an ape, I mean, she's a looker. Maybe I been around apes too long."

"How long have you been in the animal procurement business, anyway?"

"About seven years approximately."

"What did you do before that?"

"I was in the hauling business. Had a company with my brother Frank before he and I went into this animal enterprise."

"What company was that?'

"I owned it by myself at first. I wanted to call it I. Fluck U-Haul Ltd., but the government wouldn't let me use that name. When my brother came into the business with me, we applied for the name Fluck U-Haul."

"No dice again?"

"You got it. I was going to sue them. It's my name, after all, even if it is a little, ah, funny. I should have the legal right to use my own name any way I please. I mean, there's a guy called Mike Ding and they let him form the Mike Ding Car Rental Company'.

"You're absolutely right, Irving, but maybe you should consider changing your name."

"What the hell for? I like the name Irving! But then I figured, you know, the legal fees and all, and how hard it is to fight city hall. Anyway, I got awfully tired of the trucking business. I always liked animals, grew up on a farm, you see. So Frank and I decided to start up a company that would deal in all aspects pertaining to animals, especially finding animals people wanted and finding suppliers to meet that demand. Then we ended up becoming suppliers ourselves."

"Interesting. Now, can you put a guard in that ape holding room, to keep traffic out and maybe provide a quiet presence to watch over him while he recuperates?"

"You're short-handed here, Phil, you know that. And you know your budget better than I do. I don't think it's my responsibility to hire another employee. We delivered the ape alive, so it's up to the OP Zoo if you want more staff."

"Agreed. I'll take care of it. I'll have an attendant look in at the infirmary at regular intervals. That'll take care of the daytime. It's the night that's a problem. I'll hire someone as a night watchman and pay them out of petty cash or the emergency fund or something. I think the precaution is necessary."

"Just remember, when you hire someone like that, always have your security staff check them out for priors before they start working here. Gotta go now, but I'll look in on those two apes for you right now myself."

Fluck found Bamboo asleep on his straw mattress. Amanda was sitting in the corner of her cage, staring hard at him as he approached quietly.

"How come I can never sneak up on you? Take your beady eyes off me, Amanda," said Irving, "or I'll throw a bag over your head and then we'll see how come a black beauty like you isn't pregnant."

His body language, looks and tone made Amanda grimace, if a flat-faced grimace was possible. The big white-eyes made her visibly nervous; she gave out a low-pitched hoot and started thumping her chest and throwing straw around the cage.

Coming out of his slumber, Bamboo watched through half-closed eyes as the big black female ran around in a snit, with a massive white-eyes standing nearby, taunting her. Bamboo had seen him once before and now he got a better look. Bamboo himself was big, but Irving topped him by a hand span. Yet it wasn't his height, but his breadth that was really impressive—more than an arm's length across the chest, with muscled arms as big as his legs. His ears stood out from his head, and his close-set pale blue eyes roved over the room. From where he lay watching, Bamboo got an excellent look at Irving Fluck's bowed legs; and had the distinct feeling that one day he was going to have to straighten this white ape out.

8

THE ZOO

The wide green valley of the Rouge River was a pleasant location for the OP Zoo. Seven hundred and ten acres of wooded tablelands, five pavilions and a three-mile electric train ride were the major features. No dull rows of cages here, as animals were housed in spacious paddocks behind moats and fences. Animals from a particular region were displayed together in settings representing such disparate ecosystems as the jungles of South America, the swamps of Malaysia, and Africa's savannah and mountain areas.

The great apes were on public view in an outer compound, if and when the gorillas chose to go outside. The outdoor enclosure was a massive wire mesh cage with logs the size of telephone poles in various configurations, both horizontal and vertical, an attempt to simulate large jungle trees from which the apes could swing and play. The management couldn't provide real trees and foliage, since apes were naturally inclined to tear off branches, twigs and leaves, either to eat or to make sleeping nests. That wouldn't matter if a large enough area were available, or if there was a forest in which to roam, but the zoo could only do so much under conditions of captivity.

The large inner compound was enclosed in heavy plate glass, with various levels of concrete flooring, imitation rocks, more large timbers and poles for climbing, water sources and straw-like bedding material. The section between these two compounds contained individual rooms, pens, cages and sleeping quarters, and it was also the place where the keepers could get close to the gorillas and even venture among them if they saw fit.

When he arrived at the zoo, Dwart eschewed the air-conditioned comfort of the Canadian Animal Domain ride, a monorail that circled the entire grounds, choosing instead to wander among the animal element, viewing some of the thousands of inhabitants. The zoo was like a modern ark, striving to prevent the extinction of as much of the planet's wildlife as possible.

Early on a weekday the zoo wasn't crowded, and Dwart wandered into the commissary, where the animal feed was prepared. He saw slaughtered beef, special garbage drums full of mealworms and crickets, top-notch vegetables and fruits, raisins, dates, horsemeat, hay, grasses of various kinds, concentrated food pellets of all sizes, ground corn, soybean meal, oat hulls, fish meal, limestone, salt and vitamins. The commissary staff was happy to talk to him, and he learned that the food bill for the year was over half a million dollars. The backbone of the diet was about four hundred tons of prepared food pellets, but some animals required more exotic foods like sunflower sprouts, barley shoots, gelatin, herring, smelt, goldfish, skim milk powder, bananas, coconuts, live mice, hamsters and baby chicks.

He continued on to the Risible Aviary, where there were several varieties of birds whose song or call sounded like human laughter. There were Asiatic Laughing Thrushes, New Zealand Laughing Owls, South American Laughing Falconer Hawks, North American Laughing Gulls and Australian Kookaburras, or Kingfishers. What a great audience they'd make, thought Dwart, and his mood lightened considerably. He figured there should be a paddock of laughing spotted hyenas next door, and on the other side a field of hee-hawing donkeys or laughing jackasses, just to round out the set.

Spotting a furtive nut-scratcher, Dwart approached the guilty zoo attendant and asked, "Where's the chumac bird?"

"Don't have one of them, sir, what are they like?"

"They're extremely over-sexed, you might even say bordering on the nymphobirdiacal. The species is predominantly female and they inhabit jungle regions, where they fly around at dusk uttering their strange mating call in deep, husky, notes: 'Thatchumac? Thatchumac?'"

The attendant chuckled and pointed to an ostrich strutting around the enclosure. "You know how to tell if that's a male or a female ostrich?"

"No," replied Dwart, "but I'll bite, how do you tell?"

"You tell the ostrich a joke. If he laughs, it's a male. If she laughs, it's a female."

"Touché, but do you mind if I don't remember that one?"

Another keeper appeared on the scene, and the first one said, "Why don't you join us for a coffee in the staff cafeteria? It's our break."

"Okay by me, thanks," said Dwart. "My name's Dwart. And you are...?"

"Sam, and this is Ralph." They shook hands and proceeded down a walkway, skirting a large building.

"What do they do in there?" asked Dwart.

"That's the pool building," replied Sam.

"For polar bears and penguins?"

"No, for genes, it's a gene pool. You got your gene and sperm storage in there. Officially it's called the Centre for the Reproduction of Endangered Species."

"How does it work?" asked Dwart with genuine interest.

"Well, a lot of species are disappearing, so in there we have scientists, geneticists I think they call them, anyway, guys who are trying to save animals."

"By reproducing them?"

"Yeah, through animal genes and cells, and sperm. They freeze it, actually. Some people call it the Frozen Zoo. Then they can share the stuff between zoos in artificial insemination and reproduction. Like rhinoceros sperm, for instance. Ralph here, that's one of his jobs—collecting and storing rhinoceros sperm."

Dwart pulled up short and did a slow take, looking in awe at Ralph. With a note of new respect in his voice, he asked, "You jerk off rhinos?"

"Well, not by hand. You think I want to live that dangerously? We use auto-ejaculation equipment to take semen samples and store it. The cost of shipping a rhino to another zoo in North America, let alone anywhere else in the world, just to get the beast laid, well, it's just too damn high. Even then you couldn't be sure it would take. I think they have to do it in a lake or something."

"I don't even want to think about how they do it."

"It's a lot cheaper to use artificial insemination. And those jokers at customs at any border you want to cross. Ever try to go through customs with a rhinoceros? They could become an endangered species before you got through the red tape. I swear to God, those customs peckerheads are without doubt the most miserable—"

"I know," Dwart interrupted, "I've been back and forth a few times, but if you don't expect people to be reasonable you'll save yourself a lot of disappointment in life. I've always tried to take my old dad's advice. He said, 'Never deal with idiots, because if you do, you have to deal with them on their own level, and they're so good at it, they'll beat you every time.'"

They crossed a brick-paved patio with trees and benches, then turned into the cafeteria, where they picked up mugs of coffee and sat at a window table.

"Lot of animals you haven't got here," commented Dwart.

"We got four thousand. How many do you want?" replied Ralph.

"More to the point, what ones haven't we got?" Sam asked.

"You haven't got an ooh-aah bird, have you?"

"Okay, I'll bite this time. What kind of a bird would that be?"

"I'm glad you asked," said Dwart, with a laugh. "The ooh-aah bird has many peculiarities, one of which is that it lays square eggs. While producing a square egg from its round primary orifice, it screeches 'Oooooh!' When it's finished laying the egg it says 'Aaaaah!' Hence the ooh-aah bird."

"You're trying too hard, Dwart."

"They can't all be gems."

"No, but some of them should be."

"Say, fellas," said Dwart, "are there any jobs around here? I could use something to sort of fill in the pocketbook." Dwart suddenly sniffed the air. A terrible stench had reached his nostrils.

They were joined by a good-looking youth.

The other two keepers shifted uneasily in their chairs and began to gulp their coffee.

"Maybe you could get Finster's job," said Sam, introducing the young man. As he sat down, the stink became nearly unbearable.

"Ah, well, now that depends. What do you do, Finster?" asked Dwart.

"I work with the elephants," replied Finster, "I'm in charge of keeping the elephants regular. If they get constipated, they get sick. So I have to give them enemas."

Ralph and Sam couldn't suppress their laughter. Dwart asked Finster, "Just how would you accomplish that?'

"It's like, you gotta get a tub of warm, soapy water, a stirrup pump and a ladder. You fill up the stirrup pump with the water and run up the ladder and inject it up the elephant's butt."

"This is a job?" was Dwart's amazed reaction.

Finster continued, "But no matter how fast you try to get down that ladder, the elephant lets go all over you before you can get down and away. And after you've been on this job for a while, no matter how many times you shower, you can't get rid of the stench."

"For Pete's sake, you look like an intelligent fellow, why don't you quit and get another job?" asked Dwart, holding his nose.

"What, and give up show business?" Finster rose from his chair and walked away, to the immediate relief of his tablemates.

"I've done a lot of odd jobs in my time," said Dwart, "including cabin boy on a Greek Vaseline tanker, but this beats all, masturbating rhinos and giving enemas to elephants. I'll take a rain-check, thank you very much."

"They're not all that bad, Dwart. Look, go over to the zoo office and see the administrator. His name's Phil Travers."

"Not a bad guy," added Sam.

"And try to get to see him personally, not one of his assistants. The zoo's often looking for part-time help."

"Good idea. Thanks a lot. And if there aren't any jobs, I can at least canvass him to see if I could entertain at your annual banquet or shindig. Where's his office?"

"Just go due east down that paved path over there to the next set of buildings near the gate. You can't miss it."

PHIL LOOKED UP AND SAW AN OLD MAN STANDING in his office doorway, flipping a loonie in the air, then catching the coin and rolling it along the knuckles of his right hand. He wore an old cream-coloured raincoat, probably no longer water-proof, and an even older wide-brimmed fedora pushed to the back of his shock of grey hair. He leaned against the door jamb, his left hand in his pocket. "I've got some Old Highland Scotch Swallow stashed in the boot of my Stutz Bearcat. If you can use a case here at the zoo, I'll have one of my boys bring it in."

"Okay, let me guess," said Travers, smiling, "Edward G. Robinson in Little Caesar?"

"One more guess, and get it right this time or no hooch for this zoo," and the visitor rolled the coin more prominently.

"George Raft in Scarface?"

"You knew it all the time."

"You had to be a gangster out of an old Prohibition movie, and then I remembered the coin-flipping bit."

"You'd be good at Trivial Pursuit, I'll bet."

"We do play it now and then. I'm Phil Travers, zoo director. What can I do for you?" Phil extended his hand and they shook.

"I'm Dwart Farquhart, not gainfully employed at the moment. Likely you can't do much to alleviate that situation, but then again, maybe you can."

"Please have a seat. What do you do when you're working Mr., ah..."

"Farquhart. But call me Dwart, if you like, or Farky—that's the name I go by when I'm working, doing after-dinner speaking, stand-up comedy and the like. Say, could the zoo use someone like that at their next banquet and beer fight for employees? I can do zoo jokes."

"The annual beer fight, hmm. That about describes it. Not that I know of right now, but I could keep it in mind, Mr. Farquhart."

"Just thought I'd ask, as it's the line of work I'm nearly out of," said Dwart.

"Nearly?"

"Oh, I still get some jobs, but it's a younger man's game these days. I do appear at the Pink Pussycat some Saturday nights. True story."

"That's a sort of burlesque show, isn't it?"

"It'd be more accurate to call it a strip-o-rama. There's not much real burlesque left in it."

"There's a difference?"

"Sure is. I could explain it to you, but I don't want to take up your time. However, if I could get some kind of a job here, then I could enlighten you about burlesque at your convenience."

"You really should see the personnel department about that. And I don't think we have any openings at...wait just a minute now, there may be something."

"Look, I refuse to give enemas to elephants."

"Did Finster quit?"

"No, but it's good training for a career in politics. I met him, thank God only briefly, in the cafeteria. Just as a matter of interest, what do you pay him for that?"

"Not enough, I'm sure," replied Phil. "We couldn't get anybody, let alone Canadians, to do that job before the recession."

"There seem to be a lot of wild, weird, but not-so-wonderful jobs around this place."

"Things happen in a zoo that you would find hard to believe, Dwart."

"Yes, I've been having coffee with Sam and Ralph."

"Have you? Rhino Ralph, they call him. He's in charge of protecting the rhinos."

"He didn't tell me about that. Rhinos need protecting?"

"They do. They're hunted savagely in East India and Africa. The Chinese are to blame, really. It's not as bad here, but even in captivity there is some danger to the animal."

"Why would that be?" asked Dwart. "Here in Toronto. I don't understand."

"The whole of Asia has this obsessive faith in the alleged aphrodisiacal and fever-reducing qualities of rhino horn, and this extends, although to a lesser degree, to the rest of the poor animal's body."

"How do you mean?"

"Well, if they can gouge a chunk out of the animal's horn when no one's around, slice off an ear, or get a piece of his hide—anything will do—they'll try to get it."

"That's terrible, especially when you consider that the belief is bullshit. Or is it? Have you ever tried it?" asked Farky with a grin.

"I'll never tell, but to some Asians, that belief is unshakable. If you want to try a rhino byproduct and are interested, for, shall we say, aphrodisiacal or longevity purposes, Ralph can arrange it."

"He can? I thought you said..."

"A practice to which we tacitly give permission. We just pretend we don't know about it, mainly because it involves a byproduct which would otherwise be entirely wasted; and by selling it, the demand for rhino-based aphrodisiac is met and the rhinos perhaps protected from bodily assault."

"What is it?"

"Ralph does a good local trade in rhino urine. Do you want to try some?"

"You've got to be kidding. Torontonians drink rhino piss?"

"Torontonians, Asian or otherwise, will drink anything. Ralph collects the stuff at intervals and bottles it. He'll sell you enough to fill a beer bottle for fifteen dollars."

"Hell, I can get a case of real beer for that price. I wonder if I could tell the difference?"

"Don't knock it. We have some men in the zoo who are close to retirement, but look half their age because they drink a full pint of rhino urine twice a week."

"You don't say!"

"They tell me that's the reason for their continued good health, youthful appearance and high potency."

"Come to think of it, you look kind of young for your age yourself."

"Not that young, thank you. Look, Dwart, this talk of strange jobs has reminded me. We do have a job that just came up, and it's very specialized. I think you could do that job; you're ideally suited, in fact, and I doubt if it's even that dangerous if you don't get too close."

"What do you mean, dangerous?"

"I shouldn't have said that. No, not dangerous, but different," said Phil, laughing.

"What's with the big ha-ha-ha routine? What's the job?"

Phil sat for a moment or two, struggling with a job description, then said slowly and clearly, "Gorilla sitter."

Dwart didn't surprise easily, but he didn't answer for about ten seconds, and then all he could manage in reply was a weak: "What?"

"A gorilla sitter," the zoo administrator said. "Actually, we've never had one before and it's not as bad as it may sound. We have this new male gorilla from East Africa. He's had an operation on his throat." Phil gave Dwart the full story on Bamboo.

"So he's in a cage and and you just want me to watch him, babysit him and yell for help if he gets obstreperous?"

"Yes, that's the general idea. We're okay in the daytime and until early evening, but in what you'd loosely call the graveyard shift, I haven't got enough staff to assign a full-time zookeeper to Bamboo, so I was just about to look for a part-time gorilla sitter when you walked through the door. You're it if you want the job."

"Jesus H. European Christ! When I was young I had a beer taste and a rainwater income; as I got older I developed a whiskey taste and a beer income. When I did real well, which I did for a time, I had a champagne taste and a whiskey income. I've been back on the rainwater income for some time now and I do need walkin' around money. But a gorilla sitter!'

"Take your time. Think about it."

"Strangely enough, Phil, I've always had a fascination for those animals, so it's odd you should offer me this job. Come to think of it, every time I worked in a city where there was a zoo I'd go, and very soon I'd find myself visiting the apes. And when you get in close proximity to apes, it's hard to escape the feeling that they're watching you as closely as you're watching them.

"There was this one gorilla in San Diego. I visited him quite a bit, and he looked at me with so much curiosity and amusement that I began to wonder what he thought of me. I found myself wanting to talk to him, because I know he was thinking, 'What kind of a strange creature is that?' In fact I did try to talk to him—his name was Mbongo—maybe you've heard of him. He was well-known in the San Diego Zoo for his intelligence. This was back in the forties, before your time, but I've never forgotten him. If I showed up and called his name he'd come over and we'd stand there staring at each other. He seemed just like a primitive man to me. Ever hear of that gorilla? There haven't been that many in captivity in North America."

"As a matter of fact, I have. That's very enlightening. Makes me certain you're the ideal man for this job."

"I wonder what ever happened to Mbongo?"

"I know that, too. All zoos keep records on these things, and that helps other zoos with their problems. He died after a brief illness that baffled everybody, but the autopsy showed it was caused by a fungus that destroyed his lungs. Humans get it too, from soil or heavy dust conditions. They figured Mbongo got the disease from spores contained in clods of earth that yahoo visitors throw at the gorillas to make them jump. You know, you have to watch people all the time. They'll throw rocks at animals worth seventy-five thousand dollars, and they wouldn't give a damn if they put out an eye, as long as they could see the beast jump. And they certainly wouldn't know if a clump of earth was host to a deadly fungus. It's called San Joaquin disease."

"Damn it all. I'm sorry to hear that. We're a pretty mean lot on the whole, aren't we?"

They both sat in silence for a moment. Phil broke it by asking, "Do you want the job, Dwart?"

"I'll take it," Dwart said, "even before I see this dandy. That is, as long as the wage is not insulting," and he added as an afterthought, "and that it's understood that if I have to do a show, like this Saturday night, that I can take the time to do it."

"That'd be fine. I'm not necessarily looking for one hundred percent surveillance, and the wages will be reasonable. Anyway, it's a job of indeterminate duration, just until we get this beast acclimatized. We place new animals in quarantine. You could play it by ear. Do anything that will keep him calm, like talk to him, sing or something, but just keep watch over him to see he's not getting sick or too excited. Oh, by the way, you'll have other company in there for a while. We've decided to keep a female ape called Amanda in the same room, in another cage."

"I watch two for the price of one."

"Why not? It'll make it more interesting for you. As for Bamboo, if he's asleep, monitor his breathing and watch his chest carefully from time to time."

"Do I have to take his pulse?"

"No. Just watch what he does. You can report to my office if you see anything that strikes you as out of the ordinary."

"I get it—watch for agitation, see if he thrashes around in his sleep, make sure he's breathing because of the throat operation, just use common sense."

"Right. Now let's go over to the infirmary and take a look at them." Travers got to his feet and ushered Dwart along the hallway.

"Can you start tonight?"

"Why not?" answered Dwart as they headed out to the main door. "What time should I be here?"

"Let's say an eight-hour shift, and try ten to six. Eight dollars an hour plus free breakfast. Any other meals while you're at the zoo would be whatever they charge at the cafeteria. They have some good prices there for employees."

As they walked down the infirmary corridor toward the room containing the apes, they met Irving Fluck coming out. Dwart stared in awe at the ogre, while Phil merely nodded and asked, "How is he, Irving?"

"He's okay; they're both okay, except we gotta get that Amanda in the family way."

"Irving Fluck, meet Dwart Farquhart," said Phil.

Dwart tentatively stretched out a hand toward Irving. "Farquhart and Fluck, now that'd make a good name for a comedy team, or even a law firm," said Dwart. They shook hands and Dwart tried not to wince. "Well, okay, make it Fluck 'n Farquhart, then, I don't mind."

"I'm hiring Mr. Farquhart as temporary gorilla sitter for Bamboo, ten to six on the graveyard," said Phil. Then, remembering his previous conversation with Fluck, he added, "He starts tonight, unless security has any objections."

Irving surveyed Dwart for a moment and quickly decided he was a harmless old man, a mistake a lot of people made about Farquhart in particular and old people in general. "Leave your social security number and vital stats at the security office. They'll do the rest."

"Glad to oblige," replied Dwart, and as Travers moved off he followed him into the apes' room. He saw Bamboo lying in one cage and Amanda squatting in the other, and decided they looked less dangerous than Irving. He watched as Travers went close to Bamboo's cage and peered at the ape, paying particular attention to the plastic collar on him.

"It's going to be touchy getting that off," said Phil, "but we'll manage." Turning to Dwart with a sly smile, he added, "With your help, of course, Dwart. Okay, let's go. I'll show you how to punch in before you come back at ten."

"How do you feed him?" asked Dwart as they walked back to the main administration building.

"Bamboo? Well, at the moment..." Travers began.

But Dwart was referring to Irving, and although he didn't say it, he was thinking, If it was me I'd sit him in a corner and feed him with a slingshot. I bet if you looked up ugly in the dictionary, you'd find a picture of Irving.

DWART GOT OFF THE SUBWAY A FEW STOPS FROM his building, mainly so he could walk through the park. This time old Bill Bumphrey was there, sitting alone on a bench, looking as if he was convalescing from an accident. The stray mutt he'd picked up in the park was nowhere in sight.

Bill, being originally from Oklahoma, had decided to call the dog Sooner, but Dwart had suggested he call it Later. The dog answered to both names, but whether Bill called it Sooner or Later, the dog came whenever it damn well pleased.

Dwart joined his friend on the bench. "Got a job today, Bill."

"Good ! Where at?"

"Out at the OP Zoo."

"You don't look too overjoyed about it, Farky. What's the job?"

Dwart hesitated. "I'm going to be a, uh, gorilla sitter."

"A what?"

"A gorilla sitter."

"How do you spell that?"

"I said sitter."

"Why would you do something stupid like that?" exclaimed Bill.

"It runs in my blood."

"Gorilla sitting runs in your blood?"

"No, stupidity runs in my blood," said Dwart.

"Well, it's a job, anyway, Farky, so maybe don't knock it."

"Yeah, keep looking on the bright side."

"That's the spirit. It's a stroke of luck that'll keep your hand out of the dog's mouth for a while."

"Say, Bill, I looked for you this morning when I was passing this way. I haven't seen you for ten days and I was getting worried. What happened to you, anyway? I didn't want to mention it, but you look kinda beat up."

"You're right, I was beat up."

"You mean it?"

"Yeah, I got beat up, rolled and like that, but the real bad part was that I didn't even get laid."

"How much did you lose, Bill?"

"I'm not exactly sure, but about five hundred dollars."

"That much?"

"I'm not jockstrapping you, Farky, it musta been about that. I'd had a few beers over the eight, so I don't rightly remember. Her friends threatened to beat me up worse if I didn't give 'em all I had on me."

"Drinking at your age is only going to confuse your mind."

"You still drink, so what're you talking about?"

"I'm not near as old as you are, and nowadays I stick to one drink only—two ounces of scotch and two drops of water."

"That's a little weird, ain't it?"

"You see, I can still hold my liquor but I can't hold my water. Look, Bill, I'm no pimp, but you've got to stop trying to get laid on your own. With your luck you could fall into a barrel of tits and come out sucking your thumb. There has to be some geriatric-type hookers that you can trust in T.O. somewhere. Let me look into it, will you? I'll ask around at the club."

"Okay, if you say so, Farky, but there's no rush. I don't feel too good right now and anyway, I gotta save up."

"Right. So long for now. This gorilla job starts at ten o'clock tonight and I want to go home for a few hours first. Why don't you go back to that Mount Pleasant Care Home or whatever they call it and hole up there for a while? You need more rest. Say, aren't there any old hookers staying up there?"

"Not so's I'd noticed, Farky," Bill replied, 'and the matron sure hates to give me my own cash if she knows I'm going out lookin' for a wife for the night."

"I'll go up and see her for you, Bill. You need some kind of help, because you can't keep getting rolled like this."

An attractive dowager, on the buxom side, passed close to the bench where they sat. Bill tried to goose her, but missed.

"For God's sake, stop that. If you'd have connected she coulda had you up for sexual assault."

"What're they gonna do to me, put me in jail? I'm in one now."

"Bill, nowadays women are very conscious of their rights, their equal rights with men."

"She can goose me anytime she wants."

"They don't want to be treated as sex objects by men; that's part of what the Women's Liberation Movement was all about."

"What about men's liberation? Ain't we still got the right to goose women? I thought that was—what do they call it?—inalienable. It used to be part of the bill of rights, didn't it? I thought John Diefenbaker put that in."

"Listen, personal experience once taught me a good lesson—don't yield to those impulses—and I've refrained from doing so ever since."

"You tellin' me another story, Dwart?"

"It's a true one, Bill, it happened to me. I got punched in the nose by a woman and it was my own fault because I acted on impulse. I was embarrassed, I can tell you. It was in this self-serve cafeteria in Vegas."

"What happened?"

"In line right ahead of me was a heavyset, I might even say huge, gal, one of the fattest I've ever seen. It was a really hot day and she was wearing a cotton dress. I noticed that her dress was, ah, tucked into her rear decolletage."

"Her rear what, Farky? De-col-a-what? Speak

English, I never heard of that word."

"Her rear end. Her ass!"

"Why didn't you say so?"

"Well, I'm a Virgo, and Virgos are very neat. They've got to have everything in place, see? So I just reached forward and pulled the dress out."

"Out of the crack in her ass. You son of a gun. Is that when she punched you in the nose?"

"No, that's not when she hit me. She turned around and cussed me up one side and down the other. Called me every name in the book. So when she turned around again, I figured, well if she's that upset about it, I'll just tuck her dress back in her ass again. And *that's* when she broke my nose."

9

APE SITTER

Dwart checked back into the zoo and went to the infirmary office just before ten o'clock. He'd brought along a book, and the office gave him a pillow for the easy chair they placed in the room harbouring the apes. The gorillas sat in their respective pens looking at him and he reciprocated. The Mexican stand-off was disconcerting, so Dwart tried reading, but his attention was always drawn away from the book by the gorillas. The situation seemed somewhat ridiculous to him. He didn't have a clue what the apes thought of it, but he assumed they felt as uncomfortable as he did.

"Look, you guys," said Dwart, "do you want to talk about it? We've all got our problems, you know. Bamboo, you've got that damn collar to contend with, but don't go into shock about it. They'll take it off soon, I'm sure." Dwart paused. How the devil would they take it off? he wondered.

"Amanda, try to lighten up and get laid, that's

my advice. But I promise you, nobody's going to make a pass at you, not while I'm around, anyway. Unless, of course, you say okay. I'm not going to argue with a lady, and they just want you to have a baby to increase the gorilla population at this zoo. You've probably got your reasons for not wanting to bring a kid into this world. It isn't against your religion, is it? No hanky-panky on the first date, is that it? You don't want to lose your figure? W.C. Fields once said, 'Anybody who hates kids can't be all bad.'"

The apes picked up a bit when he talked to them. They moved away from the far side of their cages and came closer to him. Dwart hunched his chair further forward so he was nearly between them and at close quarters.

"Look, kiddies, I'll read you some from the book here. That'll help pass the time, eh? Now, this isn't the Good Book; I'm not trying to convert you to some religion. Missionaries have likely called on you already in the jungle; they've been pretty well everywhere by now. So you're saying to yourselves, 'Oh, no, not the Bible bit again.' And you're right, this isn't the Bible. Actually, it's not even a smutty book, although the title might make some people think so. It's a treatise called Sound Sex and the Aging Heart, by Scheingold and Wagner. I'll read a bit of that later if you like, more for my sake than yours. I'm only reading it to brush up on the symptoms of atherosclerosis and how it could affect my love life.

"If I did have the Bible here I would read and sayest unto ye, from my mouth, 'Wise up and get thee some wisdom, incline thine ears toward my words, and keep shut thy faces. For have ye not fallen among Philistines? And if ye wouldst keep in good health, and figuratively speaking, not become the central figures in the ass-kicking contest that constitutes this zoo in which ye find thyselves, then again I say unto you, harken unto my pearls of advisement, for ye are not swine, but Mighty Great Jeezly Apes.

"And so, verily I say unto you, when thou findest thyselves in the city, be it named Rome or Toronto, do as the Torontonians do—screw! And I tell you, dearly beloved, if thou canst no longer fight nor flee, then go thou with the flow, for those in charge are heading down the road in a horse-drawn aircraft without a pilot, and there are more horse's asses in the human world than there are horses, and that's a fact, Jack!

"And remember the words of Adam as he said unto Eve upon the first occasion he did cast his orbs upon her after eating the apple: 'Stand back, Eve, for I knowest not how big this thing gets, and you might get hurt.'

"Now I sayest in conclusion unto you both, why dost thou not laugh? Because these are the jokes. And I also sayeth, am I going too fast for you?

"How did you like that, kiddies?" asked Dwart. He couldn't tell whether he'd caught the apes' interest, because he couldn't read the facial expressions and body language that formed such an important part of their communication system.

"The Bible wouldn't teach you how to speak in the modern manner, now, would it?" Dwart remarked after a pause. "It's too archaic by half, and anyway, it might just be a good way to learn about the ignorance of past ages, who's to say? I suppose the real thing that separates man from animals is mindless superstition and senseless routine. Phil says to talk to you, so I will.

"The Bible does talk about animals. It says, 'Do unto others as ye would have them do unto you,' and that's its basic truth and value. Now, by the others, Jesus might have meant apes, right? And therein lies the rub. There's talk of unfortunate animals in the Bible too, and you Bamboo, are nothing if not one unfortunate victim of circumstance.

"I bet you can't tell me the name of the physically afflicted animal mentioned in the Bible. No? An affliction is something like what you have, Bamboo. You don't know, of course, do you? I'll give you a hint. It had to do with an animal's eyesight. Give up? Okay, I'll tell you, then. It was a bear, and his name was Gladly, get it? Gladly the cross I'd bear! Oh, God, I'm telling bad jokes to apes."

On reflection, he decided that was nothing new. Dwart realized he'd taken on a tough job, and that once the novelty wore off, it could get pretty dull. *Poor bastards. This is no life, really. What'll I talk about next? Tell 'em my philosophy of life? Is this an English-speaking audi-*

ence? I'd like to get a seat out there myself, so I could listen to this. Maybe at least the sounds were soothing. Dwart couldn't tell, so he carried on to pass the time.

"Man is born of woman, he grows through childhood and reaches puberty, becomes a man himself, takes unto himself a spouse and has children of his own, who grow in turn while he ages and his body deteriorates, until finally he dies and his bones are interred in the grave. And the grave is in a meadow and ashes to ashes and dust to dust, his body disintegrates and enriches the soil. The grasses in the meadow send down their roots into the soil and they grow luxuriant. And a horse wanders through that meadow and eats the grass, and through natural bodily processes the horse digests the grass and takes the nutrition from what he eats and defecates the rest back upon the ground.

"The moral of this story, my friends, and my philosophy of life is: As you walk through the meadow of life, never kick a horse turd, it may be your uncle."

Dwart looked inquiringly at the apes. "How do you like those horse apples?" he queried. "What do you know, a silent sitting ovation from the audience! They're even lying down. Great. Look, all a guy can hope for is harmony in his old age, but he's unlikely to get it, because no matter how good his intentions are, he usually ends up kicking horse turds down the road of life and causing consternation in waves among all concerned. What the hey! No use sweating it."

The apes had fallen asleep, and Dwart spent the rest of the night dozing or reading the book on the sexual proclivities and problems of the aged.

He felt he had to get Bill Bumphrey fixed up with some kind of female contact. There had to be some sexual solution for a guy in his eighties who still had the urge and figured the Wright brothers couldn't get it up the first time, either. The book said that the average for sex among the over-seventy crowd was 0.9 times a week. *How do you go about getting 0.9 of a piece of tail? That must be why they call it a piece, 'cause nobody gets all of it.*

When six a.m. rolled around, he shuffled sleepily into the cafeteria, where he got his free breakfast of two eggs over easy, a side order of bacon, brown toast, marmalade, a large glass of grapefruit juice and a couple of cups of coffee. Not enough egg yolks if you were to believe the bullshit in the Weekly World News, but a damn good meal nonetheless. Then he dropped by Phil Travers' office. There was no one there that early in the morning and he had nothing to report. Spotting a blackboard on the office wall, he wrote in chalk:

> 7 a.m. Thursday
> - *Down in the cages something stirred.*
> - *Was it a gorilla stirred?*
> - *Yes!* D.F.

TEN DAYS AFTER THE OPERATION, THEY WERE READY to take the plastic Elizabethan collar from Bamboo's neck. Everyone was anxious to see whether all had gone well with the operation; only time would tell regarding his internal condition. Travers was there with Gil Brodeur, zoo veterinarians Paddon and James and four security guards led by Irving Fluck.

"Okay, guys, what's the plan?" asked Travers as they stood outside the infirmary.

"The collar is held at the base by a heavy strip of padded plastic which we melded into place when we finished the operation," said Gil. "You have to get at that with these pruning shears, snip the strap, and the collar will snap open, because it's hinged to make that possible. The shears aren't pointed at the ends and the tips are covered in plastic, to eliminate the risk of cutting the animal. The strap doesn't have to be severed in any particular place, so just get under it with the shears and cut. I'd say the back would be safest and easiest. Let's try to do it in one motion, if possible."

"Who are you talking to? Who's going to do that?" a chorus of voices asked.

"That's why I brought Irving," Phil said with a smile, "He's responsible for the delivery of one great ape in great shape and he's responsible for security. So it should be his job. What's your plan, Irving?"

Irving scowled. "We have these soft rope snares," he replied, "and we're going to use four of 'em. It's like a fishing expedition. He's sleeping, so now's the time to start. Let's go."

"That's what these poles and thingumajigs are—snares?" asked Gil.

"Right. See this noose?" said Irving, indicating a lasso on the end of a rope that was hooked loosely onto the end of each pole. "We try to snare all four limbs at the same time, and we eventually have to get a noose around each arm. That's the minimum. Do that right away before he gets too excited and starts to move around a lot."

"It's going to be tricky," commented Brodeur.

"You're damn right, but it works, I've done it before," continued Irving. "Remember, guys, as soon as you get the noose over the hand, arm, foot or leg, you pull on the rope and you have the limb lassoed. Then we'll pull him over to the edge of the cage where that semi-window hatch'll be open, so we can get at him easier. Try to keep his back to the mesh and his arms stretched wide to each side. I'll have the shears and reach in and snip that connecting strip that holds the collar in place."

"I'm sorry we have to do it this way, people," offered Travers, "but the vets don't recommend knocking him out with more dope. You can't keep giving them too much of that stuff, it could have harmful side effects."

"Even if we can't get the collar off ourselves, if we can get the strap snipped, he'll soon take it off himself, without our help," said Paddon.

"Let's give it a try and hope it works," ordered Irving, and they all quietly entered the building.

It did work, after a fashion. After a quick but strenuous tug of war between the great ape and the guards, it ended in a tie. Bamboo sensed they were trying to do something to help him and weren't trying to kill him, but he put up a remarkable struggle just the same.

Fluck's role was the most dangerous. He managed to snip the strap on the collar with the shears, just as Bamboo jerked one arm loose and swung his hand through the hatch with all his might, striking Fluck a terrific blow across the left forearm. The follow-through caught Irving squarely in the testicles. He let out a scream of pain and involuntarily clutched at his groin with his good right hand. Unfortunately, it still held the pruning shears and he stabbed himself in the left thigh just under his crotch. The plasticized points saved him from serious injury, but blood began to blotch his khaki coveralls as he lay doubled up on the floor, groaning. One of the guards slammed the hatch shut. Everyone dropped their snares and gathered around Fluck. The guards half-carried him out and down the hall to the emergency room of the veterinary hospital. Fluck screamed imprecations at Bamboo all the way: "I'll get you for that, you son of a bitch, if it's the last thing I do!" he howled.

"I hope he didn't mean that," Brodeur remarked to Travers, "I thought we were trying to save the gorillas."

"Ah, I don't think he did," replied Phil hastily. "After all, what would you say just after you got cracked like that in the family jewels? And his arm looked like it was broken, too."

"Don't think I wasn't thinking about that possibility and worse when I was operating on him," Gil observed.

Once the excitement had died down, Brodeur noticed that Bamboo had pried the collar from around his neck and shoulders and tossed it into a corner. The incision site was completely healed.

WHEN DWART SHOWED UP FOR THE NIGHT SHIFT in gorilla city a week later, Bamboo was a much improved ape. He'd gone through trying and traumatic times, but both his pain and the strange, irksome collar were gone. He'd lost weight, but was starting to eat a lot more of the ample food provided.

After a week of observing the apes, Dwart had come to appreciate the wide range of feelings they could express through gesture: disgust, jealousy, vanity, joy, you name it. He'd also become acutely aware that intonation was a highly developed skill in gorillas, that there appeared to be a universal language among them based on pitch and tone.

Dwart knew he had to establish some form of meaningful communication with the gorillas, or the job would become a bore, and he didn't want to take the zoo's money just for sitting there. He'd read somewhere that people were trying to talk to apes and chimpanzees by using common symbols that both the ape and the human would punch into a computer. Dwart figured he could do something like that, make up a series of everyday requests the apes could use, then break those requests down into nouns and verbs like apple, banana, give, and make. Maybe he could get a book on Ameslan and teach them sign language for the deaf. It would certainly help pass the long nights. That decided, he settled back in his easy chair and he and the gorillas slept.

There were a dozen apes in the Ontario Provincial Zoo compounds. Most of the adults were about the same age, and Charlie, a huge silverback, was their leader. Barney was twelve years old, maybe more, and the father of Catherine, who'd been born a year and a half earlier. The mother was Caroline. The other males were Pauncho Grande, an ape the guards called Xerox; and another they called Assenich because he was always scratching. The females were Josephine, Julia, Tabitha and Samantha. The keepers called another female Igga Lou because she was best able to withstand the cold. Samantha, a teenager the same age as Tabitha, had a baby called Natasha.

When Amanda was three and a half years old, she was part of a group of young apes in the Cincinnati Zoo that had received sign training. The program was cut back before she became proficient, and it wasn't continued when she was transferred to the Toronto zoo.

Bamboo's voice and ability to communicate with other apes had been impaired by his wound and operation, and he still found that his efforts to do so sounded strange to his ears. How he sounded to

Amanda he didn't know, but from her body language and her replies, she was having some difficulty understanding him. He couldn't seem to control the exact nature, pitch or tone of the sounds that were leaving his throat and mouth. His brain started them out one way and they came out another. Nevertheless, they managed after a fashion.

"Old White-Eyes is asleep," said Bamboo, "why him come here night, watch, make noises?"

"Friendly," replied Amanda.

"Yes, not hurt like some others," said Bamboo, glancing sharply at Amanda to see if she understood his statement. He felt she did, and continued: "Ugly him, not strong." Bamboo got this across with the aid of a lot of gesturing.

"Them are all ugly, but none as ugly as the big one," noted Amanda bitterly.

"Mean. Hurt him bad. No mean us soon."

"Watch out for that white-eyes, or..."and she signed a slash motion across her throat.

"You here longer me. This all this place?" he asked, waving his hand around the room.

Amanda explained that it wasn't, that there was an outside where they usually stayed and that it was like where she came from, only much smaller, no jungle, hardly any trees, but grass and some other apes. There were some hard, thin vines around it and also a hard substance you could see through. When it was hot they were usually outside; but for long periods it got very cold, and then they were herded into the smaller enclosure with a roof, where it was warm.

"What them like, white-eyes?" Bamboo asked, struggling to get that meaning across to Amanda.

Some signs were universal. Amanda made a yakkety-yak dribble mouth gesture with one hand and pointed to her rectum with the other.

Bamboo stared and then broke into ape laughter for the first time since his capture. Amanda joined him in a chuckling sound not unlike a suppressed, heaving, human laugh.

THE APES WERE ASLEEP WHEN DWART LEFT AT six; he hadn't talked to them much that night. He finished breakfast and by eight-thirty he was at the Mount Pleasant Care Home in downtown Toronto, talking to the supervisor.

Patricia Stacker made impatient movements with her large, expressive hands as she succinctly described Bill Bumphrey's problem and her concern for him.

"He's not capable of making sound decisions where either his finances or women are concerned," she said.

"Who can?" murmured Dwart in reply.

"For example, Mr. Farquhart, he recently withdrew five hundred dollars from his savings, went into town and got beaten up by a prostitute and her friends around Yonge and Jarvis streets. He was brought back here in an ambulance, broke. And that wasn't the first time. Once he withdrew two thousand dollars, travelled to Montreal, and when he was sent back from a men's hostel a week later, he couldn't account for any of the money."

"What about his family?" asked Dwart, "do they—"

"A couple of cousins only, and they've given me to understand that they don't want to be in charge of his money," continued Ms. Stacker.

"Now that is unusual," observed Dwart.

"They do suggest, and I agree, that the Public Trustee and Guardian's Office of Ontario handle his affairs."

"Financial or sexual?"

"Mr. Farquhart, please! People should learn to age gracefully! An old man like him has no business trying to—."

Dwart leaned forward and interrupted her: "That's a lot of bull, Ms. Stacker. Yes, that's what I said. Nobody grows old gracefully, as you put it. Some oldsters bottle it up and die inside. That's a mistake. Guys like Bill are yelling out that they're trying to live right up to the date they have to pay their dues to life. You have to give him credit for trying. It's not over till it's over."

"I suppose I should take a less severe attitude, Mr. Farquhart," she said, taken aback. "I'm sorry, I guess his attitude is better than those who become so appalled at the changes in their bodies that they just give up."

"Right on, Ms. Stacker. May I call you Patti? I don't agree with the Jonathan Swift quote, when he said, 'No wise man ever wishes to be younger.' I'm more inclined to agree with the Abbess Brantome when she said, 'Old ladies take as much pleasure in love as do the young ones.' I can only presume she might also have been referring to men."

Giving him a searching look, Stacker said, "I'm glad we had this talk, Mr. Farquhart. And may I call you Dwart?"

"By all means," said Dwart pleasantly, 'and you let me know when you get old. Meanwhile, back at the ranch, Bill Bumphrey still has a problem."

"Yes, and he deserves some help from his friends. The Public Trustee and Guardian's Office must be approached."

"Please, let me write to them," Dwart offered.

Stacker thought this over. "Fine, and I'll back you up," she declared, clapping her hands. "Maybe they'll listen if friends as well as officials ask them to look into the situation."

"I'll do it right away and send you a copy, Patricia. Good-bye for now, then. But I'll be seeing you again. We have a date."

Dwart wrote the letter that very morning, in longhand, and one of the secretaries at the zoo typed it up for him.

To: Public Trustee and Guardian's Office,
Toronto, Ontario.

Re: William Bumphrey, Mount Pleasant Care Home
Dear Sir or Madam:

More than a few long-term supporters of the government, including yours truly, are concerned about the financial and physical welfare of the above-mentioned party.

Mr. Bumphrey is in his eighties. Supervisor Patricia Stacker of Mount Pleasant will have the details and I believe your office has dealings with her from time to time.

Several times a year, Mr. Bumphrey accumulates his extra funds and goes into Toronto or Montreal looking for a wife for the night. A few days later he is returned in poor physical condition, having been beaten and robbed, and with nil funds left upon his person.

Would this happen if he lived in Climax, Saskatchewan? Likely not, but it happens here. What position does the public trustee take in these instances? Would you suggest it was up to the relatives to take the legal action necessary to name some party like the Public Guardian as a committee to see that he doesn't misuse his funds? I presume, for instance, that you or I will be entitled to blow our funds as we see fit when we're in our eighties, unless some doctor is prepared to say we're non compos mentis and incapable of handling same. And the way doctors invest their money, I'm not sure they should be the ones to decide such things.

In the case of Mr. Bumphrey, all interested parties, inclusive of the care home, his friends and his two distant cousins, are genuinely concerned for his physical and general welfare. The relatives do not wish to handle his funds, whose amounts I believe are small to medium. Again, the Care Home will have the details.

Perhaps the Public Guardian and your office could look into providing genital hookers in these old-age care homes, so that these old men wouldn't have to travel into the wilder parts of Toronto, Montreal, or Climax, in an attempt to obtain the services they require.

Your advice appreciated, with copy to Ms. Stacker.

Yours Sincerely,
Dwart Farquhart.

10

THE PINK PUSSYCAT

The building had existed for a long time, by Canadian standards. The bricks froze in the icy six-month winter and roasted in the heat of summer. In the sometimes harsh springs and falls they cracked with every temporary thaw, antiquing the facade till it looked like an old citadel. The edifice exuded a sleazy elegance.

In its early days, "Dive" might just as well have been written over the wide front entrance door, because that was what the prudes had called it then. The Baptists probably coined the term den of iniquity, while the Episcopalians used haunt of debauchery; both descriptions of the place constituted good advertising for the upholstered sewer on Dundas Street. The one-time nightclub was still serving a purpose in society as the Pink Pussycat Strip Club.

The front door still featured brass fixtures shaped like mammary glands. To its earlier regu-

lars, the establishment was known as Knockers.
Visitors grasped a breast and knocked, and the
bouncer would slide open a panel in the door to
see who sought admission to the ornate foyer.
Nowadays the bouncer was called the lounge
superintendent and nobody had to knock to get
in. The standee customers still drank at the raised
bar which ran the length of one side of the
lounge. Behind the bar, antique mirrors were
interspersed with old pictures of nude ladies of
the evening, draped in various poses across chaise
longues and loveseats. The old-fashioned bar was
the club's best feature. Patrons could feel yester-
year when they put their foot on the brass rail and
ordered a pint of the best.

Overhead, the ceiling was painted dark blue
with small inset lights that twinkled, when they
worked, like stars in a midnight sky. A strobe light
shot bright reflections around the room. Booths
and tables encircled a dance floor, now greatly
reduced in size from the big band days. Fronting
this whole scene was an old proscenium arch
stage, raised high above the floor, that sported
faded red velvet curtains.

A lot of nostalgia here, thought Dwart as he
entered. But the Pink Pussycat, like nostalgia,
wasn't what it used to be, entertainment-wise, and
not necessarily because it was now a strip club.
Some strippers were highly skilled dancers and
talented exponents of the fine art of striptease.
The Pink Pussycat hadn't been hiring too many of

those in recent times. Instead, it had degenerated
into a joint, presenting a never-ending succession
of run-of-the-street strippers. Well, except for one,
the headliner, who called herself Little Else.
Dwart liked her, as she was one of the minority
who injected some comedy into her routine.

Else used black light and wore a long, black
velvet dress. A light wooden rod was sewn along
the bottom hem of the widely flared skirt. The
rod broke into two sections that could be snapped
together quickly at mid-point like a break-down
pool cue. This break was necessary to enable the
dress to hang more naturally during her opening
movements. When Else seized both ends of the
lower portion of the rodded skirt and raised her
arms overhead, a fluorescent painting of a bare-
breasted girl with outstretched arms and tassels
hanging from each nipple glowed in the black
light. Else could easily twirl these tassels by slight
rotations of the overhead rods in her own unseen
black gloved hands. When she turned her poste-
rior to the laughing audience, she displayed two
white gloves sewn to the buttocks of her panties,
simulating men's hands. Little Else was also good
at quips and asides as she danced before the audience. The act went over well and made her a hit
in stripping circles.

The club was under new management: Burr
McClintock, an experienced and tough operator
and an old acquaintance of Dwart's, had acquired
an interest in the place, and Dwart had hopes that

better times were to come in the form of more varied and talented entertainers.

Dwart was standing in for the regular master of ceremonies, but this wasn't burlesque anymore. He'd gotten in on the tail end of the real McCoy: America's raunchy, sawdust-on-the-floor, vaudeville-oriented version of the much older music halls of England. Burlesque played to a rough trade, through blue smoke with blue jokes. The buffoons and comics wore loud suits and loud make-up. The talking ladies, though not entirely naked, were a bum and tit show, and the chorus lines were flashy and hardbitten. It had been noisy, raucous, uninhibited entertainment based on sex, booze and taboos, and therefore wonderfully popular and successful. The bumps in the night business had its discomforts and heartaches, its rewards and compensations, but in the final analysis, it provided the sheer joy of performing before real live audiences, making customers laugh and in some small way, contributing to their happiness. The modern stand-up comedy club had taken over the legacy.

There'd been no strippers in the early days of burlesque theatre as Dwart had known them, and the comedy elements predominated. The stripping had gradually increased at the expense of the comedic talent, at which point true burlesque began its slow decline into a lengthy succession of prolonged and never-ending versions of female disrobement. A few strippers could make

undressing a form of Terpsichorean art, but Dwart
felt that the constant repetition became boring,
because modern strippers didn't seem to understand that the sex act is basically funny. They
tended to confuse stark nudity with titillation.
Genuinely sexy women left something to the
imagination, and that didn't include bare beavers
in the spotlights viewed from gynecology row. In
their defence, however, he knew that strippers
understood the large part that movement and
bodily gestures played in the sex game.

On the English stage after World War II, the
censors used to allow full frontal nudity if there
was absolutely no movement by the girl. If she
moved, then she and the establishment could be
charged with conducting an obscene performance. What the censors meant to prevent was
too much excitement in the male observer.

Dwart figured that good burlesque or music
hall required as strict a discipline as any other
comedy form. The comedian anywhere was the
tightrope artist of laughter. Comedy was a risky
business fraught with flop sweat and it needed discipline to make it work. Burlesque, being a
wilder, farther out and broader type of humour,
had to be calculated that much more precisely.
Dwart had decided long ago that if you analyzed
humour too closely, it wasn't funny anymore, so
he left the theories to the professional types and
to the critics, who usually couldn't find their ass
with both hands.

Dwart changed into his old tux, in the one feature of nightspots that never seemed to change—the cubby-hole dressing room that he figured must once have been a broom closet. Then he checked in with McClintock, who was the manager, head barkeep and bouncer. Burr was a big, friendly limey whose jacket always looked too tight because of his muscles. He was slow to anger but most people were careful not to get him riled. He had a body like the old heavyweight boxer Two-Ton Tony Galento, the Jersey Nightstick, and a sociable and weather-beaten face with an RAF moustache that hid his mouth entirely. Dwart felt safe when he was around.

"You're lookin' sharp, Farky," Burr greeted him.

"Should be, I've had a shit, shave, shower, shoe-shine and shampoo, plus a change of shirt, shorts and socks."

"Like to be a goodly crowd here tonight," opined Burr, "that municipal G-string bylaw caused a forty-percent drop in business, but the courts said it was unconstitutional. Here, read this," and he handed the newspaper clipping to Dwart as he slid a pint of house draft in a frosted mug across the bar.

The story headline read *Zing go the G-Strings off dancers' parts.* Dwart read it as he sipped his beer.

TORONTO—The playful twang of G-strings snapping off is sounding through Toronto strip bars in celebration of a court decision that permits exotic dancers to bare all. The Court of Appeal overturned a lower court

*decision quashing a local bylaw that compelled strippers
to cover their lower extremities with bikini bottoms or the
demure patch of sequined material known as a G-string.*

"Proves the justice system still works in Canada," said Burr.

"Great news. Glad it helps you."

"One other thing, Fark. I'm spelling off the strippers with a rock n' roll band. Just so you know."

"Jesus, Burr. Not rock n' roll."

"What's wrong with it?"

"What isn't? The decibels'll deafen you, and it's just plain boring. What happened to Lou Lolla and His Lollapaloozas? They played real burlesque music. The girls don't want to strip to rock n' roll."

"I switched to tape for the strippers. Just as good and cheaper. Rock brings in a younger crowd and everybody drinks more. I lowered the price of standard drinks and put in a shooter's bar."

"You can get an awful hangover with shooters."

"Sure, but you and I know enough not to drink 'em."

"Ah, well, everything changes. Hook-and-eye became zipper, which became velcro."

"Right. And we're not only relying on a bunch of drunken jokers who want to stare at vagina from Regina. We're going to have wrestling in jello, wet T-shirt contests, and male strippers for Ladies' Night."

"I suppose the next thing'll be table dancing: bare beavers at point-blank range."

"That's an idea. But this week I hired some feature dancers, and they quiver the muscles that'll make your muscle quiver. Cost me some more dough, but I think it'll pay off. Check 'em out, you're the one who's gonna be introducin' them."

"I will," replied Dwart.

"One more thing I should tell you, Farky. Lately we been gettin' some bikers in 'ere. Call themselves the Bandits. I'm kinda worried about it, but it hasn't been bad for business so far. I try to talk to 'em in their own language."

"Knew some bikers in California. Do these guys wear Levi's that look as if they've been left under their bikes every night to soak up crankcase drippings? Are their denim jackets and colours so ragged they're barely functional? Are we talking real bikers?"

"Nah, these guys wear silver-studded phantom leather jackets. I'd be more worried if they wore beat-up starvation army fur coats or ratty Nazi uniforms. They don't even have B.O."

"Sounds more like a leather fetish cult—the Brando or Dylan type. A real biker would call anybody chicken-shit who rode in leather."

"All I'm sayin', Farky, is don't start in on them, just don't provoke 'em."

"They aren't going to beat up on an old fart like me."

"Don't be too sure. Anyway, I don't want the place busted up, I don't want to have to call the cops and I don't want a biker revenge party."

"I'll keep that in mind," Dwart replied, and headed backstage.

Bikers weren't what he was worried about

when he performed; his secret concern was the possibility of suspended forgetfulness on stage, an inability to remember the exact lines of a joke, especially if he tried new material. He knew the lines but he couldn't always remember them quickly enough. On stage a few seconds could seem like an eternity. This wasn't an old man's game. You had to be fast, so why was he pushing himself? *Well, hafta make a living.*

The Pink Pussycat's customers didn't always listen politely. They paid for drinks and a raucous good time, and a comic had to work his ass off to make them laugh. That was the bottom line, make 'em laugh. But sometimes his brain didn't want to be bothered. Was that a clue that he should quit? Young comics had a ton of energy pouring out of them, effusive and infectious. He could only compete with them because he was experienced.

Most of the stuff you worry about never happens, thought Dwart. I'm not ready to quit yet, so screw them all but six and save them for pallbearers.

The girls invited him into their dressing room, where he always felt like a one-legged man in an ass-kicking contest.

He saw Little Else in one of the mirrors and she asked after his health. "Haven't seen you in a couple of weeks, Farky."

"No, but I've been thinking about you, Else. Matter of fact, I dreamt about you only last night."

"Did you?" asked Else.

"No—you wouldn't let me!" replied Dwart, and

she laughed. "Any new acts I should know about?"

"Aha, yes, we got a couple of Asians. Claim they're twins, but who knows? They strip at the same time, choreographed in unison."

"Sounds good. I like working with Asian girls. Once you work with a Chinese broad, an hour later you want to work with her again."

Dwart spent some time with all the strippers, making notes on their stage name, background, alleged place of origin and the nature of their speciality. He didn't have to know a lot, just something other than the fact that they were going to take it all off. They were performers and wanted to have their vital statistics correct in the introduction.

"You gonna be hot tonight?" Else asked as he was leaving the dressing room.

"Remains to be seen, depends on the crowd. Say, maybe we could have coffee and a bite after the last show. I don't like to go home to bed right away."

"Neither do I. See you at the Chances R after the show, then."

It was Saturday night and the crowd would soon build from fair to full house. The tapes on the P.A. were belting out a medley of *Night Train* and *G-String Twist*, and when he heard the last bars of *Girdles Away*, Farky strode out to the mike and started his warm-up.

"Ladies and gentlemen, and I speak advisedly, my name is Dwart Farquhart, and I'm pinch hitting for your regular emcee, Lord Lovas. He couldn't get out of a sick bed to be here tonight...his girl friend has the flu. Matter of fact, my best girlfriend is in bed with laryngitis. Damn those Greeks! Why don't they get their own women?

"I worked this club earlier in the summer and I think I'm going to be hired again next winter, because I heard the owner say, 'It's going to be a frosty Friday when this guy comes back again.'

"Uh-oh, is this going to be a tough crowd! Over here we have some drop-out nuns...and there's some Jehovah's Witness conventioneers...the best seats are right up here in front, and we've got a proctologist and a member of the Audubon Society sitting there already. Do we have any celebrations going on tonight? Is that your wife, sir, or a shack-up? There's a guy over there with two broads: double your pleasure, double your fun, shack up with two broads, instead of one! One of you girls is going to have it pretty soft...

"This the first time you've been here, sir? Well, the Pink Pussycat is the wildest and most provocative show in Toronto...you may've read about it in Watch Tower, the Christian Science Monitor and the Catholic Digest...they all said not to come. So that's why you're here? I can see right now that you're allergic to bullshit...So what was I talking about? Oh, yes, any celebrations, wedding anniversaries, anyone expecting? Anyone hoping to be expecting...clean underwear, divorce? I don't believe in divorce. I believe every three years the licence should expire. Divorce—it's like buying oats for a dead horse...you can't even get a ride anymore. And alimony—that's the screwing you get for the screwing you got..."

A woman at the bar laughed heartily.

"Ladies and gentlemen, here, to the Pink Pussycat, is where you come to study the science of stripology—the science of disrobing in public, where you see a lot taken off little by little. The way a woman takes off her clothes reveals her feelings about herself, the man she's with, love, and sex. We have all styles of girls here tonight...we've got señoritas, frauleins, the great comic stripper Little Else, an Oriental twin act, the Bride of Dracula, Bubbles LaTour the Fou-Fou dancer, and a French demoiselle. Oh, yes, and I guess you heard that every once in a while we have a streaker named Desire...

"Now, the first young lady out here onstage tonight is going to disrobe to the music of *Must Be Jelly 'Cause Jam Don't Shake Like That.* She's the energetic bombshell type; if you give her a little hand, folks, you're liable to surprise her...so let's give her a big hand and scare the hell out of her...Miss Fifi LaTouche, the French Canadian Connection!"

In response to Dwart's exhortations the early evening drinkers came up with a desultory round of applause. Fifi stuck her lovely tush through the break in the curtains and gyrated her buttocks onto the stage, as the quadraphonic amplifiers began to play *Paradise*, signalling the commencement of another evening at the Pink Pussy.

When she finished baring it all to sparse applause, Farquhart went back out to the mike. "I see there are some members of the P.T.A. here tonight. You know what that means, don't you? Poon Tang Anonymous...I'll just tell a couple more jokes and then we'll all take off our clothes and run around the room a bit...good clean fun. Then we can sit around naked and criticize each other...No?...Well, it would sure as hell surprise the next stripper who comes out here...

"Hope you've all got good seats. It can get real crowded in here. A party of sixty-eight walked in here just the other night—drank a lot, too—I never saw a guy sixty-eight drink so much...

His woman fan let out a high-pitched hoot.

"Have we got some girls here for you tonight! Speaking of girls, you know, there are two types of women. There's the hedonistic type...pleasure is the only good. This type says, 'Let's go make love in the park'...but this straightforward approach doesn't appeal to the cultivated man. 'No', he says, 'Let's go make love in the art gallery!'...this way he can satisfy his libido and still remain cultured...Then there's the narcissistic type...loves only herself...in bed she's hungry, at the table she gets sexy...and when you're passing a motel she never says she's sleepy..."

Carrying on in this vein, the Old Fart did the job he was paid to do, gradually warming up the audience, who began to respond with appreciative laughter.

Suddenly a hush stole over the crowd, starting

at the rear and expanding like ripples in a pond. Dwart squinted through the spotlight and felt a little wave of adrenalin speed through his arteries. Trailing in and upsetting the neighbouring patrons as they did so was a group of black leather-clad bikers, accompanied by their leather dolls. From the colours they displayed, they had to be the Bandits that Burr had warned him about.

A sense of menace preceded their approach, as their overall appearance was somewhere between sinister and bizarre. Whatever else you could say about them, thought Dwart, you couldn't accuse them of modesty. One was sporting a pointed beard and a blue derby hat, another's beard was dyed purple, offsetting a gold earring, a nose ring and blind-man black glasses. Hard to tell the women from the men because they all wore black leather.

Were they really battle-scarred veterans of beer hall punch-outs, or merely emulators of a style that fascinated some people in their struggle for self-expression? Dwart didn't see any greasy denim vests or chequered shirts with sweat-stained armpits. These bikers looked mean, but the odds were they were bust-outs from the workaday murk, who got their kicks from jolting people by their appearance. Just out for the evening to suck up some beer and make noise. Live and let live, he thought, they haven't started anything yet. A pause. "Where was I?" Dwart asked.

The laughing lady in the audience yelled, "Love!"

"Yes, we were talking about love. Love, or was it sex?—there is a difference—I'll always remember the first time I had sex, back in the 1930s, in the back seat of a Chevrolet...it would have been a lot more fun if I hadn't been alone...I really should tell you that before I got married the first time, I'd been dating my wife for about five years. Then one day I went around to see her father. I looked him right in the eye. He said, 'Hello.' I said, 'Hello.' He said, 'What do you want?' I said, 'I've been dating your daughter for five years.' He said 'So what?' I said, 'I want to marry her.' He said, 'I thought you wanted a pension.' And then he said, 'if you marry my daughter I'll give you ten acres and a cow.'

At that point Dwart took a long pause, then said, "You're absolutely right: I'm still waiting for the ten acres...

"Well, you don't get this old without having been around a bit, and I've been married twice and divorced twice. Both divorces were as a direct result of travelling to Las Vegas. I travel a lot—with this act I have to. We took a holiday in Vegas and my first wife followed me and caught me coming out of a motel with a midget broad from Circus Circus...I tried to tell her I was just cutting down...Well, you have to say something, man, you can't just stand there...I took my second wife to Vegas one time and we were gambling, and it was, like, two in the morning, and she says, 'Dwart, I'm just plain wore out, I'm going up to the room.' I said, 'Okay, I'll be up there in a little while.' An hour later when I finish playing black-jack, I go up to the room. There she is on the bed, zonked out, sound asleep, stark naked, snoring with her mouth wide open. I went into the bath-room and got two aspirins and I walked over to the bed on tippy toes, and I dropped those two aspirins right into her mouth. She sat up gaggin' and spittin' and said, 'My God, what happened, what did you do?' I said, 'I just dropped a couple of aspirins in your mouth.' She said, 'What the hell for? I ain't got a headache!' Again Dwart paused. "I said, *'Good!'*..."

As he told the divorce jokes Dwart was think-ing, that isn't the way it was at all. My only divorce hurt like hell, just like any death. Smile through the tears and be done with it. Things can be desperate, but they don't have to be serious.

At the last punchline, the biker with the nose ring said, "Bullshit!"

Dwart stopped and facing left, asked into the mike, "What did you say, sir? Sorry, I didn't quite catch it. And I don't think the people over there by the bar caught it, either."

"I said, 'Bullshit!'" the biker repeated.

"Oh, good, did you get that over there? He said 'Bullshit.' You see, sir, it's tough when you're the comic. Let me explain it to you. If you're going to heckle, you have to do it loud and clear, other-wise it's hard to respond properly. So okay, gang, he said that story was bullshit. Let's clear that up. How many of you over on that side agree with him? If you do, then let's hear it from you, too. Everybody's entitled to their opinion."

A good number of people on the right side of the hall yelled, "Bullshit!"

"Fine," said Dwart. "Now this side. How many over here agree?"

A roar of "Bullshit!" went up.

"I'm glad we got that straightened out; because you're right, you know. You're very perceptive and you recognize bullshit immediately. You guys—the Bandits, is it?—are here primarily for the rock n' roll band, I take it."

"That's right," came the reply from the back.

"How could I tell? This mass of black leather comes in, must be, oh, an entire herd of cattle in that group, ladies and gentlemen, many cows died to clothe these folks..."

"Are you saying we look funny?" demanded another biker angrily.

"Well, yes and no—just different—to me, that is. But then, we're from different eras."

"Different what?"

"Eras—time periods. We don't think or dress alike, is what I mean. No problem."

A loud reply from the gloom, "Not for us. Are you some kind of a queer?"

"Not only is he a big bugger, but he wants to talk about gays. Maybe he's gay. Oh, God, I shouldn't have said that, he'll beat me up and take advantage of me...I don't care what I say up here, I'm protected by Blue Cross..."

The purple-bearded heckler came back with "Is that a toupee you're wearing or did your cat die?"

"You folks can see I'm in trouble, but I'll either fix it or make it worse. All kidding aside, fella, it's tough to believe that out of a hundred thousand sperm you were the fastest...see, folks? This always happens. Now his friend is saying, 'Did you hear what he fucking said? Was that an insult? Yeah! Well, let's get him.'"

"You could be fucking well right, old-timer," said purple beard.

"Old-timer, you say. Is that it, Mr. Bullshit? It's not me personally, it's because I'm an old-timer?"

Several of the Harley-Davidson crowd began yelling insults peppered with four-letter words.

His mind searched for a comic routine, any sequence of humour involving age. *Got it. Yeah, the numbers bit. Whose routine was that originally? Who cares? They likely haven't heard it. Get cracking, start talking right now. Good—my brain still seems to work in a pinch.*

"Old-timer? Just let me explain age to you gentlemen. We're all grown-ups here tonight. You hope so, anyway, don't you, Burr?" said Dwart, raising his voice on the last sentence and aiming it at the bar. "You know, the only time in our lives that we want to get older is when we're little kids. You, sir, you'll remember that, I'm sure. When you're younger than ten, eleven years old, you're so excited about getting older that you even think in fractions.

"If someone asks, 'How old are you?' you say," Dwight imitated a child's voice, 'Five-and-a-half.' You're never thirty-six-and-a-half." Again in a childish voice, he said, 'And goin' on six!'

"Now when you get into your teens, you're pickin' up a little speed and you go right into the next number— 'I'm gonna be sixteen' —and you could be only fourteen when you say that. Then comes the greatest day in your life. You become twenty-one...you all remember that day, don't you? And the phrase has a nice sound to it, doesn't it? You *become* twenty-one...

"Yes," and here he paused, "but you *turn* thirty...wait a minute, slow down, whoa, what's happening here? It makes you sound like rotten yogurt...'Oh, yeah, he turned thirty and we had to throw him out'...

"It's not getting to be so much fun anymore, this growing old. It's getting different, little kids are calling you old-timer. What happened?

"You turn thirty, you're *pushing* forty"...Dwart paused. "And then you *reach* fifty. Goddammit!" Dwart started to cry, then speeding up his delivery, he continued. "You become twenty-one, turn thirty—you *make it* to sixty...yes folks..." Speeding up his delivery even more, "You become twenty-one, turn thirty, push forty, reach fifty, make it to sixty. Then you build up so much speed, you *hit* seventy...

"After that it's day by day...after that you hit Saturday. When you get into your eighties, you start *hitting* dinnertime. You *turn* noon...and twenty-year-olds in nightclubs are yelling, 'Fuck you, old-timer! And fuck the horse you rode in on!'

"And it comes to us all, you see, so we might as well be friends, you and me, Mr. Bullshit..."

Dwart noted that most of the Bandits were now laughing with him.

"But there's hope for everyone. When you get into your nineties, you start counting backwards. Yeah, you've heard ninety-year-olds say," —here Dwart adopted a quavering voice— "'I was just nine-ty-two.' Now if you make it over one hundred, then you become a little kid again. 'I'm one hundred and five-and-a-half...goin' on a hundred and six.'"

"What I said, you old fart," said Bluebeard from the audience, but in a friendly tone, "was that I didn't like your fucking jacket."

"Well, thank you very much, Mr. Pierre Fucking Cardin...you'll have to give me the name of your tailor...by the way, have you met Burr McClintock, our manager, bouncer and barkeep here? He's still around, I hope," said Dwart, peering around the room, "he weighs two-fifty and he's mean, man."

Burr spoke up from the bar, "I'm here, Farky, doin' a helluva job makin' big bucks, don't bother me." The crowd laughed, including the black leather jackets.

"Thank you very much, Burr...I feel much safer now...Yeah, beautiful, Burr.." Adopting a feminine voice, Dwart continued, "Excuse me, Burr, but Farky's getting the shit thumped out of him on the stage,"...and lowering it again, "and all you'll say, Burr, is 'Oh, well, make sure he pays his bar tab before he leaves, okay?'

"It's chopped liver for you, Farky!" and the black leather jackets began to chuckle among themselves. Everyone was back in a good mood.

Dwart's body language and smile throughout hadn't conveyed animosity. He'd jumped on them quickly, he'd kept his cool, and he was out of a potentially bad situation. Maybe he'd have a drink with them at one of the breaks in the show. And although they might do some future heckling, it would always be friendly. Part of his job.

"I'd like to conduct a scientific experiment here tonight. I'll try to find out what kind of humour the rest of you people laugh at. Is this a live audience? Did you hear the one about the sixty-five-year-old man who got circumcised? They asked him how it looked and he said, 'Like Yul Brynner in a turtle-neck sweater.'"

This got a chorus of groans except for the lone woman laugher at the bar. "Would you mind moving around the room, please, madam, so it'll sound like the laughs are coming from all over? Thank you...Now we know what some of you don't like.

"But now, on with the show. A little later this evening the four Skinner Sisters will sing *If Marriage is the Road to Happiness, I'm On One Helluva Detour*. But first let's get another of our famous exponents of the art of disrobement out here on stage to entertain you. This next gal is going to show you something different. As the fly said as he was walking over the mirror, 'That's one way of looking at it.' This next young lady is going to disrobe to the music of *My Old Kentucky Home.* Yes, and if you give her enough applause you'll get to see Louisville, a little town down there in the southern part of Kentucky, where she's been working in a house of ill repute. But then they sent her to never-never land, the Virgin Islands, for recycling. She's from the U.S. of A., so put your hands together in a nice round of applause for Polly Esther, the Baby Doll of Burlesque."

And another stripper hit the stage, and so it went. He introduced the crotch-watchers to Bessie-May Mucho the Latin Bombshell, Little Orpheum Annie, Jet Crystal, and a vampire act, Fangs for the Memories, in which the gal came out of a coffin complete with fangs, blue lights and a castle backdrop. She was supposed to dance in a fog nearly up to her snapper, but the fogging machine had run out of dry ice.

Dwart did a short joke sequence before every strip, and sitting with the bikers at intermission, he pretended to buy a round of drinks, which he knew Burr would put on the house. Unless Dwart told them otherwise, the waitresses always served him straight Coke. If he was going to hang around a bar into the wee hours and didn't want to get swacked, he had to have what looked like a drink in his hand. Self-defence against those who would otherwise ply him with alcohol. Dwart didn't have the stomach for booze anymore, and if he was going to drink he liked to pick his own time, place and friends.

As the night wound down, the joint rocked and the band rolled, the last stripper revealed all. Dwart got paid, packed his ancient tux into his one-suiter bag and headed for the Chances R like a big-assed bird.

The diner never seemed to close and Little Else and several other strippers were having a late- night sandwich. Dwart sat in and regaled them, with embellishments, about his new job and the gorillas.

"Do you think they'll get it on together?" asked Little Orpheum Annie. "They sound cute."

"Probably very nice, if you get to know them. But can you communicate with them?" was Elsie's comment.

"They talk to each other," said Dwart, "but it's pretty weird stuff. I talk to them all the time for something to do and to show I'm friendly. I feel sorry for that big fella they brought in from Africa. Must be very strange for him."

"Life sure played a dirty trick on him," said Polly.

"Sure has. I'd like to be able to communicate with them. World's biggest problem—lack of meaningful communication. Did you girls ever read any of Kurt Vonnegut's books?"

"What eez eet, that he did write?" asked Fifi LaTouche.

"Well, he wrote a book called *Slaughterhouse Five*. You may have heard of that one, because they made it into a movie."

"I saw dat," said Fifi.

"In his novel, *Breakfast of Champions*, Vonnegut had a short plot about failure to communicate."

"What was da plot?"

"I thought you'd never ask," said Dwart. The plot was, and I think I can quote it nearly verbatim, that a flying saucer creature named Zog arrived on Earth to explain how wars could be prevented and how cancer could be cured. He brought the information from Margo, a planet where the natives conversed by means of farting and tap dancing.

"Zog landed at night in Connecticut. He had no sooner touched down than he saw a house on fire. He rushed into the house, farting and tap dancing, trying to warn the inhabitants about the terrible danger they were in. The head of the household, a golf pro, ran out of the bedroom and brained Zog with a golf club—a mashie niblick, I think—and killed him. Which is why earth still doesn't know how to prevent wars or cure cancer."

The girls laughed. Dwart told them that ever since he'd read that story, he'd had a strange, recurring dream, and that the dream seemed to be triggered by the story itself, as if it were true.

"And what is dat dream, Farky?" asked Fifi.

"It happens I'm also a student of the works of Edgar Cayce. Now, we don't have time to go into his theories, but suffice it to say that he figured there were thought waves which emanate from everybody, past and present, which forever circle the globe through the ether, and that certain people have the ability to hook into this stream of thought. Certainly Cayce could do so when he was in a trance. An amazing man, a seer. And now I think I'm also plugged into that river of knowledge when I have this recurring dream."

"What's the dream?" they asked in unison

"This dream that I'm gradually piecing together is that Zog has a brother called Zig. The learned creatures on the planet Margo are going to give Earth another chance, and they're sending another space craft to Earth, piloted by Zig. This time they want to be sure he's going to communicate with whoever he contacts and talks to on Earth, so that we can learn how to prevent wars and cure cancer. They still, of course, only converse by means of farting and tap dancing.

"Now it seems they're trying to get through and make contact with a large number of people on Earth by means of these thought waves in dreams. I'm apparently one of these people. The message they're sending me is that I'm to tell as many people on Earth as possible that Zig's coming, and that when he arrives, you must be ready and able to communicate with him. The message I pass on to you girls tonight is that you're only half-ready to communicate with Zig...and that you have to start taking tap dancing lessons tomorrow..."

"Oh, my God," gasped Polly, laughing with the

rest, "stop, all this laughing is hurting my lip."

"How come?" asked Elsie.

"I was picking fruit all last week on my parent's old fruit farm, and my lips and face got chapped," replied Polly.

"When I was on a ranch out near Calgary, I learned what was good for chapped lips," offered Dwart.

"What?"

"Horse manure."

"Come off it."

"Seriously, an old cowhand told me about it," said Dwart. "He said you rub it on your chapped lips: it doesn't cure them, but it sure as hell keeps you from licking them!"

"Quit while you're up, Farky," moaned Else, "that one is just too old."

"Sorry 'bout that."

"What are you doing tomorrow? I mean later today," asked Elsie, changing the subject.

"Why?"

"How about Sunday dinner? My mother would like you and she needs a good laugh. You could come before you went out to the zoo."

"Are you serious?"

"Yes, I'm inviting you," replied Little Else. "I'll drop you off at your place tonight so I'll know where you live and pick you up at, say, four o'clock?"

"You talked me into it," Dwart replied with delight. "I haven't had a home-cooked meal for some time, good, bad or indifferent."

11

SOMETHING ELSE EGAN

Dwart lounged in his pyjamas and gazed apathetically upon the state of his sordid housekeeping rooms. The mess didn't inspire him to any rectifying action. Elsie was due to pick him up later that day for the dinner she'd promised, and he was looking forward to the occasion and the change of scenery.

Like the inveterate reader he was, he'd spent the morning perusing Time, Maclean's and the weekend edition of the Globe and Mail.An Associated Press article from Indianapolis made him think of Bamboo and the progress of his throat operation. The ape had been making some very strange noises lately.

The precious gift of speech will come back to Virginia Lacey today in the form of a twenty dollar plastic and rubber device implanted in her throat.

For the first time since cancer took her larynx, or voice box, Lacey, sixty-two, of Chicago, will be able to speak without the aid of electronics.

Though the device itself is cheap, surgeons say the procedure necessary to implant it could cost as much as five thousand dollars. Many people have had their larynx removed during surgery for cancer of the throat. The larynx is a small box of cartilage atop the trachea, or windpipe. It contains the vocal cords, which vibrate under air pressure to produce the sounds of speech.

Dwart was suitably impressed.

The day was bright and sunny, with the heavy humidity that was typical for Toronto. He wished he could afford air-conditioned quarters. He waited until mid-afternoon to shower, then dressed in light blue slacks and a grey short-sleeved shirt to go with his white windbreaker. As he watched from his upper story window, Elsie's refurbished 1960 Falcon convertible, red to match her hair, pulled up under the trees in front of his building. Dwart didn't want to keep her waiting, and he certainly didn't want her to get a look at his living space, so he came out of the house as Elsie was coming up the walk.

"I don't usually see you with your clothes on," was Dwart's opening remark. "You've been down to some expensive boutiques and got you some."

"It's daytime, Dwart, that's all."

"Night or day, you are a comely wench."

"Thank you, kind sir," she said. "Your coach awaits."

"I see you got a Falcon," said Dwart.

"No. If you ask me, I thought I got a damn

good deal," was her quick reply, making Dwart grin at the play on words.

They got into the convertible and headed across town on the 401 toward Islington. Elsie pulled up in front of a bungalow set well back from the street and surrounded by trees, shrubs, flowers and a lawn.

"Thank God, no pink flamingos," said Dwart under his breath. They entered the living room as Elsie's mother came in from the kitchen. The elder woman was a strikingly slim figure in perfect form-fitting light cream slacks, matching high-heeled shoes, and a blouse of some multipasteled Indian print, with a fringe leather sash around her waist. Looking higher, Dwart noticed that gold-scaled Chinese carp of various sizes hung from the pendant around her neck. The woman was sixty-plus or minus and obviously in good shape, but it was her face and eyes that riveted his attention. A modicum of make-up expertly well applied gave her pretty features the fine colouring of a fashion model.

She smiled and stretched out her hand. Good teeth but some overbite there, thought Dwart. Nose a little on the sharp side. Some freckles, no, lots of freckles. Dwart pegged her as being of Irish stock and formerly a redhead, although her hair was now a stylish salt-and-pepper gray. Not dyed. Only the young dye good, he thought. He looked into her flecked gray-green eyes as Little Else said, "Mr. Farquhart, Farky, I'd like you to meet Something Else!"

"You're absolutely right—she is!" said Dwart in a low voice.

"That's what I said, silly," said Elsie.

"I know, but I mean, what shall I...Mrs., uh...the last name was, uh..."

Elsie came to his rescue. "Egan," she said, "she's Something Else Egan."

"It told you I agree," Dwart replied, "and you're not whistling Dixie when you say that, but how do I address your mother?"

"Just don't call me Mother, Mr. Farquhart," said the mother.

"You have me at a disadvantage, ma'am," sputtered Dwart. "While I'm prepared to admit—although frankly on such short acquaintance, I hardly think it's my place—that you are something else again. However, I, I...have to call you...well, I can't call you that all evening. Elsie, help me out here. You know I don't go around calling people Mrs. Jones for too long."

"Her stage name was Something Else Again, said Little Else, "but her full name is really Something Else Knott-Egan."

Dwart was beginning to think this was a put-on.

"Elsie, how does a ventriloquist like you manage to work so far away from your dummy, or should I say mummy? Look, let's start all over. Introduce me to your lovely mother and tell me her name," and he spun around in a circle and came back to face them.

"All right, Dwart, now listen, and listen good," said Elsie.

"Believe me, I'm listening."

"My mother had a stage name when she was in the business, Something Else Again. But in private life she hyphenated both of her real last names. She was married twice, the first time to a man called Knott, the second time to a man called Egan—hence Knott-Egan—so she is in fact Something Else Knott-Egan. Why do you think they call me Little Else Egan?"

"I never knew your last name. I know Little Else is your stage name, but that's all you ever told me."

"You never asked me."

The mother looked from one to the other and they all started to laugh. "A little confusing at first, isn't it, Mr. Farquhart?" she said.

"So, what shall I call you? Something, or Else?"

"Either one will do. Maybe Something, so you don't confuse me with my daughter. Now, sit down, make yourself comfortable and I'll get you a drink. What will you have?"

"Could I have a small scotch and water?"

"Certainly. I saw you at the Pink Pussycat several months ago when I went down to pick up Elsie. Why didn't you ask for a double scotch with two drops of water, like you did that night on the stage?"

"Because I can hold my liquor but I can't hold my water," Dwart shot back. "Jokes, yeah, you're making me feel right at home. Thanks."

"You're welcome, Mr. Farquhart."

"Please, call me Dwart."

"Sure, be right back," and she went into the kitchen. Little Else went with her.

Although Something had left the room, a faint reminder of her presence still lingered. Dwart breathed deeply and leaned back in his chair. Something's happening here, he thought, as he eagerly awaited her return. Some kind of chemistry was working on his mind and body. His heart seemed to be beating faster.

They passed the time before dinner in easy conversation and Dwart sniffed appreciatively. "Judging from those delicious odours, I wouldn't have thought that with your domestic talents you would have become a stripteuse."

"Thank you," replied Something. "I gave it up when I got married and had Elsie. And you can only strip so long, don't you think?"

"You're right," Dwart replied, "one girl told me you could do it just as long as you didn't have a big appendicitis scar."

"I got out of it when stripping became more pornographic than erotic. Sexual suggestion is one thing, healthy even. But they go too far nowadays. What can they do for an encore? There's nothing left."

"Likely Elsie learned from you. Her act is one of the very few funny ones left in the game, that I've seen, anyway."

"Finish your drink while I get the dinner on the table."

The meal exceeded Dwart's expectations.

Restaurants were fine, but a homelike atmosphere made for a memorable feast.

Dwart learned that Something had been both
widowed and divorced; that Little Else figured
there were only three kinds of guys you met in
singles bars and strip joints: jocks, weirdos and
married men; and the mother told the daughter
that you have to kiss an awful lot of toads before
you find Prince Charming.

They asked him how he was able to come up
with all the material he used as a stand-up comic.
Dwart said you just had to have the desire, some
innate talent, timing, and keep working on your
material and your memory. You had to make or
get the opportunity to perform, then gradually
learn by observation and on-the-job experience.

Elsie wanted to know if there were schools that
taught comedy. "Maybe, but they aren't likely to
work. You don't go to a proctologist for tennis elbow.
But if you don't know your ass from your elbow,
then you do. As I said, you learn comedy from experience, by observation, maybe by osmosis."

Dwart learned a little more about Mrs. Knott-
Egan. It seemed strange to him that she should
have once been in the seamy strip business, and
had apparently encouraged her daughter to do
likewise. The truth, as he pieced it together from
the conversation, was that Knott was a nut she'd
married at seventeen, with the mistaken idea that
it would release her from the welfare conditions
of a home on the wrong side of the tracks.

She'd lived with six siblings, a work-shattered mother and a dissolute Irish father who came and went without notice, providing only paltry support for his family. But the Knott marriage promised only a repeat performance of her mother's fate, so she cast about for a way out of her new dilemma. She had little education, her main assets consisting of a bright mind, a beautiful face and an excellent figure.

She happened to go to the midway of the Royal American Shows at the big-city exhibition, and was enticed by the barker into a sideshow called Harlem in Havana.

She and Dwart reminisced about the old-fashioned shows, and Dwart mimicked the candy butcher moving up and down the aisles of the big tent, giving his pitch:

"Before the curtain goes up on our scintillating extravaganza, folks, we have a special offer for this show only, a box of your favourite candy, with a prize in each and every package. There's a solid gold plated wristwatch—yes, that's right, Mac. As I was saying to you lucky people here tonight—and you truly are lucky—a solid gold plated wristwatch and dozens of other prizes of great value are yours for the taking. This is a special offer, ladies and gentlemen, only twenty-five cents, a quarter of a dollar, for the box of candies and a prize in each and every pack. This is the last call, absolutely the last call..."

Then Something Else imitated the barker out

front, with his swaggering walk, exhorting the
crowds: "and now, ladies and gentlemen, we are
pleased to present live, both comedy and our
long-stemmed beauties, plus the featured artistry
of Blue Sapphire, a real gem of burlesque, and
her number, Blues for a Lady. See slithering,
seductive, sensuous damsels shed their costumes.
See Blue and her lovely girls au naturel in this
SINsational revue. Step right up, folks, the ticket
booth is right over here."

Mrs. Egan explained that she'd paid her way in
to see the star, Blue Sapphire, spent two bits and
bought the box of candy, but there was no wristwatch. As for Blue, she was no Gypsy Rose Lee,
but she was good and she was sexy, and she knew
how to tantalize the predominantly male but
unsophisticated crowd.

After the show, Something had made her way
backstage, wanting to know more about the business. A carny pointed her toward the female
dressing area in a trailer behind the show tent.
Blue Sapphire was more accustomed to stage-
door johnnies, so she was wary when her caller
turned out to be a young woman.

"I'd like to get into this business," Something
said, "how do I go about it?"

"So would a lot of people, honey," replied Blue,
half listening, "but why pick on me? I'm not running a school for strippers."

"Then why don't you consider it? I might be
your star pupil."

"And," she told Dwart, "I eventually did study with her, as Something Else Again."

"So, that was you," Dwart said. "Now I remember the name. And I've heard of Blue Sapphire, too. What was she like?' asked Dwart.

"Blue was her stage name, of course. She had a small blue rose tattooed two-thirds of the way up the inside of her left leg. She never did tell anyone her real name as far as I know. She may have, but I don't really know. Whenever anyone asked her, she'd make up a new name, so you never did find out the truth. She played sort of a bad name game, giving herself different make-believe names."

"Sort of like what W.C. Fields used to do," interjected Dwart.

"Yes, names like Olga Schwartz, or Bertha Sherstibitoff, Delores del Smutz, Tess Tickle, or Gertrude Bustbinder, names like that. Anything."

It was late evening when Dwart suddenly realized he had to leave, and Little Else remembered her offer to drive him out to the zoo for his nightly stint of gorilla sitting. The women were keenly interested in Bamboo and Amanda and the possibility of a touching romance between the two primates.

"Could we come out to the zoo and visit them sometime?" asked Little Else.

"I'm sure I can arrange it," said Dwart. "In fact, why not, I'm their guru, aren't I? Sure, I'll lay on a visit for you."

12

GORILLA MONGERING

Dwart's gorilla-sitting job was ending, just when
he and Bamboo were beginning to communicate.
They'd progressed to exchanging the hand-to-
chest gesture that signifies honest emotion.
Despite the cage that still enclosed Bamboo, he
and Dwart stood close to each other, and they'd
once touched through the bars. These were signs
of mutual acceptance, so Dwart felt a pang of
regret when Travers announced that the gorilla
was acclimatized and his health sufficiently stabi-
lized for him to be taken out of quarantine and
placed in the nature compound on public display.

Amanda occasionally indulged in a slow, subtle
rolling of her pelvis when communicating with
Bamboo. She crossed and uncrossed her legs
when he watched her and sometimes she caressed
the inside of her knee or thigh. Of course, she
couldn't re-arrange her hair or smooth her dress;
nor could Bamboo straighten his tie, pull up his

socks or check his fingernails. He did, however, stretch his body, strut a bit and thrust his chin up and forward. The non-verbal exchanges encouraged the zoo staff's cautious hopes of future progeny resulting from the apes' mating.

Travers had come to like Farquhart and wanted to keep him on in some capacity. But it wasn't zoo policy to hire people of his age in regular jobs. Phil figured that Dwart would need some special skill in order to justify his retention.

"I could hire you as a specialist of some kind, if I could just figure out what that specialty might be," Travers told Dwart.

"How about calling me an ape monger?" Dwart suggested. The idea had just occurred to him.

"An ape what?'

"Monger. You know. It's an old Saxon word for a trader or dealer. People only use that noun in English classes now, but it's still a good word."

"One who mongers apes, I suppose," Phil replied, doodling on a pad with one of his pencils, "and then there are ironmongers and whoremongers. People have heard of them, so the terminology seems right."

"And I've been studying them, Phil. Apes, not whores. Been reading about them down at the public library. Those gorillas make a lot of noises, but what do the sounds mean? I've been thinking it's a basic language they use among themselves. Aren't some sounds common to all species? Somebody has to study that stuff, but it turns out not many people have. So who's to say who's an expert? And the people who do it could be called ape mongers."

"Yes, there are people who do that kind of study," answered Phil. "There's one group down on an island in the Panama Canal. The Smithsonian runs it. Then there's the Gorilla Foundation in California and the Dian Fossey Gorilla Fund International, based in Atlanta. I'll dig out some stuff from our library for you."

Travers swung his chair around, looking out the window at his beloved zoo. He said nothing for a few moments, stroking his goatee. "You're a fast talker, Farquhart. And you have an empathy for apes. You could have a latent talent for a job like this. I'm going to keep you on for a while as an ape monger. By God, that ought to baffle the board of directors."

"But not on the night shift, right?" Dwart interjected.

"You didn't like that, I take it."

"It was getting a little rough on rats, and interfering a little with some speaking jobs I might get. Anyway, the apes slept most of the time."

"I'll leave it up to you. But keep up the odd night. You've got a roving commission as ape monger. Let's say five hours a day maximum. That's all I can afford."

"Now that I've become an expert, I should be entitled to a raise. A salary commensurate with my title." Dwart was smiling as he said it.

Phil returned the smile and replied, "You're an expert when I see some results. I'll look up those journals for you, and as much other literature as I can locate over the weekend. And I'm pleased you're trying sign language. Amanda's file indicates she had early training in it, but no one's had time to do anything more with her."

"It's supposed to be independent of the spoken word, but they're not deaf, so you can combine signs with short, simple terms. Seems to work better, and they make noises back. They're extremely intelligent."

"They certainly are, and that becomes more obvious when you give them the tools to access that innate intelligence."

"Would their brains make it possible for gorillas to understand spoken words even though they couldn't answer?"

"It's hard to know how much they understand. But as for talking, no. Doc Brodeur could give it to you in detail, but there are too many differences in their throat and vocal cord make-up."

"But they do make a lot of different noises. I bet if I use sign language along with the same instructions in simple English, the gorillas might get to understand the words as well as the signs, even if all they can do is sign back," said Dwart.

"You may be right, although I'm not sure how it would work. My guess is, they'd have to separate their understanding of the meaning of the words from the expression in sign language, then use that perception of the separation between word and gesture. That's expecting a lot, but it may work with simple commands."

"Phil, I know I sometimes come off as just a joker; it's just a defence mechanism. But I'm serious about this. Ape mongering, or whatever you want to call it, is a lot tougher job than I ever figured, but a worthwhile endeavor. I've roamed the world but rarely become involved in a cause. That's as good a way as any to end up with the thin edge of nothing, sharpened to a point and then broken off. I want to get involved in this. I'm not fluent in signing and I'm slow, but it's a good language. Has its problems, same as most things. Takes twice as long to complete a gesture as it does to say the equivalent word, so you find yourself talking pidgin English. You start to put a premium on economy of expression, so even fluent experts would say 'shop me,' rather than 'I'm going to the shop.'"

"I understand. I only know the bare rudiments myself," remarked Phil.

"I've met some deaf people. They know all the signs and they've got patience. They'd think it was a great opportunity if one of them could be an assistant. I can get a little bit of volunteerism, but if you could see your way clear to—"

"Dwart, give me a break," Phil interrupted, "I know it's worthwhile, but...," Phil stopped, aware of Dwart's intense gaze. "Okay, I'll take it up with the board, find out what kind of financing they'd be willing to put into such a project. Now, get out of here before you can ask for anything else."

Reaching for a sharp pencil, Phil went back to work on the stack of paper on his desk.

DWART EXPLAINED HIS NEW THEORY TO

Something Else Knott-Egan over a Raspberry Fool in a Yorkville bistro. She was quite enjoying herself. Apart from the fact that she'd skip soup, salad and main course any day to have three helpings of gooseberry, raspberry or any other kind of Fool, she found her new friend both funny and attractive. She gave him a fleeting smile from beneath the brim of her monstrously large, but very elegant hat.

Dwart reached out to touch her hand, saying, "I'm going to ask you again, what do I call you? What's your real first name, or do you have a middle name?"

"I agree, Something Else is too cumbersome and confusing and it wears thin after a while." She raised her wine goblet, her sea-green eyes looking at him over the rim of the glass.

Dwart swore her eyes kept changing colour.

"If I tell you all of my name, the one I officially use, it's only fair that you tell me all of yours. Deal?"

"Deal."

"My name is Elspeth A. Egan. The A stands for Annalese, so I'm Elspeth Annalese Egan. You can call me Elspeth, but I don't let many people do that."

"I like it, but then I have to tell you that I'd probably like any name they called you," offered Dwart gallantly, as they held steady eye contact. I'm getting soppy, he thought, but she is cool classic beauty. It's the eyes, like banked fires, glowing coals under the ashes in a fireplace.

"It's your kick at the cat," said Elspeth with a grin.

"Strangely enough I have the same middle initial as you do. Dwart A. Farquhart. God, what a

moniker! The A stands for, now get this: Aloysius.
How do you like them apples?'

To her credit, Elspeth didn't laugh, but there
was a long pause before she replied, "Forget it, I
was just getting used to Dwart. But here we are,
Aloysius and Elspeth, having lunch—unbelievable.
Let's change the subject. Oh look, here comes
Elsie. It's time for us to go meet your apes."

Dwart had access to all the areas inhabited by
the gorillas. There were a few relatively private
spots where only a wire mesh separated man and
ape. That was where Dwart usually came to
attempt communication with the animals, and it
was where he took Elspeth and Elsie, who were
delighted to be so close to the gorillas.

Elsie buttonholed one of the keepers, Angie, who
had worked for several years with the gorillas, been
eyeball to eyeball with their leader, big Charlie, and
had a degree in psychology and primatology.

"I expected more of a natural habitat, more of
a jungle atmosphere, more trees."

"Trees in a small compound wouldn't regener-
ate. Too difficult and expensive," answered
Angie. "Also, the apes here are escape artists, so
we had to enclose the entire area. The inner
compound used to be open to the sky, but they
kept finding ways to get out. So they roofed the
entire outer compound with mesh."

"Has the idea of a natural environment ever
been tried?" Elsie persisted.

"Sure, on a small scale, at a private wildlife park

in southern England. At Woodland Park in Seattle, too, and then there's an organization in California that's trying to set a big one up in Hawaii. Dr. Francine Patterson runs the Gorilla Foundation. She's in charge of the project teaching sign language to a couple of apes, a form of Ameslan, really. The gorillas are called Koko and Michael. I belong to the Foundation and I keep up with what they're doing. Koko has a sign language vocabulary of nearly a thousand words," said the young guide, eager to show off her knowledge.

"And everyone knows about Jane Goodall's great work with chimpanzees. She's proven that they're capable of rational thought and simple problem solving, and can feel emotions like joy, sorrow and despair. And of course, there's the GO-APE Society, too."

"Most of the gorillas are in the enclosed compound now. How do you get them in and out?" Elsie asked.

"You see those two big windows in that building between the inside and outside compounds? That's sort of an in-between spot where you can shift them back and forth. We do most of our feeding in there. That gets them out of either compound so we can clean up. It doesn't always work, but if we really want to confine an animal, we have a squeeze cage in there. You have to coax the gorilla into a kind of tunnel cage, then you bring the back wall forward and squeeze them till they can't move very much, or at all."

"How strong are they?" Elspeth wanted to know.

"They're pretty strong, but they're good about playing with each other. When they get older, they don't play as much," Angie explained.

"Something like adult humans," Elspeth remarked.

"Yeah, they'd rather lie around and rest."

"Do you go in there with the gorillas?" Elsie asked, looking at her in awe at such a prospect.

"Only with the young ones."

"What if you went in with the big ones?"

"The females are no problem. I raised two of them from youngsters, so as far as they're concerned, it wouldn't be a fair test of danger."

"Do they remember you, always recognize you?"

"They're really affectionate. They'll come over and sit beside you and want to get scratched and groomed. They're like us that way. They even get to know regular zoo visitors, they recognize them and their voices."

"How about the males? Would they bother you?" asked Elsie.

"I'm not supposed to go in alone with them. I don't think they'd hurt me, but it's in their nature to throw each other around a bit to show who's boss. Doesn't hurt them, but I sure don't want to break any bones or get hurt. You see that group of females? That's Amanda, Tabitha and Julia. We can't get them pregnant. With Amanda, I think it's just her dominance—she was the head of the group for so long that she doesn't want to take a more submissive role in their society."

"How often do the females come in heat?"

"The females aren't receptive when they're lactating. That's their form of birth control in the wild. They can't possibly bring up more than one infant at a time; and like humans, it takes a long time to get a kid to the point where he can look after himself."

"So they don't breed unless they're in heat."

"Right; and then they're amazingly promiscuous. It's like, they supposedly belong to one male, and they'll breed with that male when it's the best time for them to get pregnant. But they don't seem to object to mating with another male in a less peak period, or if they're already pregnant. I don't know why they do that or how they figure out the times."

"Seems very human to me," Elsie commented, "What do you think, Dwart?"

"I wouldn't touch that question with the proverbial ten-foot pole," answered Dwart. "Just count me out of this conversation. Except to say that the promiscuity could be accounted for by the lack of TV. Lord knows what the North American population would be if we didn't have television. Now, if you ladies will excuse me for a few minutes, I have to give a Chinaman a music lesson. I'll leave you in the good hands of our learned friend."

Their guide said to the two women, "Now that your friend's gone, I can tell you that when these apes are younger, they make out all over the place, but when they get to the age when they could and should be having babies, they don't seem to want sex as much."

"I heard of a robin once," said Elspeth, "who

always built her nests with a hole in the bottom. She loved to lay eggs but hated having baby robins."

"We had an ape here, they called her Marilyn. She mated every month of her life for about five years. We were providing her with partners and encouraging her—I actually felt like a pimp. Boy, did she love it! But it took five years for her get pregnant. Whether she just wasn't very fertile, we don't know. Maybe it was the males; they seem to be able to get it up, but it could be their sperm count or something. Their fertility isn't understood too well yet."

"Angie, would these older female gorillas be more prepared to mate if they had a new partner, like Bamboo? Maybe I should ask Mother that question." Elsie ducked the backhander her mother aimed at her head.

"We hope so, but if nothing happens and Amanda doesn't accept him, we can try ape switching."

"Ape switching?"

"Trading apes with another zoo."

"Oh! I can see that," offered Elspeth, "maybe these females don't like the males that are here. Maybe to them it just seems like...kissing their brothers."

"I don't think it's like that," replied Angie, "not with Amanda, anyway. She was used to ruling the roost and the others were afraid of her. Now that the males are bigger and stronger, she doesn't want to admit they're dominant and so she won't act submissively, which she'd have to do if any of them were to mount her."

"Why doesn't she get on top?" Elspeth

quipped. "How about this big guy, Charlie? You must have brought him in after..."

"No, they all came in about the same time. He was little Charlie then and Amanda was bigger, so she was the natural leader for years."

"And now Charlie's the leader?"

"Yes. Well, he and Barney have been separated for maybe a year, but I assume Charlie's still dominant. Barney got mysteriously bitten one night, and we don't know how it happened, but we assumed Charlie ripped his arm open. Mr. Travers hasn't put them together ever since. I still think it was an accident, because they're not vicious by nature—it was just one bite."

"Not as vicious as humans, right?" Elsie remarked.

"Jungle males will fight hard to establish their leadership in a group. Before Charlie and Barney supposedly fought, they got along fine, and the tribe had sort of divided itself into two groups and there were no problems. That's what I'd like to see happen again eventually."

"Now you have Bamboo, a new factor."

"He's certainly new to Amanda. He was never under her domination. I think they'll hit it off. I hope so, because ape switching is a lot of work and a lot of red tape."

Dwart hove back into view and the guide said, "I've got to be going. Nice talking to you. Come again. 'Bye now."

"This is fascinating, Dwart," Elspeth told him,

"we learned a lot, and to think, I've never been out to the zoo before. That guide thought Amanda was one of the most intelligent of this group."

"And they're all escape artists," added Elsie.

"Sure, but they don't have anything here to challenge their intelligence, so that's probably why they try to escape. It's like being in a penitentiary for a human, and these apes never even committed any crimes."

"They may be smarter than some people...that I know, anyway," said Elsie.

"Yes, dear, but you know some pretty dumb people," said her mother.

They went back to the admin building. Elsie had a date, so she headed for the parking lot, leaving Dwart and Elspeth to find their way back by bus.

Lingering over their coffees in the cafeteria, Dwart mused, "Amanda's no virgin, so why is she refusing to have sex? It's strange. You heard the guide's dominance theory?"

"Do you agree with it?"

"I'm only a Johnnie-come-lately in this business, and although I don't know her motives for celibacy, I do know her modus operandi."

"What do you mean?"

Dwart didn't reply immediately. He fiddled with several swizzle sticks, arranging them in the shape of a human figure with outstretched arms and legs. He used a small salt shaker for the head. "The method by which she is able to ward off sex," he finally said.

"What are you doing?"

"Apart from wondering where you got that hat, with which I, and a good many other people around here, seem to be fascinated, these sticks, my dear, represent the present celibate condition of our friend Amanda. Now, the purpose here is this...Can you change the swizzle sticks in any manner, or move them around to demonstrate just how she managed to stay in this terrible celibate state these many years?"

"How can I do that?"

"Think about it," replied Dwart, "Just move the swizzle sticks to show how she keeps herself free of male advances."

Elspeth thought if she moved the legs into a closed position, it would be like the traditional crossing of female legs to prevent intercourse. When she reached out toward the swizzle sticks, Dwart smartly slapped her outstretched hand and said sternly, "Don't touch!"

A moment of shock, a stunned silence, then Elspeth burst into laughter. "You're right, Farky, that's how she does it!"

"This zoo's trying to get across to the animals that the humans are out-fornicating them; that they should get in on a piece of the action, no pun intended.

"No, I'm actually wrong in saying that. It's lack of production, not lack of action that plagues some of these species. If it weren't for that, their sex life would be okay. Did you know that the male lion in charge of a pride of lions may have to make love three thousand times before he could be sure that one new lion would reach maturity?"

"You're kidding me, Dwart. That's enough to make me want to be reincarnated—as a lioness," said Elspeth. "More coffee?"

"No, thanks."

"Don't worry about Amanda. She's still relatively young, she may lose her inhibitions yet."

"I agree. The older I got the more inhibitions I lost. It took the generation after us to start the so-called sexual revolution. Maybe I shouldn't ask, but how did you respond to the shifting tides of the revolution?"

"Sex is like snow, Farky...you never know how many inches you're going to get or how long it'll last."

Dwart looked a little shocked at this sally.

"Maybe I've been around you too long already. To answer that very personal question, Mr. Farquhart, in the strip business you weren't left with many illusions, but you could still have inhibitions."

"It was a good joke. I could use it. You surprised me, is all."

"Just keep in mind that ex-strippers aren't all floozies. You should know that."

"I do. Don't get your dander up. We're both grey panthers here. I know I've been declining sexually since early adolescence, but I'm not taking a back seat to anyone. The rate of decline may be steady, but it's slow."

"And just how do you account for that, sir?"

"As I would say down at the club, I take virility pills. They keep my back from petering out and vice versa...made by the Upjohn company, too, I'll have you know."

"You do a routine about that, don't you? Would you do it for me?"

"You really want to hear it?"

"Yes, I do. Please."

"Well, okay. I'll pretend you're a group of males.

"Gentlemen, these virility pills are really potent. I warn you, when you take one, swallow it fast, or you'll get a stiff neck...I had occasion to send some of these pills to my farmer brother-in-law. He inadvertently dropped some down his well. Took him two weeks to get the pump handle down, and then all he could get was hard water...I accidentally got some mixed up with some bird seed and put it out in the bird feeder. A poor little bird came along and ate one of those pills. That sparrow shot straight up into the sky, boinked two eagles in the air and chased a 747 all the way to Montreal...I warn you, fellas, don't take more than one, or you'll pole vault all the way to the bedroom..etc. etc. That's it, Elspeth."

"Thanks, Dwart, that was great. Seriously, though, aphrodisiacs are something I never knew much of anything about. I mean, is there any truth to the claims that they can cure impotence?

"Why do you want to know?" he teased her. "Say, you're not blushing, are you?"

"Don't be silly, Farky. I've been around too

long for that."

She tended to call him Farky when they lapsed into a joking mood.

"Not long enough for me; and I think you were blushing."

"Never mind that. Just tell me what you know about it."

"Since the advent of Viagra your question is rather moot. But most aphrodisiacs are just multiple vitamin and mineral tablets with added zinc, at about five times the price you'd pay for the same thing in a drug store. A couple of the ingredients might have some value along sexual arousal lines. One's supposed to come from the yohimbine tree in Africa, where they've used it for centuries. Some company mixes it with a small amount of male hormone."

"What about ginseng? I see ads about that."

"Some people swear by it, but I don't know. Do you want to order some ginseng tea and find out?"

"I don't think I need any, smarty."

"I hear that with age you women gain sexual superiority. Do you think that's true?"

"That's what I like about you, Mr. Dwart A. Farquhart. You talk about important things. Your conversation hasn't deteriorated into a morbid preoccupation with cancer, housing, heart disease and general complaints about life."

"Just trying to have some fun out of life."

"Sometimes I think there's a nineteen-year-old in this body trying to get out," said Elspeth, fiddling with a teaspoon.

"I like nineteen-year-olds. How about a date next Friday night? I hear the Squadronaires are playing at the old Casa Loma. Too bad it isn't Glenn Gray, but these guys are good."

"You're on, Dwart, I love dancing."

Dwart excused himself and when he returned, Elspeth asked, "Why do men do that?"

"Do what?'

"I've been sitting here opposite the men's room and I can't help but notice."

"What?"

"When they come out, they check their flies, some more subtly than others, but they all do it. You did it just then, too."

"Oh," said Dwart, taken by surprise, "I guess we just want to make sure that our, ah business isn't, ah, that it's done up."

"But why don't you check while you're inside the biffey?"

"It must be a reflex action, or second nature. Or maybe our mothers were always after us to do up our flies when we were kids."

"A woman wouldn't do that."

"You don't have to. What would you check?"

"So you really don't know why."

"For Pete's sake, Elspeth. You ask the damnedest questions. Next you'll be asking why we scratch our testicles. Do we do it because they itch or because it feels good? Some questions just have no answer."

13

A CON JOB

Bamboo sighed with relief at his release from confinement. The bars to his escape weren't so obvious in the compounds. As he walked on the grass and swung from the large timber poles, an exuberant sense of renewed hope surged through his body. With cupped hands, he beat a tattoo on his chest, just as he used to do in the jungle whenever he felt in fine spirits.

The hairless white and black apes watching him from the other side of the heavy mesh fence attributed this gesture to anger or alarm. Whenever Bamboo stood upright and walked toward them, they shrank back for a moment, then chattered among themselves as they observed his erect stance, his arms at his sides and the way he stepped on the flat of his feet.

Bamboo was just as interested in the visitors, and when he stood quite close to them, quietly reserved and dignified, they usually fell silent and mirrored his pose. Bamboo wasn't erratic or hysterical like the monkeys, so people would try to talk to him, just like the old white-eyes that was with him for part of most days. Occasionally, he tried some vocalization of his own. Although neither understood the other's words, they could discern each other's desire to communicate.

The situation was very different from his first meeting with the white apes. Bamboo was getting used to many new things, and he noted that the white-eyes all talked like his friend, the one who watched over him, who seemed to be known as the Old Fart, whatever that meant. He kept Amanda's warnings about these creatures in mind, but still felt a need to speak with his captors. They knew a lot more about some things than he did, and he was anxious to learn all he could.

NEITHER DWART NOR BAMBOO REALIZED IT, but their thoughts were converging. For his part, Dwart hadn't figured he'd take such an interest in the great apes. He wasn't afraid of them at all, and they seemed to sense he was an ally. He gradually came closer to the gorillas until they were touching each other, first through the wire mesh and then inside the compounds, without any barriers. In his continuing research he'd come across the work of John Aspinol of the Wildlife Park Zoo in southern England. Aspinol spent a great deal of time with a band of nineteen great apes in their large compound. He'd even wrestled with a male silverback and found the animal to be gentle, never using his great strength.

Dwart decided he'd try the same thing with Bamboo. How do you wrestle with a gorilla? Very carefully, he thought. He didn't dare try it with anyone but Bamboo or Amanda, because of their mutual trust, but the other gorillas watched and tolerated his presence among them.

Bamboo listened closely to Dwart, the zoo personnel and the humans who visited the gorilla area. When he was alone, he tried out the various sounds they made, but with little success, and he couldn't seem to speak the way he used to.

Several of the white-eyes' sounds and phrases were repeated quite often, and usually at the same place in any conversation. When they met, and often when they were just standing there looking at him, they said *hel-lo*. When they went away they said *goood-by*.

Dwart spent increasingly long periods in libraries, researching experiments in animal language and trying to understand how gorillas thought. If he was going to be paid as an ape monger, he'd damn well be a good one.

He learned that dolphins could imitate human sounds through their blow holes. Now if only humans could imitate dolphins through theirs, he thought. Smart fish, the dolphins.

What little was known about animal communication resulted from the efforts of the men and women who devoted their lives to gathering field information on the social life and habits of wildlife. Dwart felt they deserved far more credit than they were given.

He thought about man's relationship to animals in general. All God's children got souls, the evangelists said, but they never included any of the creatures called animals. Humans killed wildlife indiscriminately, for expediency, sport or on a whim.

Nature has its own savagery, Dwart mused, and no one objects to the natural order of the food chain. But when humans and domesticated animals are about all that's left, not only will the earth be a poorer place to live, it'll be curtains for us, too.

Dwart wondered whether he shouldn't just retreat into complacency and smooth out each day with a few brews, because the problems were too big. No, he decided, he had to do his part.

AFTER CLOSING TIME, DWART AND TRAVERS SAT around a table in the main building's recreation lounge. Travers' day had been filled with conferences on the landscape design of a new exhibit enclosure, including decisions on animal space requirements, orientation to sun and prevailing winds, and selection of plant materials. He needed a stiff drink.

He kept a bottle of Wyandfoking vodka in his locker, just for days like this, and the lounge had a refrigerator stocked with the ingredients for making Bloody Caesars: clamato juice, lemons, Worcestershire sauce and Tabasco sauce. A happy hour might not help, but it couldn't hurt.

"Drink?" he offered to Dwart as he set the fixings on top of the bar, along with celery salt and a tray of ice cubes.

"Wouldn't refuse," replied Dwart.

The strong, spicy drink cleared Dwart's sinuses with the first gulp. "You make a mean caesar," spluttered Dwart, "but a little less Tabasco in mine, please, if perchance we're tempted, against our better judgment of course, to have seconds."

As Dwart neared the end of his drink he began to feel a little like a Roman caesar himself and said, "People worry about what's going to happen to them, body and soul, when they trundle off this mortal coil. Do you, Phil?"

"I've thought about it, like anyone else, but I don't worry about it because no one really knows. We're still trying to find out what happened on this earth before we got here, so how do we expect to find out what will happen after we leave?"

"Maybe I'm like the guy who drove his date out to the cemetery and parked. It was so spooky she looked around and said, 'Do you believe in the hereafter?' And he said, 'Well, if you're not here after what I'm here after, you'll be here after I'm gone!'"

"Are you ever serious, Farquhart?"

"Things can be desperate, but they don't have to be serious, that's all. You sponsored me as an ape monger, and this evening I was to report to you on my progress in that field."

"Right. Let's get that out of the way. You've

been here, what—three, four, five months now? So what have you come up with?"

"Bamboo, Amanda and I have built a strong rapport, starting out with my attempts to make their noises. When I want to show I'm glad to see them, or they me, we'll go *oh oh oh oh oh*; or if something's good, everybody goes *ah ah ah ah ah*, that type of thing. It was hard to know what to expect of them. They talk to each another and use a lot of body language, so at first I tried to codify and then develop our mutual language. With her earlier Ameslan training, Amanda's been a good and persistent student, able to concentrate, although just for short periods."

"How's the deaf assistant working out?" asked Travers, getting up and crossing to the long sofa, where he assumed a half-reclining position.

"Maureen? Very well indeed. We get as much work out of her as is decent, considering the amount of money your board allowed for the project. Cheap is cheap."

"Got as much as I could. This isn't the type of research the zoo goes in for. I'm still trying to get them to pay for your courses at the school for the deaf."

"Thanks. Bamboo isn't as advanced as Amanda in the extent of his sign vocabulary or his grasp of language. So it's a slow start, but we're making good progress."

"Give me some examples."

"He comments on activities he observes, without any prompting from me. If he sees a keeper struggling with a jammed door, he'll sign *Out, out.* He can use what, why, when and where in a variety of ways and pose direct questions by signing *What good there?* while he points to a shovel or a wheelbarrow."

Dwart paused to blow his nose. "He's even signed *What?* to express surprise or innocence when someone else has signed a statement to him. I think we could develop all this a lot further if you'd let me take Bamboo and Amanda out into some more natural surroundings. Within the grounds, of course."

"You want me to let you go for walks in the woods with the gorillas?!" Phil sat bolt upright on the couch. "You have got to be joking."

"It might be a boon to them. Would show we trusted them. I think they'd follow me back inside the compound. It might take a while, but I'd be prepared to stay with them till they did."

"And if they didn't? Or if they escaped? And what if the press got hold of that? Forget it."

"Figured you wouldn't go for it. Now, what you do with apes is, you sign a suggestion, then watch for their reaction." Dwart placed his empty glass on top of his head and balanced it there.

"So now I'm an ape, you old fart," said Phil. He took the hint, however, and got up to make fresh drinks.

"See what I mean?" Dwart remarked as he accepted his caesar, "The co-operative nature of communication."

"So you've read about other experiments going on and you've launched your own." Phil paused, stroking his goatee. "Can you show me something definite?"

"Thought you'd never ask. Maybe I can show you something with Amanda. Remember what you said when I asked you for a raise: 'You're an expert when I see some results.'"

"Did I say that?" Phil countered warily.

"You damn well did, and you know I have a good memory. So if I show you what a reasonable man would call results, then I take it I get an expert's pay?"

"You want a raise."

"Yeah, but only if I deserve it. Let's finish this drink and then go down to the gorilla compound. There won't be anyone around at this time of evening."

"Fine. Do you want another before we go, you ape monger, you?" said Phil, looking into his glass, which was again running on empty.

"Not right now. You know, each ape is as much an individual, with his or her unique personality, as each human."

"Then you agree with Jane Goodall on that, and she's one of the world's leading experts on the subject of apes. You are progressing," said Phil. "I'm going to have another quick one before we go," he murmured, heading toward the bar.

"I also think that you lucked out on those two, Bamboo and Amanda."

"So do I, but why do you think so?"

"They're exceptionally intelligent. I've watched their signs, I've talked to them in signs, I've understood their replies," said Dwart. "Like most primates, they're at their best when they're signing for food or goodies."

"What method did you use?" asked Phil, settling on the couch again.

"I gave them a few tools, a hammer, a screwdriver and a pair of pliers. We have signs for each of those things and they know them, and when I give them the sign for a particular tool, they can produce it." Dwart demonstrated an up-and-down pounding motion for a hammer, a hand-twisting motion for a screwdriver and a fist-squeezing motion for pliers.

"Let's go," said Phil, knocking back his drink. "This is damned interesting. You're really into this, aren't you?"

They followed the joint red and blue trails, skirting the Indo-Malayan Pavilion and future home for Bengal tigers until they reached the African Pavilion with its peaked roofs. The pavilion was thick with triangular palms, screw pines, tamarind, kapok, papyrus, fig and banana trees.

They stopped in the area between the outdoor gorilla compound on the right and the glassed indoor compound on their left. The screeching of mandril baboons in a nearby cage disturbed the quiet. The calls of whistling ducks and other birds and faint monkey chattering came to them from further off. The zoo was closed for the night, and except for an occasional passing guard, they were alone.

"Where's Bamboo?" asked Phil.

"The weather's decent, so he'll be outside. There's a sheltered area where the keepers leave lots of straw for him. Amanda hasn't lived much of her life in the wild, so she likes to sleep inside. She's commandeered a room down here, the one with the squeeze cage. She sleeps on one of the padded tables."

When they entered her sleeping area, Amanda recognized the old white-eyes and the man she knew as some sort of silverback around the zoo.

There were friendly body gestures all around, followed by signing between Dwart and Amanda, with Phil watching closely. He actually set the example, crouching into a sitting position, aware that it made chimps and gorillas more comfortable than if people stood in their presence. Dwart talked to her in English and signed at the same time, then translated her replies to Travers.

Dwart: Do visit.

Amanda: Good.

Dwart: Happy gorilla?

Amanda: Happy me.

Dwart: What do you do when you're happy?

Amanda: Gorilla smile eat.

Dwart: What like eat?

Amanda: Love eat apple.

Dwart presented Amanda with an apple, which she immediately ate.

Amanda: Me hungry good.

Dwart: Where is apple I gave you?

Amanda: More apple.

Dwart: Where yours?

Amanda: Sorry stomach.

Dwart: Why is it there?

Amanda: Shit. Sorry.

Dwart: Why?

Amanda: Gorilla apple sandwich.

Dwart: No more.

Amanda: Apple again please.

Dwart: Stop nagging.

Amanda: Hit hit apple come-on eat.

Dwart: You threatening me again?

Amanda: Hit in mouth. Toilet toilet devil, more apple there.

Dwart explained to Phil, "She uses toilet as an insult."

Dwart: Toilet! Now you're insulting me. Where'd you learn to nag, threaten and insult?

Amanda: Eat apple.

Dwart: Do I have more apples?

Amanda: Stink bad gorilla squash.

When Dwart translated this message, Phil drew back, pulling Dwart with him. "Better not get too close, that looks like a real threat. She might bite you."

Dwart laughed and signed to Amanda what Phil had said.

Amanda: (looking at Phil) Bad. Visit nice. Good-bye.

Phil wanted to know what she'd said.

Dwart signed back and forth with Amanda, then translated: "She said you insulted her."

Amanda: Insult me teeth (grimacing).

The two men laughed.

"She certainly wants more apples, and like you said, she's good at talking about food." Phil commented.

"Yes, they're probably best on food, drink, and more. I'll ask some other things."

Dwart: What do you do with teeth?'

Amanda: Teeth bite good.

Dwart: What this (pointing to the squeeze cage and controls)?

Amanda: Wall close.

Dwart: What difference between you, me?

Amanda: You stink (imitating a human smile).

Dwart: Not true. False.

Amanda: Fake, yes.

Dwart: Show white-eyes fake (signing and pointing to Phil, without translating).

Dwart had taught Amanda a set of signs, or rather a sequence of motions. At first she'd been reluctant to mimic the motions. Gorillas could be stubborn, and Dwart had learned that they didn't like to be told what to do or made to repeat things for no evident purpose, unlike dogs chasing a stick. This was another sign of high intelligence, in Dwart's opinion. Faced with Amanda's obstinacy, Dwart had resorted to bribing her with apples or some other fruit. Eventually, although she didn't understand the replies he required of her, she learned to do them properly, in anticipation of the treat.

"Come on, Phil, let's go find Bamboo." As they reached the door, Dwart stopped Travers and turned him around to face Amanda. "Watch closely. You're going to see some real communication."

"I've already seen plenty, but lead on, MacDuff."

Dwart placed his hand over one eye, signalling the word or symbol for *I*. Then he placed his hand on his knee, signalling *need*. Finally, he made the up-and-down pounding motion for *hammer*.

"Great," Phil said, "I get it—'I need a hammer.' Now let's see what she does."

Amanda watched all this with interest. She'd already received the signal for the fake. She knew she was being tested somehow, and she wanted another apple. She placed one hand over her own eye, then, as Dwart had taught her, cupped one hand under her left breast and jiggled it up and down. Next she slapped her buttocks with one hand, then grasped her crotch with the other.

"What does she mean by that?" exclaimed Phil. "Let's see that again. I didn't understand that at all."

"Okay, I'll do it for you again." And he and Amanda repeated the exchange.

Phil was nonplussed. "You signalled 'I need a hammer,' and she's signing back—hand on eye, I, she jiggled her left breast, slapped her butt, hand on genitals—it's definite, that's good, but what does she mean?"

Looking Phil in the eye, Dwart interpreted: "It's really quite amazing...she's telling us, 'I left tit behind in the tool box!'"

"Goddamn you, you crazy old fart. You rigged the ruddy ape!"

"No, I just showed you some new results. Now do I get that raise?" Dwart walked back to Amanda and handed her a sweet newton apple.

With Phil still muttering that he'd been had, they stepped out to where Bamboo was preparing to bed down for the night. They stood just outside the fenced enclosure, right next to their protege. Dwart began talking and signing to Bamboo and translating for Phil.

Dwart: Bamboo gorilla tired?

Bamboo: Gorilla sleep.

Dwart: Visit?

Bamboo: Happy good you come.

Dwart: You know chief silverback (pointing to Travers).

Bamboo: Look good. Gorilla smile. Gimme nut.

Dwart: Nut. No nut. Dwart showed Bamboo two apples, one smaller than the other. "Which one do you want?" he said, but did not sign the question.

Bamboo: That...(pointing to the small one) That...(pointing to the large one)

Dwart: "Which one do you want?" Again, he used his voice only.

Bamboo: Those...(pointing to the two simultaneously with both index fingers). Apples (signed with both hands).

Dwart gave Bamboo the apples and everyone smiled.

Phil broke in, "He seems to understand a lot. Be interesting to know how he feels about certain things."

"Okay, I'll ask him," and Dwart resumed signing and talking to Bamboo.

Dwart:	You tell me how gorilla talk?
Bamboo:	(Beating his chest)
Dwart:	What do gorillas say when happy?
Bamboo:	Gorilla hug.
Dwart:	What difference between you and me?
Bamboo:	Head.
Dwart:	How are our heads different?
Bamboo:	(Beating on his head with open palms, harder than any human could ever do).
Dwart:	Tough you. You're very smart. Are all gorillas smart?
Bamboo:	(no response)
Dwart:	Are gorillas smart or stupid?
Bamboo:	Smart Bamboo.

"Ah, yes," commented Phil, "let's hope self-knowledge is the criterion of veracity. He could end up in politics. Let's call it a day. Those caesars are starting to get to me."

"Me too." Dwart signed good-bye to Bamboo and they turned and started to walk away.

After about twenty paces they clearly heard a strange and peculiar voice say what sounded like: "Gud...by...yoo—ugh—big...sun...uf...ah—ugh—bich. Hav...a—ugh—nis...day!"

14

LOVE AMONG THE RUINS

Gil Brodeur threw the book he'd been reading onto the coffee table and answered the persistently ringing telephone. *Interruptions, always interruptions; I should get the damn thing disconnected.* It was Travers, excitement colouring his voice.

"Brodeur, I thought I'd seen and heard nearly everything–but nothing like this!"

"Like what, for Pete's sake?"

"Like the ape, Bamboo. He spoke to Farquhart and I."

"Shouldn't that be Farquhart and me, Phil?"

"Goddammit, Gil. I'm serious. I'm telling you, that ape can talk."

Gil hesitated, surprised, but still convinced it was a put-on. "I would imagine he could tell you a lot about running a zoo from the animals' viewpoint. Better listen to him, Phil."

"I'm not bullshitting you. I'm telling you, the gorilla spoke to us. In English, and we understood him. Or at least, I'm damn sure that's what happened. If that bloody Farquhart turns out to be a ventriloquist, I'll kill him. Now please get down here, Gil, and take a look at him. Let's see if we can get him to speak again.

"But keep your mouth shut about this. If it's really true, then it's a secret, top secret. We have to be sure, then figure out what to do."

Travers hung up, leaving Gil staring at the mouthpiece in stunned silence. *Has Travers been working too hard lately? Is he just trying to get me down there for a laugh and a drink?*

Gil put on his shoes, threw some water on his face, grabbed his jacket and whipped out the door. He jumped into his old souped-up Citroën and headed down the turnpike for the zoo. As he drove, he thought it over. Could the captive gorilla he'd operated on really talk? He reviewed the operation in his mind, mulling over what might have happened in Bamboo's throat.

For ten days after the operation, Bamboo had been given antibiotics in his food, and except for some swelling that had lasted another four days, even the incision site had healed after just three weeks. It was going on six months since the operation, but there'd been no way to assess how the repair to the inside of the trachea was behaving. Bamboo had progressed beautifully, so it was hard to justify physically checking out the results of the apparently successful operation. Gil had assumed, as had everyone else, that nothing had gone wrong. Brodeur didn't see what his presence at the zoo would accomplish, unless, of course, Bamboo could speak. A small part of him hoped it was true, and that small part warred with his natural skepticism.

Gil arrived; he heard Bamboo speak. Not well, and in a peculiar voice that was difficult to understand, but undoubtedly saying words. The wonder wasn't how well he did it, but that he could do it at all.

They were back in Travers' office, with Phil pacing up and down. Finally, he spoke to Dwart, who was seated on the chesterfield. "You worked harder and longer than I thought you would or gave you credit for. This gorilla talks, and if he gets a vocabulary and understands English, you're going to be known worldwide as one hell of an ape monger."

He turned to Gil, who was leaning against the doorway. "How do you figure it happened? You operated on him, what did you do that could result in this?"

Gil eased himself into a chair, his brow furrowed.

Before he could answer, Dwart interrupted. "We could all use another drink, Phil, if you don't mind. It's not often I feel the need of a hair of the dog before the morning-after hangover starts, but I could sure use one now. Long on the mix, please. My mouth is starting to feel like the bottom of a baby's pram—all piss and biscuits."

"Good idea. We all need one."

"Phil poured the last of the vodka. "Gil, you heard it with your own ears. If Bamboo can learn that phrase about the nice day and the son of a bitch, then he can say other things, too, and maybe he can learn the language. But why do you think he's able to speak at all?"

"I talked at him all winter," said Dwart, "so did a lot of other people."

They watched Gil stare at the floor for a while. Finally he said, "Everyone figured apes were physiologically incapable of producing the necessary sounds to speak a language. You have to have certain conditions, certain changes in the throat structure to make it possible. Somehow, I brought those changes about during the operation."

"What could have happened?"

"Understand, this is conjecture. I didn't say anything to you at the time, because the injury had to be fixed in that manner anyway, but I remember thinking that there was a makeshift resemblance to a human voice-box when I finished. Bamboo's left vocalis and ventricularis muscles ended up slightly shorter and tighter, pun intended. Then the extra muscle fibres I put around the thyroid cartilage also added some form of muscle control to the area, where none had existed previously.

Now remember, the laryngeal mechanism doesn't really have to be so complex for humans to speak. For instance, they can learn to use the expulsion of air from the esophagus to produce speech after removal of the larynx due to malignant diseases of the throat. So if a human can speak without a larynx, it doesn't take a long stretch of the imagination to realize that Bamboo, whose voice-box has been altered through surgery, could manage an acceptable form of speech.

"So that could account for some of his ability to utter different sounds, if what I'm now thinking is correct. But there has to be something else and I can only wonder what it can be. You're never sure in such an operation just what will happen during the healing process, which slowly remodels the scar tissue, trying to replicate the pre-op anatomy as accurately as it can. It seldom achieves perfection. A post-mortem would be the only way to tell for sure."

"The medical reason doesn't matter to me," said Dwart, "just the fact that he can do it. He's heard a great deal of English. Lord knows I talked to him enough. Would it be possible that he realized that our language could be learned? Another thing, his vocalization seemed to change over time. He'd be talking to Amanda or the other apes in that chattering they use—weird stuff to us, just like ours must be to them—but then he'd make noises at me that were somehow reminiscent of the cooing, gurgling babble of...well, maybe little babies. No, that's not it, exactly. Hard to describe."

"Like the pre-vocalization of children," said Gil. "Interesting concept. They call it developmental psycholinguistics—the study of children's language learning."

"Whatever, but that sounds like what he was doing. I didn't know what to make of it, but it surprised me. They all have about the same sound and tone, but thinking back, Bamboo's voice was somehow different, and getting more different as time went on."

"Different how?" asked Phil, as he handed the drinks around.

"Seemed like...well...a different way of registering surprise or pleasure, or when he was questioning something, the tonal quality wasn't quite ape-like. I made a few tapes and we could listen, but I can't describe it in words."

"I trust you both agree that we have to keep this under wraps until we see what we've got here. This could be big news for the zoo, and it has to be handled right."

The other two concurred.

"I should mention," Dwart interjected, "that I tried standard methods—from reading the books, that is. Phil, you know most of what I did."

"Tell me, anyway, Dwart," said Gil.

"The Helen Keller-Ann Sullivan bit. Keller could literally be regarded as an animal till she was seven, because she had no human language. When she realized that *w-a-t-e-r* meant the cool liquid she drank, she knew everything had a name and that the name was made up of component sounds that could be shuffled around to make other words. I tried Bamboo on the water bit. He didn't get it, in my opinion. Then I tried a thing you can do with kids, and in retrospect, I think he did show that he'd understood the concept, and later tried to do something with it."

"What was that?" asked Gil.

"I'd give him a banana. After he ate it I'd say, 'All gone,' and sign the same thing with my hands. I bet that's when he got the idea, and kept trying to make our sounds, obviously in private."

"Gorillas may well have some rudimentary kind of language activation device in their brains. They would need it, I think," said Gil, "to understand their own cacophonous system of noises. But they couldn't really use it on a human language until something like this operation on Bamboo's throat took place."

"Then he got a lot of interaction with people in a new environment and he learned to use language. That's our explanation. Good, because we're going to need one," said Phil.

"As I said, it's all conjecture, Phil, what else can I say?" was Gil's reaction.

"Well, time to knock it off, fellas; but if he can talk, then I promise to work with him till he does it as well as possible. Maybe we should segregate him again, with Amanda, too, like we did before. I'll stay with him, and he won't likely get much syntax or grammar to go with the words, and who knows about his intonation, but we could get us a real live talking ape. Hot damn!" Raising his glass, Dwart toasted the other two.

"You're right, you son of a gun, Farquhart," replied Phil, enthusiastically raising his own glass. "And here's to you, too, Gil. You did something to that ape's throat, or his larynx, or whatever. This could make medical history."

"I'd sure like to know what it was," said Gil, "How about a laryngoscopic examination?"

"We'd all like to take a look at it, but no, I don't want to try it. We'd have to knock him out again."

"I knew you'd say that."

Dwart spoke up. "Maybe not. If I can teach Bamboo the language, we could just explain it to him, tell him what Gil's going to do, get his co-operation. Then, Gil, you can examine away to your heart's content. I'm presuming, of course, that he's going to co-operate."

"I would sure hope so," was Gil's quick and pale-faced rejoinder.

"I'll just tell him to grab you by the balls while you're examining him and say, 'We aren't going to hurt each other now, are we?' "

"That should work better than an anesthetic," said Phil, chuckling.

"Very funny. No anesthesia, no examination," Gil replied.

"Okay, not for now. Thanks for coming, Gil." Phil turned to Dwart. "I'll make arrangements for more intensive private tutoring lessons between you and Bamboo, Dwart. And we should include Amanda."

IT WAS LATE, BUT MAYBE NOT TOO LATE. HE'D had a few drinks and his libido was urging a meeting with Elspeth. Dwart felt he and Elspeth were being drawn together by a mutually magnetic high hormone level. The complex circuitry of his brain told him that this was the time of night when the herring began to marinate, when the salmon began to swim upstream and when an old stud should make his move.

Brodeur had offered to give him a lift and Dwart asked him to wait while he made a phone call. The line was busy, so at least Elspeth was home and awake. He realized it wasn't a good idea to turn up unexpectedly, but the drinks had made him bold.

When they arrived at the Islington bungalow, Dwart checked for lights. The living room was lit by a table lamp and the low, flickering blue of the television.

He thanked Gil for the ride as he closed the door of the Citroën, then walked toward the door of the house before he realized that he should have asked Brodeur to wait. He knocked.

After a few moments the porch light snapped on. Elspeth came to the door, opening it against the chain, a look of mixed surprise and chagrin on her face.

"Aloysius," she yawned, and he knew she wouldn't have called him that unless she was displeased, "It's a little late to be calling. You really should've let me know."

Dwart blurted out a string of excuses. "I phoned. The line was busy. Bummed a ride going past here. He took off on me. Sorry! I know it's late."

"Yes?" She didn't invite him in, but she removed the chain. She stood in the open doorway, her arms folded over her chenille dressing gown.

"Hope you're not mad. I was drinking. Not usual. Wanted to see you."

"I see."

"Could call a cab later."

"Could you? Why not right away? Looking for another drink, I suppose?"

"It'd be nice."

"Coffee or liquor?"

"Coffee'd be best."

"You came for a cup of coffee, is that it?"

"Well, I thought..."

"That this is an all-night restaurant?"

"Whatta mistaka I maka. No, not really—"

"Did you think, by any chance, that I'm an ex-stripper, that I might be lonely, and that I might be wearing round heels?"

"No, no."

"Or did you maybe just get horny?"

"Not at all, Elspeth." There was silence for a few seconds. Then Dwart said, with a touch of indignation in his voice, "Told a lie. That is possible, you know, what you said. 'Cause I'm not over the hump...if you'll pardon the pun...but I—"

"How nice for you. But what's that got to do with me?"

"Likely nothing." Dwart looked at her sheepishly. "I just thought that..."

"What did you think, Aloysius?"

"I just thought..." He paused again, removing his hat and nervously brushing a hand through his thinning hair.

"What?" Dwart could see embers starting to glow through the grey-green ash of her beautiful eyes.

"That...I thought that..." Dwart was fighting for words. "Dammit, Elspeth, even in my dreams about you I'm more daring than this!"

"Well?" Her foot began to tap.

"Look, the thought of you keeps running like honey through my heart, and...and...I've fallen in love with you! There, I've said it."

It was Elspeth's turn to be taken aback. She paused for several seconds, then backed slowly into the hallway, swinging the door open.

"You just talked your way in, you silver-tongued devil. I'll put the coffee on. No need to call a cab just yet."

15

THE SQUEEZE CAGE

Irving Fluck's broken arm and the wound near his crotch had long since healed, but his ill will toward Bamboo still festered. His brain was forever picking the scabs off the memory, and dark thoughts of revenge filled his mind. Because both had great physical prowess, Irving Fluck and Bamboo were equally repelled by each other, like the same poles of a magnet. No one had ever said it to his face, but Irving just knew that the zoo staff called him the human ape. He'd always known he wasn't handsome, but an ape! He resented that, deeply, and his resentment extended to the animals with whom he imagined he was being compared.

His obsession with apes, however, was not his biggest problem at the moment, although in a distant way it was related to what was bothering him. He held his head in his hands, because whenever he went without sex for too long, he developed a pain over one eye. He'd had a particularly long dry spell and today the pain was over both eyes, the terrible headache forcing him to curse out loud. It was a good thing it was his eyes that were affected by the pain. *If I walk around moaning and holding my head, they give me sympathy and Tylenol; if I walked around moaning and fondling my privates, they'd give me thirty days.*

Irving's urge to fulfill his basic sexual needs was normal. But while most people craved love, intimacy and companionship with their fellow humans, Irving didn't want or need a meaningful relationship; all he required was impersonal, unemotional and non-intellectual sexual action.

Irving was the product of a conflicting upbringing. He was raised on an Ontario farm, where he'd been exposed to the sexual conduct of farm animals, which his own instincts made him want to emulate. At the same time, he was brought up in the Baptist Church tradition of sexual abstention. This state of simultaneous desire and repression created a mental shock in Irving, and had a lasting psychological effect upon him, to say nothing of the tension headaches that drove him to engage in strange activities.

At first he'd furtively masturbated in the outhouse while viewing the corset and lingerie sections of mail-order catalogues. Then, driven by feelings of guilt, he'd entered lengthy periods of complete abstinence from sexual thought and deed, in keeping with his religious beliefs. At least, he'd tried to abstain, with varying degrees of success.

He did occasionally work up enough nerve to date girls. Dating was very difficult because of his unprepossessing appearance as well as the physical size of both Irving and his member. His partners had to be large and none too fussy, and such women were few and far between in the Baptist community where he lived.

He managed to date the minister's daughter, Rosie Brentwood, and get laid, just as his peers had predicted. But he found conversation with Rosie as difficult and traumatic as with girls in general. Sex entailed emotional responsibilities he didn't want to contemplate. Rosie immediately recognized Irving as a perverted bachelor, because he just came, then went.

For a time, Irving tried to take religion seriously as a means of salvation from his perplexing dilemma. But the solace he found came in a far different form than he'd imagined. One Sunday morning, Reverend Brentwood preached on Psalms 50:10 and 50:11: "For every beast of the field is mine, and the cattle upon a thousand hills. I know all the fowls of the mountains: and the wild beasts of the field are mine."

The Reverence opined that all those of Christian persuasion should love the animals of the field and beasts of the wild, and that they should be conserved and treated with loving kindness. Unfortunately for the animals, Brentwood didn't think to include a reference to Leviticus 20:15: "And if a man lie with a beast, he shall surely be put to death, and ye shall slay the beast."

Irving promptly took Brentwood's admonitions literally, feeling he'd finally found a way to resolve his conflict while satisfying his pressing sexual needs. It was clearly a case that fell under Mark 4:19: "The cares of this world...and the lusts of other things entering in, choke the word, and it becometh unfruitful."

The meaning of the Reverend's message had become confused in Irving's mind, for he immediately and religiously began to experiment with having his way with cows in the barn. Calves proved too frisky, but the older cows stood still and seemed to enjoy it. He would have tried it with pigs, but he was afraid they'd squeal.

Irving was thus able to rationalize his actions. After all, the idea had come to him through a church sermon. Furthermore, he enjoyed it immensely.

Had he been a student of history, he would have thought himself fortunate not to have lived in the days of the Puritans of New England, who for a certainty believed that all God's children, even themselves, the Chosen, were born to an inheritance of sin. A zoophiliac habit, although not uncommon throughout history in pastoral societies, was considered the most beastly of sins, and its practitioners were burned at the stake as warlocks.

Irving had never heard of the weak-minded

youth, one Thomas Granger of Duxbury, who was hanged for having carnal knowledge of a mare, a cow, two goats, five sheep, two calves and a turkey. Thomas, the fowl fucker, would have been a role model for Irving; and the death penalty would have broken him of his lustful sin against nature.

It wasn't that Irving disliked women, or even that in fornicating with animals he was subconsciously trying to abase women. He just liked animals more than humans. He was satisfying an urgent need, so his proclivities didn't bother him. He even took Matthew 19:24, about the camel going through the eye of a needle, to mean that nothing was impossible; he took further inspiration from a French saying he'd once heard: with patience and plenty of lard, an elephant can bugger a louse.

As a teenager, he was secretive about his sexual fetish, as well he might be. No way did he want to raise the wrath of his father, who was not only mean and much tougher than Irving, but a Bible-thumping religious fanatic as well. They'd never gotten along. Irving couldn't forgive a father who taunted him by saying he was so ugly his mother had to breastfeed him with a straw. It was a source of great satisfaction to Irving that when he was older and bigger, no longer a Baptist and leaving the farm for good, the last thing he did was to kick the living shit out of the old man.

Leaving the Bible-belt farm early in life and driven by his urgent zoophilia, Irving outdid

Thomas Granger and took huge risks, even though he tried to be circumspect. Like a taxidermist, he mounted animals with impunity.

Far from diminishing as he left adolescence, Irving's predilection carried on into manhood and he continued his erotic aberrations with all manner of beasts. He always sought employment where animals were involved. After a series of jobs, he decided to follow his true vocation, forming Fluck Brothers Animal Procurement Ltd., supplying domestic and wild animals to customers on demand. His work often carried him to strange parts of the world in order to fulfill equally bizarre requests for animals. His brother Frank, who preferred to live in Africa and knew nothing of Irving's sexual preferences, did a great deal of the overseas business.

Irving's most persistent animal fantasy involved the great apes, probably because of a latent desire to couple with something nearly human. It was extremely rare for anyone to get a crack at a gorilla, and he'd never had an opportunity until his contract with the Ontario Provincial Zoo. His appetite had already been whetted—he'd done it with Josephine. It hadn't been as difficult as he'd expected, mainly because Josephine thought of herself as human.

Now he lusted after Amanda, the sleek and powerful great ape with the blue-black hair, sequestered in a relatively private room in the middle holding area of the zoo.

Irving lay back in bed and began to contemplate both the situation and his chances of success. His dreaming completely overwhelmed him, his adrenaline beginning to flow at the thought of seducing the female, who was in the prime of her life. Even though society's attitudes toward sex had changed considerably, Irving knew that few people would condone the sexual activity he now envisaged, even though the practice was more prevalent than most people ever suspected.

Some men only fantasized, while others acted on their fantasies. Irving was a doer. He got out of bed, dressed, ate a three-pound steak with six eggs to keep up his strength, then headed for the zoo.

He drove past employee parking and pulled into a secluded area of the public lot, to avoid drawing attention to his vehicle. He wasn't anxious to have any of the skeleton night staff learn of his presence. Preparations for the week-long celebration of the zoo's fifteenth anniversary were nearly complete and many people on the night shift, who'd been working overtime, had the evening off.

From the trunk of his van, Irving withdrew a small CO_2-powered tranquilizer pistol loaded with a dart containing a powerful sedative. Shoving the gun into his belt, he reached into a kit bag and pulled out a mickey of rum. Tipping the bottle back, he drank about half the contents. Then, taking a circular and surreptitious route to the African Pavilion, he silently let himself in, unlocking doors as he went and pulling them quietly shut behind him.

Reaching the holding room, he opened the observation hatch in the door and looked in. Amanda lay on a large padded table near the centre of the room, apparently asleep.

In a high state of tension, Irving muttered, "They think Bamboo and Amanda are gonna get it on in this little honeymoon suite. To hell with them and to hell with Bamboo. I brought him here and he's not going to get her first. I'd like to kill that bastard ape, but he's too valuable."

Allowing his eyes to adjust to the room's dim light, Irving slowly poked his tranquilizer pistol through the small hatch and took careful aim.

Amanda was awake. As she lay on the table, her thoughts drifted to Bamboo, who had bedded down in the outer compound. Her interest in Bamboo as a mate was growing rapidly.

Suddenly she heard a low *whoosh* and felt a sharp sting in her lower backside. What could have bitten her?

She reared up and tried to see, picking at the area where something sharp seemed to have struck her. It hurt, and she removed the small metal object. Strange. Soon she became very drowsy, rolled over onto her stomach and drifted off to sleep.

Irving waited for fifteen minutes to allow the sedative to numb her immediate awareness. Then

he silently entered the room, skirting the open
door of the squeeze cage, and slowly approached
the sleeping Amanda. Her arms and legs were
spread-eagled limply over the big table. How
very convenient, he thought, as he hunted in the
gloom for the leather straps attached to the sides
of the table. The straps were intended for restrain-
ing animals, but not for the use Irving planned to
put them to. Gingerly, he placed the straps strate-
gically so that when he suddenly tightened them
around her arms and legs and over her back,
Amanda would be unlikely to succeed in biting
or clawing him. It was tricky, but he got them
ready for a quick and nearly simultaneous tight-
ening before she became fully conscious.

That done, he stood back for a moment to figure out the fastest way to proceed. He was getting
excited and anxious, but his sexual experience
with animals came in handy, as he tightened the
arm straps as much as he dared. Then he quickly
and firmly grabbed Amanda's legs and slowly slid
her back along the table until her legs hung over
the edge. She didn't wake up. He placed the main
strap across her back and cinched it firmly. She
was starting to come to, but was still befuddled,
trying unsuccessfully to roll to either side.
Rushing back to the end of the table, Irving
secured Amanda's legs with leather straps around
each table leg. She could move, but not so much
that she could effectively prevent him from carrying out his evil intent.

Amanda, still in a semi-stupor, didn't know what was happening to her, but she looked as far over her shoulder as she could and recognized Irving Fluck. Fluck returned to the door and shot home the lightweight inside bolt.

With Amanda face down and her legs hanging over the back edge of the table and securely strapped down, Irving began to stroke her. The ape, angry and confused, began to growl. She strained against her bonds as Irving dropped his trousers.

In the outer compound, Bamboo sat up in the bed of straw that served as his nest. He didn't know what had awakened him or what was causing his vague feelings of unease. He thought of the two visits that evening by his old friend, the one called Dwart, and the other silverback white-eyes. They'd become extremely excited each time he'd spoken to them with the human sounds, and then had left in a big hurry.

He sniffed the air, a jumble of human smells assailing his nostrils. Frustration made him shake his head—there were too many visitors to the zoo for him to pick out individual scents—but he thought he detected a newly arrived presence, and his jungle senses told him something was wrong.

Bamboo rose and walked into the darkness of the compound, his bright eyes darting nervously from under his heavy brows. Nothing moved near him, no sounds except the usual night noises. He thought of going back to sleep, but his nose seemed to lead him to the door of the middle compound. It was open to his touch, and there was no activity; all was quiet in the area he entered.

Thoroughly awake now, his nostrils alerting him to Amanda's proximity, he ambled in her direction. He suddenly became aware of a strange scent. The first of the doors leading to the room where she slept weren't locked. He found himself in the service area. The next door was closed and wouldn't open to his touch, but the observation hatch into the holding room was slightly ajar. Bamboo pushed it open and looked in.

His eyes took in the scene in an instant. Now he knew what had bothered him. The white ape, Fluck, stood with his back to the door, doing something with Amanda on the big table. At that moment Amanda gave out a long, plaintive wail—"*whoo, whoo, whoo!*"

Bamboo's thunderous kick smashed open the door to the holding room, snapping the light bolt from its moorings.

Not a pretty sight, but a pretty predicament, to which Irving, charged with adrenalin, responded as quickly as he could, considering that his jeans and shorts were around his ankles. Caught in the act, the rape artist's snarl of frustration was joined by Bamboo's roar of anger. Irving turned to face the charge of the great ape, who came hurtling across the room in raw rage, beating a wild tattoo on his chest. This was no charge calculated to frighten off the enemy; this one was for keeps, a game Bamboo had seldom, if ever, played.

The brawny Fluck and the ape were a good physical match. Irving tried to sidestep the charge while extricating himself from the clothing hampering his lower limbs. His hands were busy with this task, while his mind had to switch from fuck to fight, providing Bamboo with his best chance. He should have taken advantage of Fluck's predicament, for he had the element of surprise on his side.

Because of his inexperience, he was still beating his chest when he slammed straight into Fluck with his whole body weight, sending Irving ass over breakfast across the room and into the cement wall at the back. Bamboo caromed off his opponent at right angles, landing on a table standing against one wall. Two of the table legs broke and it collapsed under the sudden force of Bamboo's fall, entangling him in the wreckage.

Irving's flailing legs ripped his pants nearly in half and one leg came free, so that when he rose from the floor he was at least mobile. "I'm gonna kill you, you bastard," snarled Fluck. He sprang across the room to deliver a mighty kick to Bamboo's body as he started to rise. Bamboo went down, Irving right on top of him, and the two rolled around in a wild jumble of arms, legs, fists and teeth, amid curses, barks and roars.

In spite of their divergent backgrounds, there were few differences in their fighting techniques. One was a jungle fighter and the other a back alley brawler. Bamboo possessed more agility in his legs than Irving, and as they clutched, clawed and bit at each other, he got his feet up into Irving's belly, and with a huge heave, catapulted Fluck across the room. Irving's manhood was dangerously exposed, a fact of which he was keenly aware, and he was lucky that Bamboo's feet hadn't performed a gonadectomy on him as punishment for his attack on Amanda's virtue.

Irving landed on the rubble of the table destroyed by Bamboo's previous fall. The crash winded him temporarily, but his hand dropped onto a broken table leg. He clutched it and with vicious glee, he raged back across the combat zone. Bamboo's acrobatics in flinging Fluck away had forced him to roll backward, but he came quickly to his feet like a Japanese wrestler and renewed his own attack.

Amanda, who could only view parts of the fight, let out a loud, pulsing scream to warn Bamboo that Irving now had a weapon. Bamboo heard the warning too late as he was diving full flight toward his enemy. Fluck, using both hands on the club, swung it toward Bamboo's head, who tried to duck. It was an off-centre, glancing blow, but despite the hardness of Bamboo's head, he still saw stars and fought to stay conscious, staggering back across the holding room floor into the open door of the squeeze cage. He remained there, slumped against the bars, though not completely knocked out.

Irving, veteran of many bar fights, saw his chance and took it. In a low voice through clenched teeth, he said, "One more belt and then you go into the cage while I finish with Amanda. Then I'll wear your guts for garters." He broke into a run with the table leg raised over his head. Bamboo watched as if the action were in slow motion, his brain desperately trying to come out of its daze and deal with the situation. To what ape Bamboo owed his next break he would never know. Irving, charging toward him, intent on his main purpose, stepped in the ape shit he failed to see on the floor. His feet shot out from under him just as he reached Bamboo. He slid feet first into the squeeze cage on his backside. Either Bamboo's brain or his reflexes acted quickly and he managed to deliver a ferocious kick to Irving's head as he slid past. Staggering, but on his feet now, Bamboo slammed the cage door shut and its automatic locking feature imprisoned Fluck. Bamboo fell backward, holding his spinning head. Amanda was talking to him and he tried to concentrate on what she was saying.

Going over to her, he busied himself at her behest, trying to figure out the leather straps that bound her to the table. Meanwhile, Irving ranted and raved in the cage. When Amanda was free, she rushed at the squeeze cage, screetching ape imprecations at Fluck. She motioned Bamboo to help her, and they pushed on the back wall of the cage, as she'd frequently seen the guards do with the contraption. The wall slid slowly forward, pinning Irving's body between the wall and the front bars, so he was barely able to move. All he could do now was glare at them with black rage in his eyes.

"You'll get yours one of these frosty fucking Fridays! I'll get you for this, you son of a bitch!"

Bamboo didn't yet understand the meaning of most of what humans said, but he was now beginning to repeat the things they uttered, and to recognize the sounds they repeated most often. He could add words and phrases he'd previously heard and learned, incorporating them all into his response. He gave Irving an ape-ish grin and said, "Hav a nis—ugh—fros tee fuking fri...da!—ugh—yoo big—ugh—sun uf a bich."

Bamboo took Amanda by the hand and led her out the door. They headed directly to the bed of straw in the outer compound. The zoo's worries about Amanda were over.

Irving, badly bruised and bare-assed, fulminating with rage and imprisoned in the squeeze cage, watched them leave, his roger and bare balls dangling in the breeze.

16

AFTERMATH

Towelling vigorously after his shower, Dwart came back into the bedroom and gazed at the scene. Evidence of femininity was everywhere, and the pungent odour of lovemaking hung over the rumpled bed. Lingerie was stacked in an open drawer and a stuffed tiger sat on top of the dresser. It went well with the dragons embossed on the black lacquered Chinese folding screen standing behind the headboard. Lemon wedges and melting ice water were all that was left in the glasses on the night table. The room looked loved in.

He could hear noises from the kitchen, where a radio was tuned to a local FM station. The Mills Brothers were singing *Sometimes I'm happy, sometimes I'm blue, My disposition depends on you...*

I haven't got a toothbrush, he mused. Ah well, just some Crest and my finger will have to do. Should help the old breath a bit.

"Breakfast is ready," Elspeth called from the kitchen.

"Be there in a minute." Dwart hastily finished his ablutions, tucked his shirt into his pants and zipped up his fly.

A homey sight greeted him on the sunlit kitchen table. Elspeth had made Angels on Horseback, with wholewheat toast and marmalade, grapefruit juice and black coffee.

"Looks great."

"Sit down over there."

"Not yet," Dwart replied, giving her a hug, a squeeze and a kiss. A series of little shudders ran through his body. "Are we going to do that 'was it good for you' routine? If so, you were great."

"Not necessary. I really enjoyed myself."

"Look, I'll do better next time."

Elspeth pulled back slightly from his embrace, looking him in the eye. "Will you, now? Good."

"Well, you see...I think I got too excited."

"Thank you, kind sir," said Elspeth, dropping a mock curtsey, and in a heavy southern belle accent à la Scarlett O'Hara, added, "Fine praise comin' from a man who knows what I look like without my shimmy."

"The body doesn't always listen to the brain. I know what I want it to do, but when you're excited...I mean, you have to be relaxed for the message to get through—"

"Listen, Dwart, everything doesn't have to always be steamy sex. A hug is nice, a kiss and a cuddle are fine. Now let's sit down and eat our breakfast before it gets cold."

"I know, but just so you understand that sometimes you want to do so well that somehow...the desire to do so gets in the way of doing it. Or something like that. The brain has to be cooler, and in command, to prolong..." He felt shy talking about it. "Anyway, I think I proved I'm not past it."

"Certainly did, so why don't we give ourselves another chance? Then we can both try to do better. All right?"

"Right. Just fine with me." Dwart grinned, hugged her again and sat down to dig into the broiled oysters wrapped in bacon. *Some of these might work, and, I hope, more slowly.*

When they got to the coffee, Elspeth asked, "You told me about that old friend of yours–Bumphrey, wasn't it?–and his sex problem. Have you had any help from that government office?

"Matter of fact, there is a little progress there. The public guardian's office got my letter, all right, then phoned the matron at the Mount Pleasant old age home. Patti Stacker told me about it last week, when I went to visit Bill. She said he asked more questions about me than he did about Bumphrey."

"What kind of questions?"

"Like who I was, and get this: he asked her if I was senile!"

"What did she tell him?"

"I'll ignore that. She told me she knew this particular official and thought he was singularly lacking in a sense of humour; but she did her best to convince him that I thought of myself as something of a comedian and was just trying to be funny. She told him Bumphrey had a real problem and she certainly thought someone should be in charge of his finances, because left to himself he'd blow his wad. Ah, could I re-phrase that, please? He'd indeed spend all of his money on women."

"That's sweet. I can't think of a better way to spend money, actually," said a smiling Elspeth over the rim of her coffee cup.

"You're prejudiced," replied Dwart, "and therefore not qualified to offer an opinion. Anyway, Stacker says he's thinking about it and we'll get an answer soon. Oh, and she also let a couple of other nurses at the hospital read her copy of my letter. One of them came into her office while I was there and they had a good laugh about it. She pointed out a mistake I'd made. Well, it wasn't my mistake actually, it was a typo by the secretary out at the zoo and I never caught the mis-spelled word before I mailed the letter."

"What was it?"

"In one of the last paragraphs it said, 'Perhaps the public guardian and your office could look into providing genital hookers in old-age care homes,' etcetera. Now, I'd written 'geritol' and I meant it in the context of old hookers, geritol hookers. The secretary couldn't read my writing or maybe didn't understand the word, so anyway, she typed in the word genital. And that has got to be weird."

"It sounds pretty painful, too."

"You bet. I have to correct that error or they'll rightfully consider me to be an uneducated and senile klutz. I explained what I really meant to the girls at the care home. I suppose the only people who wouldn't think it was funny would be Bill Bumphrey and the public guardian. Senile, am I? I'll write to him again. If you get me some paper, I'll do it right now while you finish your coffee."

Elspeth brought him a writing pad and Dwart began to draft a letter, handing a section at a time across the table to Elspeth.

To: The Public Trustee/Guardian Office

Re: Wm. Bumphrey, Mount Pleasant Care Home for the Aged

Dear Sir:

Further to my letter of May 7th, the matron at Mount Pleasant asked me what I meant by 'genital' hookers.

I didn't mean some kind of curved medical instru-ment. That was a typing error and should have read 'geritol hookers.' I wouldn't want you to think that I don't understand the English language.

Of course, the use of genital hookers might disabuse anyone of all thoughts of sex, so that just might work; although the UN Committee on Human Rights might deem it cruel and unusual punishment, even torture and a crime against humanity.

No, it would be better if the Ontario government

*looked into the legalization of prostitution, à la some
South American countries. They could start with the
older pros, the geritol set, and would then be seen to be
doing something constructive regarding unemployment
and to be providing jobs for ladies of the evening in their
declining years (or should that read reclining?). If it
worked, you could extend the program to all ages, probably with the co-operation of the provincial housing cor-
poration, who have numerous foreclosed houses that
could be used for that purpose. There are some (wrong
thinkers, no doubt) who would say the government has
backed ideas of far less potential for success. This could
be a winner for you.*

*Why not give it a try? Perhaps take it up with the
cabinet? The oldest profession will always be with society, its elder members included, and they provide a service, especially for old guys like Bill Bumphrey. With
their experience, they could handle Bill in a breeze and
at far less cost to him than the $2,500 it's cost him on
the last two occasions on which he got rolled.*

*The government and civil service really ought to be
giving this proposal serious consideration. Think what
chances for advancement and empire-building there
would be in a new department called the Ontario
Hooker Control Board. But I should state right now
that if the job of commissioner of the board comes open,
I, the party whose idea this was, am going to apply for
and expect to get the position.*

*In closing, I would point out that I am not any more
senile than anyone else my age on this planet. I have
noted from time to time, even on various occasions, that*

most of Earth's inhabitants do show flashes of senili-
ty—and that's on a good day.
   Respectfully and Seriously Yours,
   Dwart A. Farquhart

"It's funny, honey, but you won't get a rise out
of them," Elspeth said after reading the letter, "if
that's what you're after. Like the lady said, they
don't have a sense of humour and are probably
deathly afraid that if they reply in the same vein,
someone higher up or in the media might see it,
and somehow they could be criticized. But if
you're determined to mail this letter, I'll get you
an envelope and a stamp."

"Thanks, but I think I'd best get it typed up at
the zoo. Sorry to have to leave so early, but I've
got some very important monkey business to dis-
cuss with Travers." Dwart got his hat and coat
from the hall closet, then took his leave after a
long French kiss at the door.

"When do I get another chance?" were his part-
ing words to Elspeth. "I think one of those oysters
is starting to work."

"Whenever you feel lucky," were hers.

WHEN DWART ARRIVED LATER THAT MORNING,
the zoo was noisy with preparations for Zoo
Celebration Week. The big parade scheduled for the
upcoming weekend was going according to plan.

As for the African Pavilion's gorilla compound,
things were in a state of confusion. Irving had

been found in the squeeze cage, in dishabille, in a
viciously foul mood. The great apes had discovered him first and thought it hilarious that one of
the white-eyes was apparently on display for their
benefit. Caroline, Barney and Samantha threw
peanut shells at him, while Xerox planted himself
in front of the cage and mimicked Irving's spasms
of outrage. Then, of course, the human attendants
showed up for work and reported it to security,
who came to investigate. They released Irving
from his embarrassing predicament, which he
refused to explain to them.

By then, word of strange happenings in the ape
section had reached Phil Travers, who hot-footed
over to see for himself, as anything to do with that
part of the zoo had now become super-sensitive
in his mind. It looked like today was going to be
as stressful as yesterday, or more so, and now he
had a small hangover to contend with as well.
The area surrounding the holding room had been
blocked off to allow for repairs to the door and
the table.

Travers summoned Fluck to his office, and he
expected a full explanation. Irving showed up in
a new set of working coveralls, looking sheepish.
Phil wondered how much Fluck knew about the
previous night's discovery of Bamboo's linguistic
ability. Probably nothing, unless he'd heard
Bamboo speak during whatever had gone on
between Fluck and the apes. Travers didn't want
to introduce the topic. Instead, he waited to see

whether Fluck brought it up.

Bamboo and Amanda were still in their sleeping quarters in the outer compound. Travers had a report on that. He knew he had last seen Amanda in the holding room as late as around eleven the previous night. Then, in the morning, Irving was found jammed into a locked squeeze cage and Amanda was sleeping outside with Bamboo, which she'd never done before. Irving's state of undress was equally mysterious. What the hell had gone on out there last night?

For his part, Irving didn't know how much Travers had surmised about the reasons for his midnight visit to the ape section. He remembered that Phil had once kidded him about Amanda, but he was sure that until now, no one at the zoo had suspected the secret nature of his interest in animals.

Phil listened to Irving's story, refraining from any comment as he did so. Fluck wasn't being quite coherent as he rambled on about doing his job, checking on the apes, hoping to catch one trying to escape, finding out how they did it, all for security reasons, of course.

Whenever he was asked to tell the truth, Irving thought this meant three different versions of the same story. He contended he'd been suddenly and viciously attacked by Bamboo for no apparent reason.

"I'm tellin' you, Phil, there was no provocation on my part. He kicked down the door for no reason I can figure, 'cause it wasn't locked, and he jumped me.

He seemed insane with rage. You know, I think there's something radically wrong with that bastard."

"It would seem he doesn't like you for some reason."

"You're damn right he doesn't He's a danger-ous beast and subject to unpredictable fits, if you ask me. He should be put down, or at least kept in a cage, before he seriously hurts someone."

"No!" Phil reacted strongly to this suggestion. "We're not about to consider such measures." Privately, he figured Irving's story to be more than a little cockamamie, not borne out by reports from others, or by any observations he'd personally made of Bamboo's conduct. Bamboo wasn't fero-cious. On the contrary, he'd become very reason-able.

Watching Phil ponder the situation in silence was making Irving nervous, so he thought he'd better keep going. "He just seemed out of his skull about something. I had to fight with him. He ripped off my clothes, and I'm telling you, I was lucky to fend him off with that table leg and get into the cage before he killed me."

There was a short silence between the men. "But why were you checking out the apes at that time of night in the first place?" Phil asked again.

"Good question. Like I told you, I was just checking that everything was all right. That's my business, that's what you pay me for—animal pro-curement, animal protection and animal security."

"You were responsible for getting Bamboo here

in the first place, granted, but now that he's in the zoo and healthy, how much concern need he be of yours? I know you don't like him and he broke your arm, but why hate him for that?"

"Maybe I shouldn't have gone there at that time. But I wasn't checking on Bamboo. I was just wandering around the entire premises and decided to check the ape quarters. You know they're always trying to escape."

"True."

"The staff told me that before you put roofs on those compounds they used to get out all the time. At one time they were putting vaseline on the walls and the apes were still getting out."

"There's no doubt that they're smart, and there are too many angles in that exhibit to keep them in without a roof. We'd tried electric wire around the top. It didn't stop them, so yes, we had to make major changes."

"Only proves you gotta keep checking, and not just in the daytime. You gotta see what they're up to when they think nobody's around watching them. That's what I was doing, Phil, spying." Irving figured he was now on the right track in convincing Travers. "Just trying to help the zoo. You people give me a lot of business."

"I want a complete report on this, Irving, in writing. This situation is very peculiar and the board's going to ask me a lot of questions about it."

"Why tell them anything? You can pass it off."

"Look, Irving, they're going to hear the story sometime. It wasn't me they found, bare balls to the breeze, locked in the squeeze cage in the gorilla quarters. It was our security expert. It's got to be investigated and that requires a report. I've got a position here, you're only on contract, which incidentally is about to expire and may not be renewed, as you always knew."

"But I was only doing stuff that was included in my contract."

"And I have to explain how the outside expert I hire as a security consultant gets outsmarted by an ape? You're not being too helpful with details, Irving, and frankly, your explanation leaves a lot to be desired. While you're writing up that report, explain to me why a security guard found a tranquilizer gun in that holding room."

"Are you calling me a liar?" Irving blustered, a nervous tick appearing in his cheek.

"No, but since your contract is nearly up, and until it's renewed after further investigation of this incident, you'd better take a leave of absence from the premises. You can leave all your keys with my secretary."

"Goddammit! That ape is a jinx. I'd like to kill that bloody monkey." Irving had been enjoying a soft touch at the zoo and now he was really pissed off, and it showed.

Phil suddenly felt the urge to be a little careful, as big Irving was working up a head of steam. He wasn't a man to antagonize at close quarters, and now looked even meaner than usual and tough enough to kick-start a Sherman tank.

"This is an example of what I mean, Irving. You're getting, ah, well, ah, a bit paranoid about Bamboo, wouldn't you say? I'm going to have to ask you to stay away from the apes altogether, and I especially mean Bamboo. If you do anything to that ape, we will sue your ass off." Phil meant business. He kept his voice hard and hoped he looked calm.

Shoving his chair violently backward, Irving stood over Travers' desk, staring hard at the administrator. "I don't like this one damn bit!"

"Neither do I. Just calm down. Good-bye for now. And you are, I presume, going to give me that report I asked for?"

Irving glared at Travers but gave no answer, then stomped out of the room and down the hall. He met Dwart Farquhart coming in, but passed him by without a word.

DWART HAD BEEN AT THE ZOO FOR THREE-QUARTERS of an hour by then. He'd dropped right into the aftermath of the Fluck-in-the-cage affair. Some workmen were cleaning up the mess in the holding room when he arrived. Dwart picked up the table leg. There was a streak of blood down one side of it, and Dwart wondered what a table leg was doing in the cage.

For some time, Dwart had been walking freely among the apes. They never bothered him and he felt no fear or anxiety in their presence. They knew him as a friend and accepted him as part of their community. Apparently, they weren't as welcoming with others.

He went searching for Bamboo and found him with Amanda in the outer sleeping section. Two things were evident. Bamboo had some bad bruises, plus a lump and caked blood on the side of his head. A torn pair of men's shorts lay in the straw near the gorillas. *What the hey?*

Dwart squatted with the apes and, using the speech, gestures, signing and body language they'd devised for communication, he got the basics of the story from their perspective.

Amanda was emphatic about some details: she'd suddenly felt drowsy and Irving had tied her down with straps.

Dwart got the picture and he was shocked. Bamboo had interrupted Fluck in some sort of sexual attack on Amanda, they'd fought, and either the apes had thrown Fluck into the cage, or Fluck had retreated there because he was losing the battle. Bamboo's condition suggested that Irving had gotten in some pretty good licks himself. Amanda, having spent the rest of the night with Bamboo, seemed in fine spirits.

This is a bad situation, Dwart thought. From what he'd seen of Irving's personality before this latest and literal embarrassment, he knew Fluck was quite capable of killing Bamboo if given the chance. The apes were on to Fluck's secret, and

Bamboo confided to Dwart that he'd spoken some white-eyes words to Fluck. Irving was also aware that Dwart and the gorillas were able to communicate to some degree. *Two apes against a white-eyes; who're they gonna believe?*

Then Dwart realized how ridiculous the notion was. The animal rights movement was getting stronger all the time, but animals still couldn't give testimony. *How could they swear on a Bible? They aren't even Christians.*

Irving had already been humiliated before the whole zoo staff. The implications of the incident, especially in Irving's mind, might grow to horrendous proportions if he thought there was enough proof of his guilt. Bamboo might be in mortal danger from the nutcase, especially if Irving's secret did involve bestiality, which was still a criminal offence in Canada and parts of the United States.

Dwart was convinced that Irving was going to pull another stupid stunt. *A knave in knight's clothing, doing his deeds in darkness. How can I prevent it?*

As Dwart questioned Bamboo again, he pondered the good and bad points of Ameslan. They were getting more proficient at it, but the sign language had its limitations.

Dwart could see now that he had a long-term responsibility toward his unfortunate fellow creature: he had to teach Bamboo not only sign language, but also to talk, to ask questions, maybe even to make jokes. Dwart was pleased with their progress in that direction. They were further along than he'd imagined was possible, and much further than he'd let on to Travers.

"Did the ugly white-eyes, Irving, did he, ah, threaten you, Bamboo?" asked Dwart.

Bamboo looked somewhat puzzled. Dwart made signs: white-eyes, pointing to his own eye, a throat-cutting motion with his finger, and asked, "Did he use a word (Dwart gave the sign for *word*) like *kill?*"

Bamboo thought, all the while puffing and pursing his lips, beating the air with accompanying hand gestures. Then he articulated, "Kill yoo, kill yoo, kill yoo." Bamboo's eyes widened and he made slicing motions across his throat with his fingers. "Kill yoo-fros tee—ugh—fu king—ugh—fri da—ugh—yoo sun uf a bich!" said Bamboo fiercely, repeating Irving's words.

Dwart was convinced. He signed to them both, "How you like white-eyes—name—Irving?"

Amanda rubbed her hands in the dirt and then pointed to herself.

"Ah, you mean dirty ape."

"Dirty toilet devil!" signed Bamboo forcefully.

Dwart signed, then said aloud, "What did you think when you got white-eyes into the cage?"

Both Amanda and Bamboo pulled up the sides of their mouths with their fingers, the sign for smile or laugh. Then all three broke into laughter, the apes with a deep-breathing huh-huh-huh sound.

Even as he laughed, Dwart knew that something had to be done about the danger posed by

Fluck, and fast, with as few people as possible knowing about it. Otherwise all they'd accomplished could be jeopardized. To Dwart it seemed that he was the logical person to do whatever had to be done, but he wasn't sure he had the guts. He resolved to plan first and worry about the danger later. He couldn't talk to Travers, either, in case his plan involved something the zoo administrator couldn't sanction.

As Dwart was signing good-bye, he noticed that Amanda was taking an interest in the badly torn pair of striped Calvin Klein shorts. *Designer shorts, yet. Who would've thought it of Irving?*

Could you get shorts in ape size? he wondered as he walked along. And if you could, why would you want to? They'd look ridiculous. He imagined the gorillas in a Calvin Klein billboard ad, in keeping with some of Klein's more outrageous underwear pitches. The slogan could be: Girls go ape over Calvin Klein shorts.

He was nearing the admin building as he wondered how much they'd pay to have Amanda and Bamboo pose in the briefs. It occurred to him that his idea might be just another way to exploit the gorillas, then decided the money could go to a trust fund to save the apes.

Entering the building, he had to step aside as Irving Fluck, obviously in a black rage, passed him in the hall without speaking. "Someone really twisted his kilt," Dwart muttered on his way to Travers' office.

"I've been out to see Bamboo," he said as he entered. "It's a bad situation. What do you propose to do about it, Phil, if it's any of my business?"

"Right now, most of my time's taken up with getting this Zoo Celebration Week under way, starting with Saturday's parade down Yonge Street. I can't think about anything else until after that."

"I sure hope that isn't too late."

"What do you mean?"

"Irving is a strange and dangerous man."

"I agree. There's something fishy about his story."

Dwart didn't tell Phil that he thought he knew what smelled. Travers was a strong ally of ape survival, but he had a position to maintain and a board of directors. He couldn't just authorize some quiet, covert action; he had to go through channels. Best not to have anyone connected with the zoo in on what's percolating in my mind, he thought.

"Well, I'll keep my eyes open," he said aloud. "Let me know if I can help. I'll keep in touch." Dwart left the busy office.

He called Elspeth from a pay phone in the lobby. "Good morning again, tiger, or is it afternoon? It's me, Aloysius."

"I know, I know."

"I'm at the zoo. Something's happened, and it's not good. I'm going to need your help. Do you still have some good connections at costume supply places?"

"Mmm...yes. At Mallabars. The owner's a great old friend of mine. Why?"

"I'll tell you about it when I see you. I've got some planning to do."

"What are you planning, Dwart?"

"I'll tell you in person. I'm grabbing a cab. Be right over."

17

THE BIG PARADE

They drove to Mallabars right after lunch and parked near the employees' entrance. Elspeth, who knew her way through the labyrinth, led Dwart to the costume room, an impressive, complex clutter of sewing machines, cutting tables and a kaleidoscope of assorted costumery. A woman of indeterminate vintage sat at a desk in the far corner of the room.

Elspeth introduced her to Dwart. "This is Dorothy Ozolinski, one of the best and fastest in the business. You want a costume, you got it."

"Ma'am, a great pleasure to meet you. I'm appreciative of any services you can render on such short notice."

"Not at all. Anything for the Egans, mother or daughter. They're old friends, and any friend of theirs..." Her face crabbed with wrinkles as she smiled. "What exactly is it that you need?"

"I need a very large tuxedo for comic purposes. I've got the measurements right here. You'll find them a little strange, long in the arm, short in the leg, with a large waist."

Mrs. Ozolinski looked over the sheet of paper that Dwart handed to her. "Yes, indeed," was her only comment, "Obviously not for you."

"You might have to take two or three other tuxedos and sort of take them apart and amalgamate them into one," suggested Dwart.

"That's my thinking, too. It'd be quicker, and for that matter, cheaper than a new one."

"New isn't necessary. Old is good."

"We always have some rental tuxedos around; in fact, sometimes we put them on sale. What colour do you want? They come in all colours. Pink, perhaps?" She gave him the crinkly smile again.

Dwart thought that over. *Maybe. Outlandish might be better, since the whole idea requires audacity.* Then he decided it was a bold enough scheme already. "No. I think just a standard black, please."

"All right, anything else?"

"Yep, I need the frilly-front shirt."

"What neck size?"

"Ah, a twenty-two neck should do. You're going to have to split a shirt down the back and add in. The sleeve measurements are written on that piece of paper. Do you have some oversize clown shoes in stock?"

"Yes."

"A pair of those, and paint them black."

"Okay."

"A cummerbund to fit the waist, suspenders, and please sew up a black tie long enough to fit the shirt. Oh yes, and throw in a cane and a large top hat. I'll get the size for you."

"You have a big friend."

"Yes, big enough, but we pad him out a lot. Burlesque, you know, trying for an authentically different look."

"I think you're going to get it," said the seamstress.

"Dorothy, can we get all this in three days, by Saturday morning, early?" asked Elspeth. "Sorry to impose, but it is important."

"Rest assured, my dear, you'll have it," replied Dorothy, "but you'll have to pick it up, I can't deliver."

"Right then, first thing Saturday morning."

They were about to leave after thanking her profusely when Dwart had a thought about the hat. "The top hat may be a tough item to produce."

"I've been thinking about that. Call me back with a head measurement and I'll slice into an existing hat like a piece of pie, then staple or sew an insert into the expanded portion."

As they left in Elspeth's car, Dwart couldn't help but comment, "Now that is one accommodating lady."

"Yes, and you can trust her to do it well and to

have it done on time. She made most of my costumes and makes all of Little Else's. Very reliable, always has been. Used to make costumes for Georgia Sothern. And for Blue Sapphire, my first stripping coach. Those were the good old days— five hundred a week, compared to the pittance you could make schlepping drinks, stuffing envelopes or babysitting.

"Did you know that H.L. Mencken thought up the word 'ecdysiast' as a fancy term for stripping? He was a friend of Sothern's, who thought public objections to strip-tease would vanish if it were known by a new and more palatable name. Comes from the zoological term for moulting."

"So that's what you were doing on stage...classical moulting?"

"It was a living, and very lucrative, especially when you became an expert, got an established name and top billing."

"You're talking to the converted, Elspeth, I love strippers. On that note, did I tell you about my Calvin Klein underwear idea?"

Dwart explained the idea to her as they drove. He told her what had happened at the zoo, what he feared might happen, and how he planned to thwart Irving. Finally, he swore her to secrecy.

THE ONTARIO PROVINCIAL ZOO'S ANNIVERSARY day had arrived, and the parade down Yonge Street was to kick off a week of special events and exhibits. For a couple of daylight hours, wild animals would take over the street where wild homo sapiens prowled by night.

There would be marching bands, floats, a few tame elephants and other animals walking with their trainers, just like the old days when the circus came to town. Some of the larger and more dangerous animals would be hauled in cages by gaily decorated trucks.

Big Charlie, Toronto's own silverback gorilla, was sure to be a hit again. Torontonians loved him as much as they did the Maple Leafs, the Blue Jays or the double-blue Argonauts.

Clowns, balloons and unicyclists would be part of the peripheral fol-de-rol. The whole hodge-podge was being assembled at the zoo, and would be transported by truck to the starting point downtown.

Dwart hung around the African Pavilion where the zoo attendants' attention was on getting Big Charlie ready for his downtown sortie. The area was full of service vehicles.

Elspeth, decked out in a fancy clown suit, sat in the driver's seat of a 1923 open Country Club touring car, loaned to her by a friend. She was parked as close as she could get to the ape holding area between the inner and outer ape compounds.

The oversize tuxedo for Bamboo and a clown suit for Dwart were in a large suitcase he'd stashed in the holding area, and he carried a smaller briefcase containing the accessories. He watched for a chance to isolate himself and Bamboo long enough to get the ape into the tux and himself into the clown suit. Watching the elephants go by and looking at the briefcase in his hand, Dwart thought of the old joke about the briefcase made from an elephant's foreskin: very handy and very smooth; you just rub it and it turns into a two-suiter.

Dwart saw his chance when a commotion erupted in the other end of the building. Perhaps the keepers were having some trouble with Big Charlie. He signalled Bamboo to follow him into the shower room.

One weak point in his plan was convincing Bamboo to wear the tuxedo. *How come they ever called this a monkey suit?* He hoped the suggestion of escape would clinch his attempts to persuade the gorilla to squeeze into the tux. That and a lot of lettuce; Bamboo loved lettuce.

"On, Bamboo. Put on. Let me do you," Dwart said aloud, signing at the same time.

"That?" asked Bamboo, pointing to the lace on the shirt.

"That's lace," Dwart voiced only, trying to remember the sign for lace. "You eat your lettuce and let me dress you."

"Sit?"

"No, I've got the shirt on. Bamboo stand."

"Pants there."

"Yes, pants. Look, watch me. One leg at a time."

Bamboo did as well as could be expected, but it was slow work.

"Hat, hat, hat that!"

"You got that right. You're a smart gorilla, Bamboo. Have some more lettuce." Finally Dwart managed to do a passable job. Nearly done, all but the string tie and the shoes. To hell with the shoes, he decided. Either they'd make it or they wouldn't.

"Bamboo look, Bamboo listen. Look, listen, hard. Will be much noise, see many new things." His worry was that the great ape would spook at all the excitement and rapid changes to which he was about to be subjected.

"Me listen, me watch."

Clown suits wouldn't likely bother Bamboo, he'd already seen zoo visitors in a gaudy array of chintzy clothes. Dwart got into his one-piece suit. But what about the masks? Dwart pulled the one he was going to wear out of the briefcase, showed it to Bamboo, and said, "Show fake. Do fake," and then put on the mask. Then he took it off. "Two face— look—two face." He repeated the action and said, "Me." Putting it back on again, he ran up and down the room beating his chest like a gorilla. Taking the mask off he laughed and said "See fake."

"Huh—ugh, huh, huh, huh! Yes, fake." Bamboo laughed too, then grabbed the mask from Dwart and tried to put it on, knocking his hat off in the process.

Dwart snatched it back and said, "No, not you, me fake. You don't need fake."

"Hat visit hair time do take off there?" Bamboo bounced up and down in excitement, trying to get his hat back on.

Dwart set the hat straight on Bamboo's head, then opening the door slightly, he cased the premises. The attendants were leaving with Big Charlie in his cage. Dwart tried to fix Bamboo's string tie again. No dice. Elspeth could fix the damn thing, women were better at that stuff, anyway. "We're going now, Bamboo—*move!*"

The two clownish figures, one the standard three-ring-circus type, the other an ape in a tuxedo, crossed the open space between the outer door and the car where Elspeth waited. The lone security guard in the area saw them from a distance, but he was much more interested in the hullabaloo surrounding Charlie than the antics of some clowns in an antique touring car, obviously on their way to the parade. He made no attempt to stop or examine them. Dwart shoved Bamboo into the back seat, talking to him all the while in encouraging tones. Elspeth moved over, Dwart got behind the wheel and their vehicle joined the throng of trucks and cars heading for the starting point of the procession.

"What do?" asked Bamboo.

"Act like a gorilla in a parade," Dwart replied.

"Name parade—what?"

"No talk. Eat those bananas." Dwart pointed to a cardboard box full of them in the back seat. "You'll find out soon enough."

The four-cylinder Model A engine was putt-putting along in fine form.

Elspeth said, "The owner told me that, despite its name, this car only stops if it gets outside the city limits into the country. So we should be okay."

They debated the merits of making a break from the other vehicles right away, but thought it might look too suspicious, so they opted for staying with the cavalcade a while longer. Before they could decide on a likely place to veer off, the parade master's convertible swung in next to them and he yelled, "Hey, that's a good lookin' rig. I want you up near the front when we start."

Dwart shouted back, "How about the rear? Good to have a strong finish."

"This is bad, Dwart," Elspeth murmured to him, "he wants to see us in this parade and he'll remember if we're not in it, whether we're at the back or the front. Can we make it through the whole thing before we make a break?

"Follow me," yelled the parade master.

"Let's wait and see, maybe we'll get our chance later on."

At first Bamboo was skittish and frightened, but his head no longer ached and he began to enjoy himself. He'd never before seen the white-eyes working with all their various contraptions.

With the police giving them a motorcycle escort and clearing the traffic ahead of them, they soon reached the starting point at the corner of

Bloor and Yonge. They tried to keep the touring car as far back in the parade as they could, but what with the parade master bugging them and no good chance to split, the big shebang was under way before they knew it.

With the bands playing and the crowds getting thicker along Yonge Street, Dwart and Elspeth became caught up in the spirit of the event, especially as they saw Bamboo watching and listening in amazement. Elspeth showed him how to properly doff his hat and take a bow. They heard a spectator marvel at how real Bamboo looked.

"Holy H. Smoke, I wonder how long this is going to take?" Dwart shouted at Elspeth.

"In a parade you have to go the route. We're in it and there's no way to predict how long it'll be. I'd say maybe an hour or so, pet. But aren't we having fun?"

The parade passed Wellesley, College, Dundas, Queen and King streets. The parade was nearly over. They could see the O'Keefe Centre looming large a few blocks ahead, along with the Royal York Hotel and Union Station. The traffic on the side streets was congested.

Dwart was extremely anxious. Spotting a sudden break in the pedestrian traffic to the east on Colborne Street, he shouted, "We gotta try to get off the main drag, Ellie, so it's now or never," and in his excitement he swung sharply left out of the parade line-up.

"I hate to say this, lover, but this is a one-way

street going west! Didn't you see the arrows?"

"Hell, I didn't even see the Indians," answered Dwart, trying to correct his error by cutting south on Scott, which turned out to be a one-way going north. He shot through Wellington against the grain, but the old car and costumes attracted so much attention that every other driver made way. He cut correctly left and headed toward the old town of York on Front Street East.

Elspeth yelled, "For Christ's sake Fark, park, before you kill us all!"

Dwart swung down Market Street and braked to a halt in a No Parking zone. Bamboo watched everything with interest, munching calmly on a banana. He hadn't had so much fun since he left Africa.

"I'd better drive," said Elspeth, and she forcefully changed places with Dwart and got behind the wheel. She drove through the traffic on Market Street. At the Yonge Street corner she signalled a right, feinted left, then drove straight ahead toward Dwart's boarding house on Markham, her automatic lane straddler working well all the way.

"Elspeth," said Dwart, when they stopped in front of his house, "this whole thing reminds me of what they said when the nun fell down on top of the court jester."

"Okay, what'd they say?"

"They said, 'This is virgin on the ridiculous!'"

"WHAT DO YOU MEAN, BAMBOO'S MISSING?"

Phil Travers screamed at the security guard, his lips turning white.

"I mean he's not in those compounds, he's not in that pavilion anywhere, sir."

Phil's voice dropped to a fierce whisper as he stroked his goatee in agitation. "And just where do you suppose he might be?"

"I, ah, I, I really don't know."

"Then find him. *Find him—or else!*"

"Or else what, sir?"

"Or else you're all bloody well fired, that's what else! Search the other pavilions. Search the woods. We've got seven hundred and ten acres out there—he's got to be o ut there someplace. I want that ape back here. He's the most val—. Just find him and get him back here in good shape. Any word, any sign of his whereabouts, I want it reported to me, personally, immediately. Is that clear?'

"Very clear, sir, but I don't think it's fair..."

"I don't give a monkey's dink what you think! Now get going and track him down." As the hapless guard left the room, Travers sank despondently into his office chair, his handsome face pale and lined with worry.

18

BILL BUMPHREY

Dwart looked at Bamboo, then at the stack of bills on the mantlepiece for vegetables, fruits and nuts. "And that's not all you eat," he said to the big ape. "How about all the leaves, grains, shoots and other goodies I purloin for you from the larder out at the zoo?"

"Me eat, Dwart, maybe sandwich, pea-nut-but-her. Good. Good. What purloin there?" replied Bamboo.

"I hate saying steal, dammit. I liberate the stuff for you, is all. It's just lying around, so I take it. They'd have to feed you anyway if you were still out at the zoo, so it's not really stealing. I take it, that's what I do, and I feed it to you, and you damn well eat a lot of it. I never really realized just how much you do eat. You know, it's time you started to earn your keep."

"What mean, Old Fart?"

"It means you've got to go to work. You have to

do something that helps bring in money, so we can buy groceries for you to eat, to stuff down your gullet."

"Bamboo love eat."

"That settles it, I have to put you to work."

"No understand work talk. No understand work, what word that? Time eat." Bamboo pointed to the refrigerator.

"That figures," said Dwart, "it shows that you're already fitting into the welfare state. Maybe I should take you down to the social assistance office and apply for benefits. Only trouble is, we don't really know what kind of work you're out of, and if I tell them you know how to do absolutely nothing, they'll think you're already working for the government."

"Bamboo love work?"

"Some do, some don't, mostly the latter. Anyway, I've been figuring out what you could do, Bamboo. You're going to make your debut in show business and I've got just the act for you."

"What, what? Work? Frown bad."

"I thought you were Bamboo, the Brilliant Gorilla."

"False."

"No, true."

"Me gorilla good forgot."

"Be patient. This is an old vaudeville routine. You don't do much talking, if any. That's good for breaking you in. And you'll be the perfect example of typecasting—you'll play a gorilla. But I need a girl, a talking lady. You come into the club with this girl and the two of you interrupt the act I'm doing. It's a natural." Dwart augmented the main ideas in sign language as he talked.

"Girl, girl—Elspeth?"

"Why not? Sure, that's the best idea. Either her or Elsie. They're used to you, you don't scare the hell out of them like you do most people when you're outside a cage. But the audience won't know you're a real gorilla, they'll just think it's a magnificent make-up job. A man in an ape suit. I'll set it up and get the script ready. I think I can remember it."

Dwart's excitement grew and his words spilled out in a torrent. "This'll be a gas. They might go for it at that Shriner's convention coming up at Maple Leaf Gardens. But a better spot would be the Pink Pussycat. Burr McClintock's always looking for something new to put in the place. A bit of the old burlesque.

"This is going to be your dee-butt, boy, and after you get better at talking, we'll register you as a landed immigrant with the federal government. You're already bilingual. We'll get a work permit and bill you for what you really are, a real live talking gorilla. When they find out you're the real McCoy and not a phony baloney, they're going to go apeshit!

"They don't have an immigration quota for gorillas, but Canada allowed you in legally, so you're entitled to Canadian citizenship. It's easy to get a Canadian passport, any foreign criminal can vouch for that. You're going to be world famous, my friend. We may save you and your buddies yet, Bamboo. Stick with me, baby, and you'll be farting through silk."

"Yes, eat, Fart, Bamboo love food."

"Look, Bamboo, I told you, you can't eat all the time. I should go out for a while and see to a few things, make some arrangements."

"Bamboo go out. Bamboo love parade."

"We don't want panic in the streets. There's no more parade. I can't take you with me."

"Bamboo love out."

"I'm sorry, you have to stay here and do whatever."

"Teeth bite good. Banana nice."

"Oh, and remember what I showed you about the toilet and how to flush."

"Rotten toy-let," said Bamboo.

"It's not like the jungle. Crap on the floor is not biodegradable. We're more civilized here in Toronto—we use sewage disposal and dump all our shit into Lake Ontario, let it float around for a while until it thins out a bit and then we drink it. That's the hygienic way of doing things.

"You don't understand all that, I know, but if I can get you enrolled in the University of Toronto, you could get a degree in sanitary engineering and then you'd know all about how to do these things. I'm working on it. I could likely get you in on an athletic scholarship. Boy, could the Blues ever use you. Their linemen usually lead the league in all offensive categories, including nose hairs. You'd never make the team at Western, though, you're too good-looking."

Dwart knew Bamboo still understood only a small part of what he said, but sometimes, being a compulsive talker, he just rambled on anyway. It seemed the friendly thing to do and he figured it should continue to be a teaching tool, since the ape had learned a great deal already merely by listening to people talk.

When he really wanted Bamboo to understand and react, he spoke slowly and was careful to use simple words, clear pronunciation and straight-forward language and sentences, often accompanied by sign language.

"Me go out. Bamboo stay. Okay?"

"Out go visit. Okay." Bamboo signed good-bye.

"You, Bamboo, bolt door. Clean up room. What would you like me to bring you?"

"Drink there."

"What?"

"Gorilla drink beer."

"We can't afford any. I told you about money, Bamboo. Is that last case all gone? If so, sorry. No beer."

"Gimme champagne," Bamboo persisted.

"Champagne! What the hey! You and me and Elspeth celebrate with a couple of bottles after the escape and now you want more. Why do you like champagne?"

"Good drink on lip there. Bamboo love."

"You've got a champagne taste and I haven't even got a beer budget. That's why I'm going out, to see if I can arrange some income."

Bamboo watched from the upstairs window as the Old Fart walked down the tree-lined street, intermittently appearing and disappearing among the foliage. Then he bolted the door as instructed and used the toilet, with a great deal of difficulty. He needed a bigger, custom-made commode. Returning to the living room, he turned on the TV and tuned in to Sesame Street.

Dwart walked through the park to see if he could locate Bumphrey and sure enough, the octogenarian was sitting on his customary bench feeding bread crumbs soaked in vodka to the pigeons. "Makes them easy to catch when they get drunk," Bill told him, "and a good squab pie ain't to be sneezed at, I'll guarantee."

Bill told Dwart that he had something strange in his possession, maybe a collector's item, but he didn't really know what to make of it. "It does require some legal action, Farky, in my opinion."

"What might that item be, Bill, and what kind of action are you talking about?" asked Dwart, always amazed at what Bumphrey would come up with next.

"Cast your orbs on this," and Bill thrust a Father's Day card into Dwart's hands. "I got this in the mail from the daughter of one of my cousins. And I don't think it's proper that such a card should be sold to a young innocent girl."

The picture on the card was of a beautiful little girl lifting her dress. She wasn't wearing any panties.

Dwart stared in disbelief and finally said, "Cute kid. I'm not known as a prude, Bill, but this leaves something to be desired, I'll agree with you on that." Bill had him baffled and worried. "So what's this action you're talking about?"

"Now, take a look at this article in the Globe and Mail, Farky," and Bill handed him a newspaper clipping.

Dwart read the news item. "For Pete's sake, Stanton's is selling this card, Bill. I can't believe it, it must be some kind of mistake. Since their first store opened these guys haven't even stocked, let alone sold, cigarettes and tobacco. And now they're selling these kind of cards to little girls on Father's Day!"

"I didn't know about the cigarettes."

"That's right, the original old man Stanton was dead set against tobacco and decreed that it was, what? An instrument of the devil or something like that. Turns out he was right. Anyway, he wasn't having any sold in his stores."

"What's he selling now? Sex?"

"Well, it's not really sex, and look what the article says. That some people are going to find the card offensive and in bad taste. They sure will!"

"That's my complaint, Farky. What happened to blue Toronto? The chicken crown counsel says the police acted on a public complaint, but that the card probably wouldn't meet the definition of obscenity under the criminal code."

"I think he's right, Bill. They've asked Stanton's, according to the article, to remove the cards from their shelves and they've done it. What more do you want?"

"To heck with that noise. Every time I got into some deep doo-doo, the cops and the prosecution counsel always said, 'Yeah, we appreciate that the excuse you're offering may well mean that you're innocent, but it's not up to us to decide. We have to charge you and let the judge decide.' And then we had to go all through that court hearing crap; and usually, like I told them, I got off."

"Bill, a charge in this case isn't likely to produce a conviction. That's what the crown lawyers are saying."

"Balls on a hen turkey! Let's you and me go down to the cop shop and I'll demand, as an irate citizen whose sensibilities have been hurt, that they lay obscenity charges. Imagine selling that card, first to a little girl, and then I have to get it in the mail from her. It's shocking! Those sons of bitches! Or we could take Stanton's to civil court."

"I know you, Bill. You're just looking to cause trouble. Settle down and forget about it. I can't help you on this one. I've got something really important to do. I can't tell you what right now, but it's big and it's going to take up most of my time. That's what I wanted to tell you. In fact, I gotta go right now and work on the situation. So long for now, see you when I can."

"Come back, Farky." Bill shouted after him. "Goddammit, I'm going to sue the bastards, tell Stanton's that if they don't play ball, I'll shove the bat up their ass. They've put me into shock, I've got nervous palsy worrying over this thing. They should pay me a million dollars in damages for mental anguish and suffering.

"I'll take this to the Supreme Court of Canada. Dammit, every time I have sexual relations now, I think of my own relations sending me that picture, and it's so incestuous I have to back off. They've ruined my sex life, they've made me an impotentate. I'm only eighty-five, I was saving the best stuff till the last. I could have gone another fourteen years; I had it all planned. Those bastards have got to pay through the nose for what they've done to me. I'll go after them in Queen's Bench."

Bill continued to rant and rave to passersby. They ignored him, which only made Bill more angry. Farky was the one person who paid attention to him.

Dwart was already across the park, but he could still hear Bumphrey's voice. Sad, he thought. We all eventually came to the end of the line. It'd be nice if we knew when it was time to get off.

19

GORILLA MY DREAMS

"It's a natural, Burr: Ape escapes from Ontario Provincial Zoo. You've seen the headlines in the papers. I don't think you'll be sorry you tried out an ape act at the Pink Pussycat, not with all the media coverage. The actor and the costume will be here in a few minutes."

"Is it a good act?"

"Is it a good act, he wants to know. Let's say it's as good as it ever was."

"And just how good was that?"

"It was a genuine burlesque act, Burr, nothing more, nothing less. It played very well in the old days. Some of the punchlines come in by bus à la Wayne and Schuster or Henny Youngman, but so what?"

"What was wrong with those guys?"

"Nothing. I'm not knocking them. Actually, they're my type of comics. You may have noticed, some of my jokes aren't exactly new."

"Yeah, I've heard a few groaners, but some people seem to like 'em, and maybe the rest just like to groan."

"You sure know how to hurt a guy. What can you say about this type of routine except that it works. People like a little corn, and the ape, he'll look real. The guy I found is an expert make-up artist, a regular Lon Chaney; he's built such a good ape suit you won't be able to tell him from a real gorilla. You'll meet him tonight."

"Okay, I'm convinced. It could give the crowd a boost, especially as we got our own zoo ape wandering around Toronto. I figure he must have been kidnapped or they would've found him by now."

"I agree with that theory," said Dwart, sipping on his draft beer, "but the zoo will likely get Bamboo back eventually. Now, I've rehearsed this guy with Little Else's mother, who's Something Else."

"You can say that again, I know her, comes around to see Little Else every once in a while. Some good lookin', too, for a bird her age. Understand she used to be in show business."

"Don't try to cut my time, Burr. I like her, so hit on some of your own dancers."

"Relax. I'm not hittin' on anybody. Screwing the staff doesn't help me run this joint any better." Burr mulled over his own statement for a few moments. "On the other hand, it might not hurt."

"You'll like the costume, Burr, it's the cat's ass.

He'll come in the front with Elspeth and they're going to interrupt my act. It's sort of an actus interruptus routine. Oh yeah, and I'm using a musician from the rock band who says he can play a mediocre trumpet. He plays behind the curtain while the gorilla pretends to play it out front—that's the finale of the act. So if you could just tell him it's okay."

"You usually know what you're doing."

"I like to think so. Anyway, you don't want the same stuff all the time. You said so yourself, 'Monotony doesn't attract repeat trade—keep it different, keep it topical, and they'll keep coming back to see what's going on.' That's what you said."

"Okay, Dwart. I'll ride shotgun at the front of the house to make sure nobody messes with the gorilla guy."

If they try, they'll get a big surprise, Dwart said to himself with a smile, but I sure hope they don't.

"Just remember, that motorcycle gang is probably going to be here tonight," Burr reminded him.

"Fine, just keep them off Elspeth, will you? You know, if they try to get out of hand with her."

"I don't think you have to worry about them anymore. They're on your side now. A few came in last week when you weren't on. Came back to the bar to see me. Made a point of askin' why you weren't on the bill. They said they'd take it unkindly if I didn't hire you more often."

"Should I take that as a compliment?"

"They're a rough crowd, but you do keep them in line somehow."

"I don't back off if they get boisterous; that's the answer. If I were a junior citizen I wouldn't talk to them that way. They're rough, but they have some good qualities."

"If this act works tonight, we'll use it every Friday and Saturday night for a while. I don't want to do any more payroll, so how's if I just pay you for the whole act and you take care of the others?"

"Fine by me, and if you can make it cash, all the better."

"Right."

Dwart left Burr fixing the mix machine behind the bar and headed backstage. Bamboo and Elspeth were in the alley, using her Volkswagen van as a dressing room, even though they'd already costumed before driving down to the Pussycat. The club didn't have enough dressing room space as it was, and Bamboo wouldn't pass close scrutiny by the backstage denizens. The plan was to hustle him into the club from behind the bar, which was part of the act, do the routine and hustle him out the back and into the van right afterward.

Dwart hoped it would work, but he was philosophical. He figured when you got over a certain age you had to keep your nerve, stay with the action and try to use it to your own advantage.

He, Elspeth and Bamboo were about to pull a con job on a society that did its best to disengage oldsters from the game of life and leave them as atrophying spectators on the sidelines.

He and Elspeth had talked it over and agreed there was little to lose by rocking the boat and putting on a show involving a real gorilla. They wanted the fun and excitement, and they didn't plan to get caught.

Bamboo had nothing to lose, unless it was the landed immigrant status he should now be entitled to. The Department of Immigration had let him into the country, he spoke better English than some Canadians, and he had a job. What else would he need? Dwart knew lawyers who had taken worse cases to the Supreme Court of Canada. That didn't mean much, because he also knew lawyers who only worked because they were too nervous to pick pockets.

They were all prepared for showtime, Elspeth and Bamboo awaiting their cue to enter. Dwart went back into the club and waited in the wings while the band played *With Plenty of Money and You*, for the enjoyment of the capacity crowd of noisy young drinkers.

The band finished and the Old Fart stepped through the curtain break, front and centre.

"Good evening ladies and gentlemen. A pleasure to be here. I see we have a cosmopolitan audience here tonight. Now, would everybody out there who isn't gay clap their hands together.

Thank you one and all. Every entertainer likes a good round of applause. I know, you're saying what's that old fart doing up there? Well, it's because that's who I am: the original Old Fart.

"Does that bother you, ma'am? According to some gals, only male chauvinistic pigs fart. You see, women don't fart, they fluff. Let's see how many male chauvinistic pigs we have here tonight. Are you a male chauvinistic pig, sir? Tell the truth!"

"No," replied the guy at the front table.

"He's saying no because he wants to score tonight, and I understand that. Let's have a show of hands, or better still, all you male chauvinists just yell out *Yay, men!*"

After a feeble chorus from a few men, Dwart said, "Okay, there's a few guys who don't want to get laid tonight. The rest of you try to act normal.

"Female chauvinists? How many female chauvinists do we have here tonight? Yell *Yay women!*

"There's a few of you, too, okay. How many ladies do we have here tonight who think that if they do the same amount of work as a man does at the same job, you should be paid the same amount of money, if not more? Let's hear it again, *Yay women!*" Most of the women obliged.

"Well, that's what we're all lookin' for later on tonight—women!

"What was I talking about? Don't tell me I've lost my train of thought already. The band was playing that song about plenty of money and you before I came on. I'll start there. Unfortunately, that describes the only two things in life that make it worth living for some people, money and sex. Notice the priorities in that song, though. D'you think maybe they got it in reverse? For their next number, I'm going to request *I Couldn't Leave Her Behind Alone* from the sound track of the Shriek of Agony."

Some groans went up from the audience, and Dwart said, "You don't like that song? Then maybe I should sing one for you myself. Sure, why not? This song is so old I bet no one here ever heard it before. I learned this song at Sophie Tucker's knee. Not a pretty sight, ladies and gentlemen, not a pretty sight. Here goes:

'Don't cry, dear Daddy, Why are you sad today,

Is it because dear Mother Has left you and gone away?

As the tears rolled down me trousers,

I said to my daughter...Jack, I'm crying because your Mother has gone...

And I'm frightened she might come back...!'"

Dwart acknowledged the applause: "Thank you for that spontaneous outburst of scattered indifference. But I digress. I should tell you how I came to be billed as the Old Fart. It's simply because of my age."

"Yours or your jokes?" asked a heckler.

"In biblical times it was considered a miracle if you could get an ass to speak. Now it would be a miracle if you could get one to shut up. Folks, I know for a fact that God has a sense of humour; and if you don't believe me, just look around the room. I prefer to think it was because of my age, but it was kind of you to ask.

"Some people think that at my age I'm past sex. Now, that's a myth, you can't prove it by me. Admittedly, I'm more into information than I am into sex—getting knowledge, as it were. You might say I'm over the hump and am now an infomaniac.

"By the way, did you hear about the sixty-five-year-old flasher? He was going to retire but he decided to stick it out for one more year.

"My doctor told me I should get a little more exercise and he suggested every day I should go out and play thirty-six holes. So I bought myself this harmonica." Dwart pulled a harmonica from his pocket and displayed it, then blew into the mouth organ, pretending to get his lip or tongue stuck in one of the holes.

"And that's what I'm going to do for you this evening." He put the instrument to his mouth again and played a ragged scale. "I bet you thought I was going to be lousy. Mouth organ music isn't difficult, it just goes blow, suck, blow, blow, suck, suck, blow." The groans were louder this time. "Look, I know this act smells, I'm closer to it than you are.

"Ladies and gentlemen, I would like to play for your pleasure right now, a beautiful tune by Cole Porter, *Night and Day*. Like the beat-beat-beat of the tom-toms, oh, I can hardly wait to hear this. I should get a seat out there myself and listen to this." He played the opening of the song using only one note.

That was the cue for the interruption. Elspeth approached the stage from behind the bar with Bamboo in tow, dressed in his tux.

"Oh, I'm so thrilled," Elspeth gushed. "How's the show going so far? Isn't that a couple of seats over there? Oh yes, I can see some. See you all later." Then, to the gorilla, "Come on, darling," and Bamboo followed her. They approached seats near the stage that had been purposely left vacant. Dwart stopped playing the harmonica and stared in mock disbelief.

"Wait, wait, wait. Just one cotton-pickin' minute here, lady. You can't come in here with that thing!"

"And why not?" Elspeth asked.

"Well, we've got an audience here. What about the smell?"

"Oh, he'll get used to it," was Elspeth's quick rejoinder.

"You can't talk to these people like that. I mean, that gorilla's gotta leave right now, before we have a policeman take him out."

"He doesn't go out with policemen."

"Well, where's he going to sit?"

"Any place he wants to, I would imagine. Sit down, darling," Elspeth cooed to Bamboo, at the same time signing him to sit, which he did.

Dwart began to plead with Elspeth. "Wait a minute, wait a minute. You don't understand. I'm trying to do an act here."

"We've seen your act, and we don't understand it either."

The skit continued with a bit about how the gorilla managed to get past Burr McClintock in the first place. Clutching his head in exasperation, Dwart said, "There's no use talking to you. Will you please sit down in front?"

Elspeth looked herself over and replied, "I'm not built that way."

"I didn't mean it that way," was the straight-man's line.

"Do you mind gorillas in here?"

"I certainly do mind gorillas in here."

"Well, would you mind this one? I have to go to the powder room." And Elspeth exited.

"Hey, hold it. Oh, hell." Dwart stood staring at the ape. "Get a haircut or something, will ya? This show's going ape. I gotta finish my harmonica solo. Cole Porter's beautiful *Day and Night*, I mean *Night and Day*." Dwart repeated his one-note tune, then he paused and said, "You can't say much for my talent, but my courage demands respect," then continued to play.

This called for Elspeth to come back into the room, and when he saw her, Dwart said, "Welcome back from the can, lady. Could you hear us in there? We could hear you in here," then continued to play.

They worked in some jokes about the quality of Dwart's playing, Elspeth suggesting he get off the stage. Dwart refused and Bamboo jumped up on the stage, ostensibly to throw him off. They faked a wrestling match, then pretended to discover that Elspeth and the ape were really in show business together and that they had a musical number they wanted to perform.

"What do you do?" asked Dwart.

"I sing and the big ape accompanies me on the trumpet."

"What are you going to play?"

Bamboo spoke up for the first time, "Gorilla My–ugh–Dreams" . . ."

The crowd seemed to be taken aback at hearing the ape talk, instead of the grunts and other animal noises he'd made until then. Then, as if reminding themselves that it was a guy in an ape suit after all and of course he could talk, they applauded.

"You mean to tell me the ape talks?" Dwart asked Elspeth meekly.

"Of course, don't they all? Say something for the man, sweetheart."

Bamboo stepped to the edge of the stage and tried the gag they'd rehearsed: "What weighs–ugh–four hundred pounds–has four legs–ugh–hair all over–ugh–and screws ants?"

Dwart, still playing the foil, said, "I don't know, what does weigh four hundred pounds, has four legs, hair all over, and screws ants?"

"My two, ugh, uncles!" Bamboo quipped.

Dwart noticed that Bamboo's *ughs* were becoming softer and and less pronounced. The gorilla's speech was improving rapidly. Dwart feigned nervous co-operation and asked Elspeth, "What do you want me to do?"

Elspeth told him to stand there and listen. Picking up a trumpet from the band stashed there for the purpose, she handed it to Bamboo, who placed the instrument to his lips as he'd been taught to do by Dwart. The crowd reacted with more laughter. At the same time, Dwart stepped forward to make the introduction, "You've probably heard of the sweetest music this side of heaven, well now we're going to hear music from the other side."

The trumpet player behind the curtain started to play a solo of *Girl of My Dreams*, and the pit band picked up the tune with a guitar and drums. Bamboo was miming the trumpet playing in front of the curtain. It was going well.

Suddenly Irving Fluck burst through the front door and charged haphazardly at the stage, weaving between the crowded tables and brandishing a forty-five-calibre pistol over his head.

"That's him right there! That's Bamboo, the ape that escaped from the zoo. Help me capture the bastard!"

Everyone laughed, thinking Fluck was part of the act, but Dwart, Elspeth and Bamboo froze.

Bamboo stopped miming, his playful body lan-

guage and gestures gone, as he adopted a crouching cross-armed defensive posture, and the audience picked up on the menace inherent in his
stance.

Dropping the trumpet, Bamboo tore open his
tuxedo shirt and thumped his chest, letting out an
unmistakable animal roar. A shot from Irving's
gun sang past his head and ripped through the
curtain, literally tearing the real trumpet from the
hands of the musician behind it, ending *Girl of My
Dreams* in mid-note as the man let out a yell of
surprise and fear.

The crowd suddenly realized they were dealing
with a real ape and a real killer. They stampeded,
pouring through, around and over the tables in
the general direction of the exits.

The bikers, however, loved a brawl. Irving
fought against the flow of the rushing crowd,
pushing his way toward the stage. He couldn't get
a clear, well-aimed shot at Bamboo. Just as he
broke free of the crowd, the bikers closed in. Like
pro linebackers, one hit him low and another hit
him high with flying blocks to the body. They all
went down in a crush of tangled humanity. At the
same time, Burr McClintock, coming around
from the front the bar, managed to get between
Fluck and the stage. He leaped into the pile, looking specifically for Irving's gun hand. He twisted
Fluck's wrist and the gun discharged into the ceiling as he wrenched it free.

The crowd had nearly cleared out. Irving,

stomped on at the bottom of the pile of bikers, was pushed, shoved and dragged, fighting and cursing, into the street with the last of the spectators. Burr, throwing the handgun into the sink as he ran past the bar, jostled the last of the crowd through the main door, then slammed and bolted it shut. Even the band, the minuscule stage crew and the strippers had fled through the back door.

The thespians still stood transfixed onstage, looking at the trashed and empty room in stunned silence.

The small group left in the Pink Pussycat could hear the snarling sound of police sirens converging from several directions. Someone had wasted no time in calling the cops. Dwart signalled that they should head for the van, but when he opened the back door, a cruiser was already coming up the alley with its lights flashing. He slammed the door shut and locked it.

Returning to the main body of the club, he sat at one of the few upright tables and held his head in his hands. Bamboo came and squatted beside him.

"Please don't tell me to have a nice day," said Dwart, putting his hand on the ape's shoulder. "We didn't get away with it. The act was going so well, too." Then he signed, "That rotten toilet devil Fluck!"

Burr McClintock joined them. "You didn't level with me Farquhart, and I am mightily pissed off about that. We'll talk about it later. This is your fault, not his, whoever he is," Burr continued, "and I take it he's the escaped ape. We haven't been introduced yet."

"Sorry 'bout that, Burr, this is Bamboo. Yes, he is the escaped ape. Bamboo, I'd like you to meet Burr McClintock."

"Good, Bamboo love shake hands, ugh, please meetcha," and Bamboo stuck out his huge hand, which Burr took gingerly, and they pumped their appendages up and down.

"What happens next?" asked Elspeth, joining them at the table.

"Ah, well, if I knew that...! But it's bound to be very interesting—" Before Dwart could finish, the sound of a voice amplified by a bullhorn came from beyond the Dundas Street entrance, "Come out now with your hands up, and nobody gets hurt!"

20

TURDUS MIGRATORIUS

"Get off your butt, Robin, and get down to that Pink Pussycat Strip Club. It's somewhere on Dundas near Jarvis, isn't it? I just got a tip. All hell's broken loose out there, looks like it's about that escaped gorilla. And get back to me fast. I want the story for the eleven o'clock news."

The Latin name for the common robin is *turdus migratorius*, which was why his fellow television news reporters called Gaylord Grabas the Robin.

The clothes covering his short, plump figure had a a rumpled look, as if they were in constant need of pressing. He had a round cherubic face and quick, darting eyes that twinkled when he smiled. His friends regarded that smile as candid, but his detractors called it smarmy. A thick shock of brown hair fell over his forehead. Long side-burns failed to impart the intended macho look. His voice was high-pitched and exuberant, and he laughed too often. He alternated between unsophisticated, honest simplicity and an impudent brashness, a combination that got him through many doors.

He'd do anything to get a story, and had a particular fondness for scooping his competitors.

"Bamboo's escape is the hottest story in town right now! If they've cornered him, it's big news."

"Right, so get going, Robin, we'll get a camera out there as soon as one of the guys gets back."

"Okay, you're the boss." Gaylord the Robin grabbed his trench coat and hat and jogged to the elevator. C-JOY was the last word in Toronto TV broadcasting, and the latest station to which he'd hired out his migratory reporting services. The station's commercial jingle played in his head as the elevator creaked its way to the ground floor: *Hear joy and feel joy on C-JOY. You're nobody till somebody loves you, and C-JOY loves you!*

Robin took the subway, got off at the Dundas station and hurried over to the crowd milling around the Pink Pussycat. Several police cars were also in evidence, and an ambulance was just pulling away, its sirens wailing. Robin had a nodding acquaintance with the police sergeant in charge.

"What's going on down here, Sergeant Snarfley?" Robin inquired.

"Looks like a bit of the old St. James Infirmary Blues to me," said the sergeant.

"Meaning what?"

"Meaning this isn't exactly what you'd be

inclined to call a friendly crowd. There are some pretty bad apples in this neighbourhood."

"So who's inside? Is it true you've got that escaped ape trapped in there?

"Could be, we don't know yet. It's either a real ape or a guy in a gorilla suit. Could just be a publicity stunt."

"Why do you think it could be Bamboo?"

"Well, if it is a real ape, it couldn't be anybody else, now could it?" said Snarfley.

"No, I guess not."

"The big guy they just took to the hospital, name of Irving Fluck? He'd been stomped pretty good before we got here. He kept telling me there was this bastard gorilla Bamboo in the strip club dressed in a tuxedo, and that the ape, some old fart and a woman were doing a vaudeville routine onstage! Can you believe that? The guy could be out of his head, a basket case for all we know."

"Was he the only one injured?"

"Looks that way, other than a few bruises and sprained ankles among the crowd from when they tore out of there in a panic. Something sure spooked them, and we're trying to figure out what."

"Maybe this guy, what did you say his name was?"

"Fluck, Irving."

"Maybe," said Robin, writing down the name, "he was telling the truth. But as you say, it could be a publicity stunt put on by the club."

"They're always trying something and I'm getting really sick of it. There's still a few people in there. We're trying to get them to come out, but they've locked themselves in. They've stuck a speaker from their P.A. system out that upper window, and someone in there's saying he's Bamboo and he wants to negotiate a peaceable exit."

"Let me get this straight. You're telling me—"

"No, someone in there's telling me."

"Okay, so—"

"So there's a monkey, an ape, a gorilla, in there and he's talking to us. Now what would you call that?"

"One helluva story!"

"Sure. If it ain't a hoax."

"Even if it is. Who else is in there?"

"Well, this old comedian, the woman who was with him, the manager of the club and maybe some strippers. We really don't know."

"Who's the comedian?"

"Nobody I ever heard of. Supposed to be somebody called Farky the Old Fart."

"I never heard of him, either. Any corroboration on Fluck's story?"

"Are you some kind of ambulance-chasing lawyer, Grabas? You're starting to talk like one. Corroboration, he wants."

"Just trying to get the facts, man. We get enough flak at C-JOY for half-cocked reporting."

"I'll bet you do." Just then someone hollered at

Snarfley from a cruiser and he started toward it with Robin at his heels. "Matter of fact, maybe we do have some corroboration."

"How d'you mean?"

"There were some members here from that bloody motorcycle gang, the Bandits, when we got here. I figure they were the ones who kicked the shit out of Fluck. We got a couple of names—Mouldy Melvin and Soup Campbell are the monikers they go by. Those bikers don't talk to cops much, but they did say Fluck had a gun, that he seemed to be trying to take out the ape, and that they heard the ape talk from the stage."

"Maybe the comedian's a ventriloquist. Did the bikers know this Fluck person?"

"Said they didn't. I did ask them, because Fluck might have been there doing some kind of drug deal or something with the bikers. But I've had Fluck checked out and neither vice nor the drug unit's got anything on him. Big, mean and ugly would be the shortest way to describe him. Must have taken lots of big guys or a gorilla to beat him up."

"I see."

"Then you see more than me, Grabas, 'cause we don't really know the whole story yet, or who exactly we've got in there, or what they want. But I'm going to talk to them. So that's all I know, and I don't know why I told you that much."

"I appreciate it, Sarge."

"Now get out of my hair while I try to get this situation cleared up."

Robin Grabas circulated among the crowd. He found more than one person who'd been in the club audience, and on questioning them he was impressed by their firm conviction that the gorilla was no fake and that he'd talked.

"You shoulda seen him," said one, "when the big guy tried to shoot him. There's no actor or mime artist I ever saw who's that good. That was an ape, man, and I'm not talking Tarzan, you better believe it."

"What exactly happened in there?" Robin persisted.

"If the crowd hadn't figured it was a real ape, they wouldn't have panicked like that. I was near the back. I didn't see too much after everybody started tearing outta there; I had to go with them or get trampled. Maybe it was because of the guy waving the gun. Of course, that could've been part of the act.

"Anyway, that was some excitement, real virtual reality. Everybody split, you couldn't stop them. Now they're saying it's that escaped gorilla from the zoo in there and he's got a gun."

"Did you think he could talk?"

"I heard him, or thought I did, and at first I thought it was phony. But it looked and sounded so real. He was on the P.A. system just a few minutes ago. Says he's Bamboo the ape and wants to talk things over."

"Talk what over?"

"He wants to talk terms, give himself up to the

cops and go back to the zoo. The cops got no reason to kill him, but you can't trust them, you know? They don't even know he did anything wrong, just that maybe he's dangerous and should be back in a cage."

"And he doesn't want to go."

"Right. Would you?"

"Can't say as I would." Robin had heard enough. He headed for the C-JOY camera van which was just pulling up to the edge of the crowd. The crew quickly swung their cameras into action, scanning the crowd scene in front of the Pink Pussycat. He jumped into the truck and got onto the phone link with the station.

"Okay, Robin," his editor barked, "what's the story? We're getting close to deadline."

"I think we've got a dandy, and better yet, we're the only media here."

"Good. Give me what you've got."

"It's gotta be the escaped zoo ape, Bamboo. He and some kinda gang—we don't know yet which protest or terrorist group is going to take credit for this—have locked themselves inside. This is the club whose main attraction is Girdles Lovejoy— hey, we should get her on C-JOY—who says she's plenty hot and gives it all she's got. Anyway, the cops think the gang led by Bamboo is armed and dangerous, and that members of the motorcycle gang the Bandits are involved, too. At least two shots were fired inside the club, and one person was beaten up. Looks like the guy who got hurt rushed in with a weapon, panicked the crowd during an act involving the burlesque comedian Farky the Old Fart, the ape Bamboo and one of the strippers."

"Is that it?"

"What more do you want? But no, there's more. Get this: people are saying Bamboo can talk. He speaks some English, and doesn't want to go back into captivity. He's negotiating with the cops. And there's enough liquor and food in the place to last them a long time. We don't know yet whether any of the gang's drunk or on drugs."

"Shit, Robin! How sure are you of all this?"

"Well," and Robin paused, "I gotta say I'm not positive of any of it, but if you want a story for eleven, you gotta decide right now whether we're gonna go with it."

"So level with me, what have we really got?"

"Barring some element of horseshit, I'm maybe seventy-five percent sure. But we have a way out if the ape can't talk. It may be a publicity stunt the club's putting on, so we won't look stupid if it turns out we got taken in, too. Either way, it's an exclusive."

"What's our follow?"

"Well, whoever they are, they're still in there. The place is cordoned off by the cops, who are about to start negotiations with the gorilla, or the Old Fart, or whoever. So we can say this is all we know for now, we're following developments and will have regular bulletins later, the usual routine."

"All right, we'll roll it. Damn, this is a good one. Now, get ready to give me a stand-up with the stuff you just spouted. We'll go with it live as the main feature and beat every other goddamn station and newspaper in Toronto."

"Gotcha."

"And stay on it."

"Are you kidding? You couldn't get me off it."

That night, C-JOY, the Sunny Side Up News Station, scooped the lot.

SNARFLEY GOT ON THE BULLHORN AGAIN, yelling at the dark building, whose shadowy gothic windows eyed him blankly in the night. "You people in the Pink Pussycat! Let's talk this over. We all want to go home to beddy-byes now, don't we? So why don't you all just come out of there with your hands up, and I promise you, nobody'll get hurt."

Several minutes of silence from the building, then Dwart went to the stage mike, which could be switched into the outside speaker.

"This is Dwart Farquhart. We want to talk to Phil Travers, the administrator of the Ontario Provincial Zoo. He knows a lot about apes, and he also knows why we're in this predicament with Bamboo. If you bring him here, we can likely get somewhere. Over and out."

His announcement over, Dwart joined the others. They righted some overturned chairs and sat down at one of the tables.

"How do you think this thing'll work out for Bamboo?" Burr McClintock asked Dwart. "Will they go for it?"

"I'd have to say an unqualified maybe. I hope they go for whatever proposal we make. Then Travers can maybe talk the cops into meeting the terms. He's got some clout with some high-powered people. It's not as if we planted a bomb in the subway system or hi-jacked a jet."

"Or we were some half-assed country's terrorist group trying to obtain the release of their buddies in exchange for hostages," said Elspeth. "What are we going to propose, Dwart?"

"That's our main problem. We don't want to ask for something that's impossible, but I haven't got that far in my thinking yet."

"I'll see whether they've got anything about this on the box." Burr flipped on the television over the bar. They were immediately rewarded with a view of the crowd out front and a voice-over describing the night's action at the Pink Pussycat:

'It's not clear whether terrorists or some other group are responsible for this incident, or whether they're holding the escaped ape Bamboo against his will. The group has not made any demands in exchange for Bamboo's release. Reporter Gaylord Grabas is at the scene."

Robin's image filled the screen and he launched into the story as previously related to his assignment editor, adding a tag at the end:

"I've just been handed information to the effect that Dwart Farquhart, better known as the Old Fart, the emcee at the Pink Pussycat cabaret, has demanded to speak to Dr. Phil Travers, the zoological expert and administrator of the Ontario Provincial Zoo.

"Farquhart wants Travers to be the go-between in negotiations for the release and subsequent treatment of Bamboo. They rejected an offer to use Girdles Lovejoy, one of the star attractions at the club."

The camera zoomed in on the picture of a nude Girdles in the display case on the outside wall of the club. The shot faded out and the newscaster returned. "In other news, more deaths in the Middle East today, as bombs exploded—"

Elspeth, who'd been pacing the floor, said "Please turn the damned thing off, Burr, we've seen enough," and flopped onto a chair.

Burr complied and returned to the table. "Let's all try to relax, okay?"

"Just look at Bamboo," said Dwart, pointing to the ape, "he's beaten us to it." Bamboo was already sleeping on some polyfoam mats, stage left. "He's not likely to kick off from the stress factor, that's for sure. Eat and sleep, that's what he does best."

"Let's try to do the same, at least till Travers gets here," said Elspeth. "What's on the menu tonight, Burr? I say we turn off the lights and just use some of those table candles. We could have a party. I was having so much fun tonight. I'm hungry."

"How about Planter's peanuts, beer nuts, Old Dutch potato chips, taco chips, pepperoni sticks and pickled eggs? Lots of those, but anything more substantial or hot comes from the Chinese joint next door. I set it up that way so I wouldn't have to contend with kitchen staff."

"As long as I don't have to eat those twisty orange popcorny things. The colour alone is enough to make you want to throw up," said Elspeth.

"Maybe they'll let us send out for Chinese."

"Kinda doubt that."

"Okay, I'll bring a selection of munchies and draw a pitcher of draft."

"Nothing heavy for me, Burr. Maybe some Coors Lite," said Elspeth.

"Sounds good," agreed Dwart. Burr proceeded to pile the table high with standard bar hors d'oeuvres. There would be no meal to follow, but Robin was right, they weren't going to starve while they waited.

WHEN TRAVERS GOT THE NEWS, THE PORTION of his brain that governed hindsight immediately told him he should have known where the ape had gone. Dwart hadn't acted quite worried enough at Bamboo's continued absence. That should have alerted him. He got into the police cruiser that had come to his house to fetch him. Luckily for his blood pressure, he hadn't tuned in to C-JOY's eleven o'clock news, because he got the story more slowly and with far less hype from the police officer who drove him downtown to the Pink Pussycat. It was now after midnight, and the city's finest had cleared out most of the crowd who hadn't drifted away of their own accord.

Robin Grabas and one camera operator sat in the front seat of the C-JOY van, half-asleep but waiting to see what else might develop that night.

Snarfley latched onto Travers the moment he arrived, and as they sat in the sergeant's car, he briefed Phil on what he knew. Travers digested it all before he said much of anything.

"Nobody in there is really going to cause you much serious trouble, sergeant. Let me go in and talk to them."

"You agree that a gorilla named Bamboo is in there?"

"I'm sure he is."

"And you want to go in and talk to him, you say?"

"That's right."

"You're levelling with me and you're not afraid?"

"Sergeant, that ape in there is an extremely valuable animal, and I don't mean just as zoo property or a freak; I mean he's valuable to humanity. To you, as well as to me. That ape has learned to talk, as a result of a throat operation. We have a unique opportunity here to talk to what was very recently a wild animal, and gain a tremendous amount of knowledge that will help us in our dealings with other species of life on earth. I want your solemn promise that no matter what happens, you will not harm Bamboo. Your officers may consider him to be a dangerous wild beast and get trigger-happy. I'm telling you that we're dealing with a personality, a person. Do you understand me? You've got a job to do and I appreciate that. I'll give you every co-operation, but please, do the same for me. Technically, he's our great ape, and there are no charges against him, are there?"

"No, nobody's said he's committed any crime. Not even disturbing the peace, because the people I questioned said it was this Irving Fluck who did that. He was also unlawfully carrying a firearm and attempting an assault likely to cause bodily harm; maybe attempted murder. Add causing a disturbance in a public place, discharging a firearm within city limits—come to think of it, we can probably throw the book at Fluck. And I will, 'cause I'm not going through all this for nothing."

"Then, just so there's no chance of error, could you order all of your police officers here to take the ammunition out of their guns? That way, no one can get nervous and make a mistake."

Snarfley thought this over. "On the whole, that's probably a good idea. You're going to have to take the responsibility; but that won't help me if something goes wrong."

"You'd get more flak if something happens to Bamboo. Just send me in there. I'll talk to them and come out and tell you their side of the story, why they won't come out and what they want." Travers nearly said "what we want," because he knew that he was inextricably but willingly on the side of the alleged little gang inside, and that together they'd have to work out a solution to the standoff.

Robin Grabas knocked on the cruiser window and Snarfley rolled it down. "I take it this is Dr. Travers, Sergeant?"

"That's right. Philip Travers, administrator out at the OP Zoo. This is ah, ah..."

"Gaylord..."

"Yes, Gaylord Grabas, of C-JOY TV. You may have heard him on the air."

"Occasionally. How do you do?" Travers said coolly, for he knew of Grabas' reputation for hype.

"May I ask you some questions?"

"Why don't you wait till I come out?"

"You're going in there now?"

"Grabas, he's going in to negotiate," Snarfley said slowly. He removed his hat and stared fixedly at Robin, "So butt out for now."

"May I go in with you?"

"No, you may not," Phil and Snarfley snapped simultaneously.

"Then will you talk to me first when you come out? I mean, before you talk to any other media.

Whenever you're ready. After all, I was here fast and first."

"That seems fair enough. Sergeant, would you escort me to the front door, please? I'll knock and tell them it's me. I'll try not to be too long, so we can all find out what's happening."

Travers slid out the passenger door and waited while Snarfley went around to his officers, ordering them to unload and holster their weapons. Then he and a constable escorted Travers to the front door of the Pink Pussycat.

Burr opened the door and locked it once Travers was inside. He ushered Phil to the table and offered him a beer. The deserted nightclub made Dwart and Elspeth look pale and lonely, with a what-do-we-do-now? look in their eyes.

Dwart broke the silence. "Phil, I had to do it without your knowledge. I figured for sure Irving was going to try to kill him. And Irving has proved me right. I felt I couldn't get you involved because I didn't want to get you in trouble. You got me into the ape mongering business, what more can I say?"

Burr poured a pint of draft for Travers and placed it in front of him. There was another silence as Phil stared into the mug, then took a deep swallow. "Worrying about Bamboo hasn't done that much for my health, and I'll admit I was bloody angry when I first heard you'd engineered the escape. In fact, I still am. But I can understand that your motive was legitimate, particularly in view of Fluck's actions this evening. So let's forget it. The question now is, what do we want Bamboo to demand as the condition of his peaceful surrender? Is he supposed to be holding you here as hostages? That's hardly credible."

"No, they sure wouldn't buy that," replied Dwart.

"We have to devise a scenario that'll fly, not only with the police outside, but with the North American and worldwide public. We've got the world's first talking gorilla on our hands, and as we've known since we first found out about it, that's big news."

"Whatever we come up with should benefit Bamboo first and the zoo's interests should come second. You represent the zoo. What do you say?"

"I agree, but there's no reason why those interests can't be in harmony. By the way, how has his speaking ability progressed? You've had him stashed somewhere and have been working with him for several weeks."

"He's doing very well. And I've had this idea bubbling on the back burner of my brain for some time. What is it that we were all trying to do with Bamboo? What's the zoo's goal, what are you trying to achieve as a zoo administrator, and why did I become what you and I call an ape monger?"

"We want to save the great apes of Africa from extinction as a species."

"Can it be done?"

"It's doubtful, but possible."

"What would help?"

"Publicity—lots of publicity. Attract the public's attention, interest and participation. Get funding from individuals and governments, and their co-operation."

"Then let Bamboo make a speech to the United Nations!" said Dwart.

Travers sprayed the beer he'd been about to swallow across the table. Elspeth ducked sideways.

No one spoke for what seemed to be a long, long time. Everyone knew the idea was outlandish, with great potential but low probability, yet if it could be pulled off, it would help accomplish their common goal.

The very audacity of the idea seemed to fit the requirement for maximum publicity potential. They all began to speak at once, wondering whether it would work, was Bamboo up to it, and would the UN agree?

"Could Bamboo do it, Dwart?"

"Yes, Phil, he could. But you know the old saying, 'It's not how well he could do it, the surprising thing is that he could do it at all.' We'd need a little more time. We could get that, and he could be coached."

Another silence, then Dwart asked, "Where do we go from here?"

"The answer's just outside this door," said

Travers, "A fellow named Gaylord Grabas with C-JOY TV. Give him an exclusive on all interviews with Bamboo or us, and I think he'd work tirelessly to give us the publicity build-up we need so the story doesn't die before we get what we want and Bamboo needs."

"We've just heard him on TV," said Elspeth. "Flamboyant, but he does a good job of grabbing your attention. I've seen him before. He's outrageously full of hype and embellishment. Some people say nothing spoils one of his stories like an eyewitness."

"But in this case we know the story's true," Dwart added.

"All right. If you all agree, I'll go out and talk to the police, then give Gaylord his interview. I'll tell them the situation can be worked out satisfactorily, which it can, that Bamboo is in here and that he is in fact a talking ape. Also that the owner of the Pink Pussycat agrees the club will remain closed while we negotiate the terms of surrender.

"And most important, Bamboo will come out and return to the zoo if it's agreed that he'll be allowed to speak to the United Nations. I'll ask them to post guards to keep the public away, along with lunatics like Fluck."

"If we're going to milk this for publicity, we can't just come out right away," Dwart interjected. "We'll have to pretend we're under some sort of siege. You know, maybe Fluck did us a favour after all, breaking up our act."

"I haven't seen the act," said Phil.

"I have," Burr cut in, "and believe me, Fluck did them a favour."

"Goddamn critics, always on your ass. Luckily, I never read the reviews anyway. If I did, I might quit. To hell with you, Burr," Dwart continued good-naturedly, "I was just going to ask what you and the club were going to do while this was going on. The club's going to lose money."

"Not necessarily," said Burr, shaking his head, "look at the free publicity I'm going to get. You couldn't buy it for any price. Anyway, you don't need to think I'm not willing to do something for conservation and endangered species. I kinda like that big ape already."

"I'll see Grabas privately, right after I give him an opening statement tonight. If we promise him exclusives, he'll go for it. He and I will tee up a plan to maximize the publicity. You people make the best you can of things tonight, and we can all look into the details tomorrow, while Grabas and I figure out how long we should prolong the negotiations."

Onstage, Bamboo woke up, trying hard to remember where he was. Often when he awoke and found he wasn't in some nest of moss in a familiar jungle tree, he'd panic at his strange surroundings. But when he realized he was still in captivity, in some sort of slavery, the panic in his mind diminished to anxiety and despair.

He always tried to fight down the rising sense

of doubt that he'd ever get back to familiar surroundings and the old way of life with which he'd
been so comfortable. The doubt wasn't surfacing
as often, with so many new and sometimes enjoy-
able experiences in the strange world of the killer
ape race.

The lights were off in the Pink Pussycat and
Bamboo heard voices from the main room.
Rubbing the sleep from his eyes, he approached
the apron of the stage and silently dropped to the
floor. There was one candle-lit cabaret table near
the bar seating four people: Elspeth, Dwart, the
big silverback who ran the place, and the man he
occasionally saw at the zoo, the one who only
showed up in times of crisis in Bamboo's life. The
small table was piled high with human edibles
and the drink they called beer. Dwart kept some
of that in the cold box in his apartment and
Bamboo liked the taste.

He'd removed his costume. His padded feet
made no sound and his body instinctively missed
every chair and table as he slowly wound his way
through the debris of the room. He emerged from
the dark to loom over the table.

Even though they all knew who it was, there
was a suppressed but instinctive collective gasp
from the group. Bamboo stuck his big, paw-like
hand toward Phil and stated, "Doc Tor...Trav
Vors, ugh, I, ah, ugh, presoom!"

21

U.N. SNAFU

The negotiations lasted five days. The Travers-Grabas combo alleged great controversy as to the conditions under which Bamboo would come out peaceably and return to the zoo. Bamboo's fate was the lead story in all the major media, but C-JOY, billing itself the centre of the broadcasting world, was supplying most of the information to other reporters, thanks to Travers' deal with Grabas. The two became the main intermediaries between Bamboo and the zoo, public authorities and the media. They arranged the live interviews with Farquhart, Bamboo, Burr and Elspeth inside the club, giving North American audiences their first glimpse of the cast of characters involved in the drama.

They heard Bamboo say a few words, but only once, as Robin didn't want to overplay the gorilla's speaking ability. All he wanted at that point was to prove the ape could speak, so they could begin to sway public opinion in favour of Bamboo's demand to speak to the United Nations General Assembly on behalf of the disenfranchised animal kingdom.

The zoo brought in all the basic foods for Bamboo, while sympathizers and wellwishers among Toronto's restaurateurs and gourmet chefs sent in more food than the little gang could possibly eat. The Stone Storage Store, the largest single outlet for furniture sales in Eastern Canada, shipped in their best posturpedic mattresses for the entire group, including Bamboo, and advertised the fact in the major dailies. Dwart didn't get to use his own mattress very much, but Elspeth's saw double duty.

The store also offered a five thousand dollar donation to the Bamboo cause in exchange for a promotional photo of Bamboo sleeping on their product. The fundraising possibilities, at least while Bamboo was in the public's mind, weren't lost on the occupants of the Pink Pussycat.

"There's no doubt we could book him on a world-wide speaking tour, and that we'd get the backing of a ton of sponsors," said Robin, already imagining himself as part of the world tour.

"But not until he's done the biggie, the one at the U.N.," was Dwart's response and Phil backed him up. "That'll give him global credibility."

"I wasn't suggesting otherwise, and I agree wholeheartedly," rejoined Robin.

"Now, just a minute, gentlemen," said Elspeth,

jumping into the roundtable discussion, "to even start thinking that way seems like a mistake to me. You aren't considering Bamboo's best interests. How much of your world tour could an animal— I mean Bamboo—take, without suffering ill effects? Think about it."

"Not very much, I'd say," Phil remarked.

"I guess it would put a big strain on him, and on his voice," agreed Dwart.

"Why don't you ask him what he wants? That is, if you seriously believe he has rights. He's sitting right over there," said Elspeth. She joined Bamboo, who was eating some gorilla-sized coconut and apple cookies loaded with raisins, a gift from a Toronto bakery. "Bamboo, tell them what you'd like to do."

"Me speak what gorilla want. Bamboo want save gorilla. You speak better me. You say what kind speak get gorilla want."

"Well said, Bamboo," cried Elspeth, giving him a hug.

"After speak, like go home. Amanda go me— smile, good. Okay?" said Bamboo, trying to hide a big grin behind his hand.

Elspeth thought this was the sweetest thing she'd ever heard. But not Phil. "And there would go my two best apes," he moaned. "Not so fast, Bamboo. We spent a long time trying to get Amanda in the family way. This is a good job we have for you here in North America—studding."

Dwart helped out with some signing, and after

a pause while Bamboo assimilated the content of the message, he said, "Same job me home."

"Nice work if you can get it," the Robin interjected, "and I had to end up in journalism. It's not fair."

"Listen to me, Bamboo, and the rest of you, too," said Phil, looking the ape in the eye. "When we get better at communicating with you, the Old Fart can explain this to you better. I want to make a fine home for you, Bamboo. I believe zoos shouldn't have individual cages any longer. We need to create whole ecosystems, big enough to contain as many compatible species as possible, monkeys, deer, birds and reptiles. Our outdoor area needs a lot of work, but I want to expand it into one large cage that encourages natural behaviour from those animals that have to be confined.

"You have to remember, gorillas born in captivity have never seen their homelands, never seen a rain forest. Bamboo, you're the only ape in my zoo who's ever lived in the wild, but if you go back, you'll be in extreme danger.

"We can develop a natural setting for you, with a mix of live trees, plants, vines and undergrowth. I envision a place with an artificial lake and stream, maybe, or a waterfall and a watering hole, with fish and mud banks. A place that'll give you freedom of movement and some privacy when you want it.

"It'll cost a lot of money, but with you as the

promoter and major attraction in our campaign, we can make it happen, and be that much closer to saving a host of endangered species.

"So I'm asking you, for your own good, stay and help us. I want you to think it over," and Phil signed, "Please!"

"Let me get this straight," queried Grabas, always in search of a story angle. "The idea is to create safe places for gorillas, in zoos or somewhere else, where they can't be exploited or destroyed. And to get humans to change their thinking about the importance of that goal to the overall quality of our own lives."

When Phil nodded eagerly, Gaylord added, "Then we need to convince the United Nations to support such projects. They have to change from managing the status quo to becoming a catalyst for international problem solving."

"Is that possible?" asked Elspeth.

Grabas shook his head doubtfully. "I've covered U.N. stories—not an easy task, believe me—and it just seems the massive bureaucracy defeats anyone who tries to get anything done there. But we have to try to find a solution."

Burr was a newcomer to concerns about endangered apes and was listening carefully. "The United Nations is going to have to do a lot better than they have up to now."

Dwart jumped enthusiastically to his feet, "Come on, Bamboo, get back up on that stage and we'll start rehearsing for your speech at the

U.N. First things first: we'll get to work on the text right away so you can learn the new words you're going to have to use."

"You can say that again..."

"Now cut that out. You know you have to improve your vocabulary if you're going to become an educated ape, don't you?"

"No, but hum a few bars, I may get it."

Everyone laughed uproariously at these old burlesque saws, which seemed fresh when Bamboo uttered them.

"Did do right?" asked Bamboo.

"You're going to be just fine. I wish I'd had you as a partner back in the good old days."

"Well, it's been fun," Gaylord broke in, rising abruptly, "but I gotta run. Got work to do at the station. I'll leave you folks to turn your singular talents to the problem. Keep me posted, okay? Where's my sports jacket?" It had slipped off his chair and lay on the floor with one sleeve in some spilled beer. "Damn, that's my best jacket," he groaned as he headed for the door.

"Could you ask Elspeth to coach Bamboo for a while, Dwart?" asked Phil, looking hopefully in her direction. "You and I should have a little talk about the speech. What he says will be very important, and then there's the technical problem of just how he's going to say it."

"Fine by me, boys. Come on, Bamboo." Elspeth and Bamboo slipped behind the red velvet curtains onstage.

"Apart from grammar, word order and sentence structure, I think it's a question of comprehension," said Dwart, taking a small notebook from his breast pocket. "I've been keeping a record. He understands a lot of things, really, and a lot of words. So much so, that sometimes you don't want him to know what you're saying, and Elspeth and I have used the time-honoured device of spelling rather than saying the key words. But somehow he's figured out that c-a-n-d-y means one of his favourite treats, so now we have to use more artful dodges. We're now trying pig Latin."

"Let's talk elsewhere," said Phil, loosening his collar. "I'm not used to the air in these bars. I'm used to zoo smells, but this place reeks of stale beer and cigarette smoke."

"Whatever you say. Nightclubs are for night owls. When the regular customers have had a few, they don't notice it. I'm used to it. Let's try the dressing rooms, I think there's an air vent into the alley in there."

Dwart led the way to the rear of the club and they entered the strippers' dressing room. Dwart sat down in a chair facing the mirrors, put his feet up on the counter and began combing his hair. Phil, unused to such premises, scanned several articles of feminine attire hanging from the walls and over the lighted dressing tables.

"Seems some of the girls forgot their costumes in the rush to get out of here," Dwart remarked, smiling at Phil's interest in the items.

"Some of these things look as though they threw in the sponge some time ago."

"End of the ball game for that baby over there," said Dwart, pointing to a particularly dilapidated and raunchy G-string hanging from a burnt-out light bulb. "That one could do a show by itself."

"There's a much better smell in here, but I can't put my finger on it," said Phil, sniffing the air, "What is it?"

"I'll give you a hint. They mention it in the name of the club."

"Oh! Ah, yes," said Phil, his face flushing as scarlet as the lingerie that surrounded him, "Is that why they picked the name?"

"No, I think it was because they figured that a big cat can really hurt you, but a little pussy never hurt anybody. We may as well stay here, I suppose."

"Why not?" Phil agreed enthusiastically.

"Okay, but try to keep your mind on the speech."

Phil stopped sniffing and replied thoughtfully, "Ah, yes. Well, Bamboo's smart all right, but no genius. Grammar would take him too long to learn, if it's even possible. Even a human child has to learn it gradually. Bamboo's at an early stage and only time will tell how well he'll grasp the language. He's done beautifully so far, but he may have gone as far he's going to."

"The date of the speech is a big factor. We haven't got much time," said Dwart, watching

Phil study a wall calendar featuring a spread-eagled stripper wearing only high heels and long black silk stockings. A large red rose protruded from her vagina.

"She must have removed the thorns," said Phil.

"Did you notice it's a 1983 calendar?"

Phil turned back to face Dwart. "So we have to be pragmatic. We have to decide what he's going to say. After that we'll decide how he's going to say it, then we'll break that down into simple terms."

"Let's not sweat it, we don't have much choice except to let him say it the best way he can on the day we get there."

"Maybe he could memorize a bit; and we can keep teaching him new words. It would be best if he understood their meaning, if it's going to be a good speech."

"A good speech always helps, but the fact that Bamboo can talk at all should get us by."

"What would we tell the United Nations if either of us was giving the speech?" Phil asked. "I'll bet there's no stem on that rose, it's probably just taped on."

"Yeah, well, we'd have to think about that, now wouldn't we? Sit down and write out the speech."

"Then why don't you make up a first draft, Farky? Put down what you would say if you were giving it yourself. Then we'll all brainstorm it, add, delete, whatever, and cut it down to a string of ideas."

"I see where you're going, Phil. Then we go over the ideas in as simple language as possible with Bamboo. Find out what he understands and what he doesn't, and see how he words his replies.

"Right now what he says comes out in that sort of pidgin English, kind of related to sign language. It does get the idea across. Not in standard Oxford English, but syntax isn't the only component of speech. If he knows what he's saying, he'll also have gestures and body language going for him."

"We'll end up with a string of ideas that he gets used to, and that will be his speech. To me, that's the best approach."

"It'll come down to his attention span, I figure," said Dwart.

"You know, that calendar is a collector's item."

"You're right on both counts."

"He hasn't really had a chance to demonstrate how long he can concentrate. So we can only hope."

"I'll get working on the draft, what the hey!"

"Try to keep your flights of imagination down to a minimum, will you?"

"Why? You and Grabas will be blue-pencilling it anyway. Like I said, I'll just sit down and write up what comes to mind."

"I think we can have you out of the Pink Pussycat in about forty-eight hours. Grabas and I are flying down to New York early tomorrow to confer with the U.N. officials," said Phil, "so I'll be on my way. There are some things to take care of at the zoo before I go." His eyes strayed to the calendar again.

"Phil, take the ruddy calendar with you. They'll never miss it."

ALTHOUGH NOT WITHOUT HIS OWN SKILLS, Travers knew the human jungle was full of all manner of tigers, asps and hyenas, and he was glad to have Robin Grabas along. Experienced media types, like criminal lawyers, were professional cynics, well aware that even friendly witnesses lie. Travers hoped Grabas' grittiness would help bring about the desired result.

Gorillas were low on the U.N. priority list, so they were shunted off to a junior official. Dan Haggerty was a trougher who'd been promoted two levels above his ability. His capacity to resist introducing useful knowledge into a situation commanded profound respect in bureaucratic circles.

Before his migration to civil service at the state, then the federal and now the world level, he'd tried his hand at law. As a student, he'd agreed with every dissenting opinion in case law, an attitude that guaranteed his failure to pass his first-year exams. He switched to politics, but gained neither nomination nor election. At that point he decided to dedicate his life to public service.

Haggerty greeted Travers and Grabas in his office, and after feeling each other out with small talk, they got down to the main point. Phil explained Bamboo's background and the discovery of his speaking ability. Then he described the the situation in Toronto and their plans for the proposed speech.

Haggerty wasn't buying. "This sounds rather high-flown. There are no animals, gentlemen, no African apes, allowed in the U.N. Assembly. No provision has ever been made for them. This situation is without precedent."

"Technically true, but it is an excellent way of stating the case of the apes, and that of animal rights," replied Phil.

"It's very noble of you to try to save the apes, but I really don't see where the U.N. enters the picture, except perhaps with funding through the usual channels. Perhaps I can refer you to the environment section."

The start of the runaround. "No thank you," replied Grabas emphatically, "we'd prefer to see the Secretary-General. This is important."

"Important to whom?" Haggerty asked.

"African apes. In the wild and in every zoo in the world."

"You're talking about funding for endangered species, and that's up to the environmental division," Haggerty repeated.

"If somebody wants to give money later, fine. Right now we need your help in arranging for Bamboo to speak," said Grabas. This guy was beginning to bug him.

Haggerty took off his horn-rim glasses and began to polish them. "And I take it this Bamboo is their only spokesman, since you're telling me he's the only one who can talk."

"Correct."

"A single spokesman, I see. Now that would constitute a pleasant change at the United Nations. But really, gentlemen, do you seriously propose that we entertain an ape?"

"That was the intent. You do have guest speakers, do you not?" asked Gaylord.

"Certainly," said Haggerty, "V.I.P.s address the Assembly from time to time, and major world figures are invited to speak. The last such person we had from Canada was Brian Mulroney."

"So a great ape shouldn't be too far out of line," quipped Grabas. "Wouldn't you consider the first and only talking anthropoid to be worthy of V.I.P. status?"

"I certainly would not. Fortunately for your cause, I don't have the final say in this matter. However, I do have a great deal of influence, and since I was placed in charge, I presume my recommendation will carry a lot of weight. Your argument is that the animal talks and this makes him unique and important. But you haven't convinced me that there's no physical danger to anyone, and that's my chief concern. Does talking alone take him out of the animal category? I don't think it does, and I don't think animals have rights."

This did not sit well with Travers. "The apes are man's closest living relatives on earth. Surely that means they merit our care and protection."

"Does he want to form another African nation?" asked Haggerty. "I really think we have enough of those already."

Sarcasm already. Is this guy for real? wondered Grabas. How'd he get into the U.N. and why did we have to draw him?

"Well," Robin stalled, "we hadn't actually thought of that, but that doesn't mean it's not a good idea. Let's run with it for a moment. The United Nations deals more with nations—sorry, obvious statement—gives nations more status than they do to individuals, is that right?"

"That's the way we're set up, of course. Although we do deal with individual human rights around the world and how people are treated in various nations, in addition to doing research on world problems."

"Why don't we propose to the U.N. that they create a new nation, just like they did with Israel? Why not set up a little one for the apes? Just a little duchy in the Virunga Mountains. Call it a sanctuary or a protectorate, like you suggested in the first place."

"Did I?" said Haggerty with a laugh. "Then their national anthem could be Carry Me Back to Old Virunga."

Phil and Robin laughed politely, not wanting the interview to deteriorate any further. "You're right, Mr. Haggerty," added Travers, picking up on Grabas' ploy. "The U.N. could buy the territory from the surrounding countries, who do have some humane and conservationist feelings in the matter. Let all the nations contribute to the kitty. Or if it won't work in Africa, let's use the money for a sanctuary in some place like Hawaii. The apes could be more easily protected there."

"Nearly all governments spend huge sums on far less useful projects," added Gaylord.

"It wouldn't work, gentlemen," said Haggerty. "Around here there's always a catch-22; always lots of problems when you're trying to reach consensus on anything. It wouldn't work."

"Why not?"

"Because of human stupidity and obstinacy, because the nations never deviate from their own priorities, and because this isn't a priority for any of them."

As the discussion wore on, Haggerty finally accepted the videotapes the other two had brought, along with reports and expert opinions on Bamboo's case. Travers pointed out that the true mountain gorillas had lived in the Virungas for at least four hundred thousand years, and should at least have squatter's rights.

Grabas found himself thoroughly absorbed by the issue. Taking a personal interest in a long-term cause was a new experience for him.

"I don't think the creation of an independent park in those countries would work," Haggerty maintained, "and in any event, the United Nations wouldn't do it, so why waste everybody's time? Even if you could buy the land, the people running the country would divide the money among themselves. After that you'd have to grease the palms of the local authorities, pay off the poachers, the cattle grazers, the farmers and the fuel gatherers to make it worth their while to stay away from the park. But that would only be a one-shot deal. They'd only abide by their part of the bargain while the money lasted, then they'd be back for more.

"You'd have to provide a fenced buffer zone around the entire area and get well-armed troops to patrol it. You'd have to use foreigners, to prevent local guards dealing with their own relatives and friends behind your back. They're all poachers. This isn't just my opinion, it's based on United Nations experience in similar situations. And now you tell me there are only a few hundred of these gorillas left. Somehow I thought there were more than that in the world."

Travers was eager to enlighten Haggerty. "There are probably over 100,000 gorillas in the Central African region, comprising three subspecies. The western and eastern lowland gorillas, spread throughout the Central African Republic, the Congo river basin, Gabon, Equatorial Guinea., Cameroon and Nigeria, are the most numerous.

"The third subspecies, the mountain gorillas

who inhabit the Virunga volcanoes, nearby
Mount Visoke and the surrounding inland area,
are the most endangered—there are only a few
hundred of them left.

"The difference between these three groups is
similar to what you'd find among humans of different races. There's no physical problem with
inter-breeding, and I think we'll be able to manage it with Bamboo and Amanda. But their offspring won't be pure mountain gorillas. If the
mountain gorillas were to die out, it'd be, in
human terms, as if there were no more Swiss."

"Are we finished, gentlemen?" Haggerty was
determined to bring the meeting to a close. "I'll
write a report on our discussion and pass on my
conclusions and recommendations to the agenda
committee."

"Please remember, Mr. Haggerty, at this point,
we're only consulting you about a speech to the
Assembly by a talking gorilla," said Gaylord.
"The rest was just conjecture. We're serious about
this. I, for one, have decided I don't want to live
in a world which has maybe eight billion people
and no exotic animals left, just another four billion cats and dogs defecating in the streets. This
isn't just another newspaper disaster story to me."

There was an awkward silence as they shook
hands. Travers broke it by asking, "When can we
expect a decision? We need to know as soon as
possible. Especially from a news standpoint. Mr.
Grabas has to get on with the next phase of the

publicity, where we promote the speech to the Assembly, providing, of course, that you and your committee decide in our favour."

"Reams of publicity around the world," added Grabas, "think of it—great human interest, good for the United Nations.'

"I can't give you an answer in less than a week. I'll call your station before noon next Wednesday, or Thursday at the latest."

Out on the street, literally and figuratively, Robin said it first, "He was one of them, all right."

"One of what?"

"What the Irish call black-hearted, a man who opposes everything for the sheer joy of being agin' it. In my book he's a real son of a bitch."

"Yes," Phil agreed, "he's going to recommend that we be turned down, and he has the power to sway the decision. If he says yes to a proposition, then it's all over and done with. By saying no, he not only demonstrates his power and self-impor- tance, he continually re-establishes the need for his own job, because he can keep the negotiating process going, creating more work for his own department. On the other hand, if we just accept no, he saves himself a lot of work."

They flew back to Toronto, having no reason to be pleased with their day's work. They reported in to the Pink Pussycat headquarters that evening, the two constables on duty outside waving them through.

After hearing the doleful news, Dwart recognized the need for some levity. He ordered the specialty of the house for all, except Bamboo, who said eagerly, "Gimme beer sip."

"You know we don't have a house specialty," said Burr.

"But you should have a house drink. Every class joint should feature a house specialty, like the Singapore Sling at the Raffles Hotel. The house will now entertain motions from the floor as to what we should now imbibe and christen as the house specialty."

"I move it should be gin, orange juice and Phillips Milk of Magnesia," suggested Phil.

"And what might such a beverage be called, then, eh?" asked Burr.

"A Phillips screwdriver."

"Grabas, what's your motion?"

"I'd go for a mix of vodka and that pink lemon-ade called Tang, but instead of putting an onion or cherry in it, I'd use a prune."

"And you'd call that?"

"A Pink Prunetang. Two of those and you feel it. Drink three and anybody can feel it."

"What's your entry, Elspeth?" asked Dwart.

"I'd call it Spantran and you fellas could all use a drink of it, I'm sure."

"Okay, what's a Spantran?" said Burr.

"Half Spanish fly and half tranquilizers. Two glasses of that and you go out looking for it, but if you can't find it you couldn't care less."

"Okay, Burr decides. And the winner is—sorry,

Burr, I don't have an envelope."

"I gotta go with the Pink Prunetang."

"Why?" they all chorused.

"If we're gonna name a house drink for the Pink Pussycat Cabaret, it has to have the word pink in it. I'll mix up a batch right now, minus the prunes. I'll buy some of those as soon as we get out of here."

22

JESUS SHAVES

By the time Travers and Grabas returned from New York, Bamboo had returned to the zoo and Burr had thrown the doors of the Pink Pussycat open again. The club was drawing huge crowds every night, and the Bamboo gang continued to use the premises as their headquarters.

"Let's find a power button, go over his head, do something and do it fast," said Dwart when he heard about the U.N. visit and Haggerty's attitude. "Bamboo has got to make that speech."

"Persistence and determination, that's what I like to see," said Gaylord, "but what can we try next?"

"I felt we gave Haggerty a thorough presentation," said Phil. "We have to get the idea past him but I don't think we were successful. Maybe we should have sent a different delegation."

"No, you two were the best, Haggerty's just bein' a prick." Burr McClintock didn't say much, but when he did he came right to the point. "I see a lot of his type in my business, and there's really only one way to handle 'em—you get just as miserable, or more so. I oughta know, I can get pretty miserable at times. "

"He's right, there," Dwart chimed in, "I've seen him in action."

"Gentlemen, we aren't talking about violence, are we?" Travers asked, alarmed.

"If it were in my bar, yes, but we're in Haggerty's bar, so to speak, so we have to use psychological violence. If he's a true bureaucrat, he'll react to it.

"Mind you, it's kill or cure. Because if it doesn't work, you're dead in the water."

"So just how would you go about it?" asked Dwart.

"Who's the most miserable prick you know, Dwart?" Burr replied.

"No contest. Irving Fluck."

"And what's Irving doing right now?"

"Time. He's in jail waiting for his preliminary hearing. He can't raise the bail the court set, and he may even still be in the prison hospital recovering from that shit-kicking you and the Bandits gave him."

"Then let's pay him a visit. I got an idea in mind, and if he's willin' to make a deal, then we'll bail him out." Burr suggested.

"For God's sake, why?" asked Travers.

"Good question," said Grabas. "I don't know

him at all. You people do, but from what I've heard, he's a psychotic. He hates Bamboo. So what's the plan, Burr?"

"We've tried the legitimate approach with Haggerty. Now I'm talking about a fake one, and we need a real heavy like Fluck to pull it off. Let's talk to Irving, and if he goes for it, I'll lay out the plan in detail."

"But how do you intend to use him?" Dwart insisted.

"Scare tactics. You'll just have to trust me. He's as ugly and mean as a bouquet of rectums. I'm no Robert Redford myself, but with Fluck and me along, this idea just might work."

"Irving doesn't like me. I don't think he likes anybody. But he needs help, especially from us, or he's going to do quite a bit of time," said Phil. "It's worth a try."

"Phil, Gaylord, can you arrange another meeting with this Haggerty before he makes his decision?"

"Probably."

"Chances would seem good."

"Do it. Dwart, will you go with me to see Irving?"

"The only way I *will* see him is with you."

"Okay, we're going to send a new delegation to the United Nations; but right now, Dwart, let's go see your pal Fluck."

IRVING WAS SUFFERING FROM AN INTERNAL hemorrhage. His other wounds and sundry abrasions had healed, although he still sported a few red scars and scabs. He'd been in serious turmoil, battling with police investigators and the attorney general's department. While in the prison hospital, he'd hired a lawyer who went over the charges against him and explained the penalties he faced if he were found guilty.

The lawyer had checked the police report and held out little hope of an acquittal. He'd suggested a variety of defences. Irving felt they were a crock, especially for the money the lawyer was asking. Sure, he could plead not guilty and string it out. Maybe the prosecution would get sloppy, maybe they'd make some technical errors he could hang his defence on. Maybe they'd fail to prove their case. And maybe all the witnesses would die and pigs would sprout wings. Irving knew he was facing three to five.

The lawyer suggested a temporary insanity plea, but Irving figured he'd rather take his chances in the slammer than in a psych ward. *They'd ask me a lot of embarrassing questions I don't know the answers to.*

Irving's main problem was that he was guilty and he was going to have to pay for his frailties unless he could find a way out. The authorities would confine him in a cage, just as he'd done to so many wild animals; he could die inside, like some of the animals did.

Stop thinking that way, he told himself. You'd only be doing time for the Pink Pussycat, nothing else. He felt reasonably sure they wouldn't find out about his compulsion, so he had to stop thinking about what happened to sex offenders in penal institutions. Still, it tormented him and he was desperate for a way out.

Then one night he dreamed about his father. To Irving, the old man had always been a Bible-punching bastard, but in the dream he treated Irving in an unaccustomed kindly manner, taking him to the old rural Baptist church where the Reverend Brentnell was preaching. They both seemed to be trying to tell him something, but he couldn't quite figure out what.

His brain wrestled with the dream. *I am Jesus little lamb, yes, by Jesus Christ, I am.* The words of the hymn he'd been singing in the dream sped through his mind. Maybe Brentnell and his old man were trying to get him to return to religion.

Irving went with that thought and weighed the odds. Would they believe him? Could he act convincingly enough? He'd had some practice in his youth, so maybe he could pull it off. Worth a try. Others had accepted Jesus into their lives, why not him? *Jesus, here I come, I'm ready to walk with thee.* If I have to throw myself on the mercy of the court, thought Irving, I'm going to need all the help I can get.

As if in answer to his prayer, Irving got a visitor the next day. The Reverend Edmund Pringle of the Unity Pentecostal Church was a dedicated Christian who tended to those unfortunate, forlorn souls who found themselves sick in mind and body and incarcerated in the prison hospital. His mission was to listen to their life stories, their trials and tribulations, and to bring to them the redemptive answer to their anguish.

The Reverend was a defrocked barrister and solicitor who'd found the Criminal Code too explicit for his ready understanding of the law. He'd switched to the Bible, where he'd found he could easily manage the vagaries of its text, including the Ten Commandments, which allowed for a far greater latitude of interpretation. Irving listened carefully to Pringle and was born again, ready to go to heaven and back in a wheelbarrow.

A HOSPITAL ATTENDANT LED THEM THROUGH the corridors. They stopped outside Irving Fluck's room. Dwart and Burr were ushered inside while the guard remained outside, where he could observe through the small window in the locked door.

Irving eased himself out of his chair and a smile creased his face. His visitors glanced at each other in surprise.

"I'm surprised and delighted to see you, Dwart. It's good to see someone I know. Who's your friend?"

"Actually, I'm one of the guys who put you in the hospital," Burr said.

"And rightly so. But I thought there were about

ten of you. That's what it felt like, anyway." Irving looked Burr over. "Although you're a pretty big fellow yourself."

"I didn't think you'd be glad to see us, Irving. I had my doubts whether you'd see us at all," said Dwart.

"No hard feelings. I guess I was off my rocker. Retribution is mine, sayeth the Lord."

"We won't argue that point. I run the Pussycat and I thought you'd kill several people for sure, and I said to myself, not in my place, if I can help it."

"I got your message. Didn't tell my lawyer you were coming. He'd probably advise against it, but I figured I should find out what you want. You'd have no reason to just pay me a social call."

"True enough. We all have our problems," said Dwart as he looked around the room: single bed, old dresser, table with battered top and one chair. "And you certainly have one here."

"And we have one with Bamboo," said Burr, "and the idea came to me that if you wanted to help, we could maybe make a deal."

"Even though you obviously hated him. It never made sense to me, Irving, and frankly, I was afraid to come here by myself."

Irving was slow to answer, but then he said, "I've recently come to the conclusion that when there's a problem there's usually a solution. So let's talk. That's why you're here, right?'

"Right." Burr laid out his proposal. "If you

show remorse for tryin' to kill Bamboo by helping the campaign to save the apes, it might make
things easier for you at your trial. The zoo would
pitch in to help you; they'd even put up your bail
if you promised not to skip."

"You sure you're not trying to make a deal with
the devil?" asked Irving with a toothy grin.

"You might put it that way." admitted Burr.
"You're not the nicest guy we know. But that's just
why we need you."

"What do I have to do?"

"Just act like yourself one more time," said
Dwart. "This is a definite case of typecasting. We
need a mean, miserable, scary son of a bitch."

Irving looked them over, the smile disappearing from his face. Burr took a half a step in front
of Dwart.

"You're too late, friends," Irving said sadly.
"You're too late."

Silence.

"Could you be a little more specific? I don't
understand," said Burr.

"I don't do that shit anymore, not for money,
not for vengeance, not even to help myself." He
sounded convincing, even to himself.

"Isn't there something you'd do it for?" asked
Dwart.

"Yes."

"What, then?"

"I'd do it for Bamboo and the cause of endangered species."

"You amaze me, Irving," said Dwart, but he was skeptical.

"Why? What makes you say that?" Irving paused and faced them squarely with his hands spread wide in a supplicatory gesture. "I have become a born-again Christian and I have accepted Jesus' admonition not only to forgive, but to love my enemies. So just tell me what I have to do to help Bamboo and I'll do it."

They had their doubts about Fluck's sudden about face, but Fluck's co-operation was what they'd come to secure, and it seemed they had it, so they told him the plan.

PHIL AND GAYLORD PERSUADED HAGGERTY TO meet with a new delegation. The date was set for first thing the following week.

This time, the delegation included Dwart Farquhart, who cut an imposing figure in his new togs; Elspeth Egan, in a stylish but austere suit; Burr McClintock, whose look was more casual and outdoorsy; and Irving Fluck in a black suit one size too small, with his chest nearly bulging through his shirt front.

They appeared at Haggerty's office at the appointed time, and when they were announced, they marched resolutely in.

Burr took one of the three seats arranged in a semi-circle around Haggerty's desk. He motioned Dwart and Elspeth to take the ones to his left. They sat in unison, while Irving remained stand-

ing behind them, glaring at Haggerty. The
bureaucrat spotted a bulge under Fluck's coat,
near his left armpit.

Elspeth opened her attache case and pulled out
a small tape recorder, which she handed to Burr.
Placing the machine on Haggerty's desk, Burr
punched the record button and spoke: "This
recording is being made in the office of Daniel
Haggerty, executive assistant at the United
Nations, on July 25, 1998. Staring directly at
Haggerty, Burr added, "I am making this recording to avoid any subsequent misunderstanding
about what transpired in this room."

Haggerty sat goggle-eyed. What was going on
here?

Burr, dead-pan, spoke again in a low but precise voice. "Now, sir, please state your case as to
why you oppose the idea of Bamboo the gorilla
addressing the United Nations General Assembly
on behalf of his species and the endangered animals of this planet."

A flush started at Haggerty's shirt collar and
gradually suffused his face. He stared at the tape
recorder as if it were a poisonous snake. He
looked at Irving and for a moment thought they'd
actually brought the ape. The man's size and
demeanor frightened him. Finally, he decided to
answer, but he was obviously rattled.

He stumbled through the same litany of excuses he'd given Dwart and Phil the last time, until
Burr interrupted: "And that's your case?"

Haggerty growled his reply, "Yes!" Regaining some of his composure, he demanded, "Just who the hell do you think you are, anyway?"

"This individual," said Burr, jerking his head toward Fluck, "is with the Environmental Vigilantes. Insisted on coming along." He turned to Dwart. "Mr. Farquhart here is an attorney who has joined our cause, and this is his associate, Ms. Egan. Phil Travers, who you met, asked me to head this delegation. Phil Grabas, our media relations man, who you also met, couldn't make the trip, but he's waiting to hear the results of our meeting with you. Do you have our legal research and opinion ready, Mr. Farquhart?"

Dwart nodded to Elspeth, who removed a sheaf of paper from her case and handed it across to Burr, who flipped casually through the pages. Rising, he dropped the sheets on Haggerty's desk. "I hope you're familiar with these precedents referring to the protocol involved in dealing with human—and animal—rights as they pertain to the U.N. Charter."

Haggerty, deciding on a policy of plausible denial, picked up the papers very cautiously, as if they were hot. His eyes couldn't seem to focus properly, and his brain couldn't seem to take in the words. He looked up and saw Irving, who'd taken a step closer to his desk. Haggerty's face suddenly turned pale. "I'm not a lawyer. I can't be expected to digest all of this."

Burr replied, "Mr. Farquhart here happens to

be a good one. Since you're opposed to protecting endangered species, I feel I must inquire as to
your expertise in that field."

Burr checked the tape recorder, then barked
his first question. "How long have you been in
this department?"

Haggerty, now completely picked off base and
wondering whether to try to run back to first base
or try for second, muttered, "Ten years."

"And what did you do before that?"

Haggerty stammered for a moment, then
refused to answer any more questions.

"Fine. Mr. Farquhart, in light of Mr. Haggerty's
refusal to co-operate, what is your advice as to our
next step?"

Dwart leaned in to make sure the tape recorder
picked up his voice. He declared Haggerty guilty
of discrimination against animal rights, jeopardiz-
ing the long-term survival of endangered species
and moral laxity regarding the humane treatment
of less fortunate creatures. He ended with the
clincher—that a suit be commenced under a man-
damus motion to obtain a court injunction to permit Bamboo speak to the U.N.

"Should damages be included as well, Mr.
Farquhart?" asked Burr.

"I think somewhere in the millions. After all,
his negative decision may well cause the extinction of an entire major species. This is a class
action and there is entitlement to so ask."

Burr turned off the tape recorder and returned

it to Elspeth, who replaced the device in her case and snapped the lid shut.

Dwart, Elspeth and Burr rose abruptly and filed out, but Burr turned back at the door. Irving was still standing, staring at Haggerty.

"Mr. Haggerty," Burr said, "Mr. Fluck would like to say a few words to you. I'll leave him with you for a few minutes."

There was nothing Dan desired less than a private audience with this brute, who looked like a hit man.

Irving sat down uninvited in the chair vacated by Burr. "They're not always so nice, Mr. Haggerty, but then they're dedicated to their cause. Just as I'm dedicated to mine. And I wouldn't want you to get hurt."

"Are you threatening me, sir? If you are, I'll have to—"

"By no means, Mr. Haggerty, because I want to be your friend, I really do."

The sudden change in Fluck's demeanor and tone caused Haggerty further consternation. He dropped the eyeglasses he'd been fiddling with and stared suspiciously at Irving.

"You see, we have a mutual friend. One who can help us both make the correct decision on the best way to help God's creatures, the gorillas."

"And who might that be?" Dan was interested. Maybe there was a way out of this without losing face.

"Jesus Christ," said Fluck. "Have you ever really met him?"

Haggerty groped for an answer. He was a staunch Roman Catholic and attended mass regularly. "That's a very personal question, Mr. Fluck, but I have to say, yes, I think I have. I think I know why you ask." The bureaucrat thought he'd spotted a chance to vindicate his position regarding the gorilla's speech, but Irving interrupted him.

"Would you be surprised if I told you that I had met Jesus?"

"Frankly, yes."

"I want to tell you something, Dan. There are two sides to me. You might be surprised to know that I'm the man who tried to murder Bamboo. I won't go into the reasons why, but when I take a dislike to someone I can't always control my emotions. Recently I was born again, and I hope the good Lord Jesus will take care of me and prevent me from reverting to my former sinful ways."

Irving reached for the bulge under the left side of his coat. Dan flinched.

Fluck pulled out a Bible and intoned, "Let neither of us be guilty of the sins of pride and self-conceit, because it leads us into other sins, including the failure to treat our fellow creatures with fairness and goodwill." Irving recited a Psalm, then remarked, "I'm not good at this yet, but would you like us to pray together and say a particular prayer for Bamboo and the apes?"

Startled but calmer now, Haggerty replied,

"Ah, sure, I guess so." If praying would get rid of Irving, he was all for it.

Fluck bowed his head and leaned forward in the chair, his eyes emitting the fanatic gleam of religious fervor. "Lord," he began, "do not forsake the great apes; be warm to their cause, just as you have been to me. We pray for Bamboo and his band of endangered gorillas. We pray for Dan Haggerty, that you may open his heart and show him the light and the way to help Bamboo's cause.

"And we pray for me, Irving Fluck, to prevent me from backsliding into my former ugly tempers and acts of violence against those who frustrate both you and I in my attempts to make amends for my former sins against Bamboo and the cause of your animals. By the power of the Holy Spirit vested in me I pray to the dear, loving God of all creatures to make Dan Haggerty and I His agents; and God, through him let your will be done, and keep me from malice toward my fellow men, even if they should abuse your trust. Amen."

Irving rose quickly before a half-bemused Haggerty. Leaning across the desk, his menacing face only a foot from Dan's, he thrust out his giant hand and shook Haggerty's so hard it brought tears of pain to the bureaucrat's eyes. "Good-bye, Dan. Let us hear from you soon. Thank you for the interview. I must rejoin my other friends."

Irving Fluck left the office. Haggerty noted that

he had to turn partially sideways to fit through the door. Dan remained limp in his swivel chair, not yet a born-again Christian, but beginning to see the light.

"I think your part could clinch things," Burr told Fluck as the group waited at the airport for the departure call for Toronto. "We might have scared him enough to get his co-operation, but finishing with the Holy Joe routine makes it a dead cert."

Irving, his eyes sparkling, grabbed Burr by the arm. "Come on, brother. Come into the bar. Praise the Lord. What we all need is a drink, and I'm not talking a stiff Shirley Temple."

They all trooped into the lounge. When the waiter appeared, Irving ordered: "Straight scotch all around. Chivas Regal. Make those doubles."

"And who's going to pay?" asked Dwart.

"The Good Lord will provide, Brother Farquhart, of that I'm sure, with the aid of one of you, who I hereby appoint as His agents. It went smooth folks, real smoo-ooth. You'll hear from Mr. Haggerty soon and the news will be good."

The drinks arrived. Irving stopped them as they reached for the glasses. "Wait. Do you know why it went so smooth? Because I meant what I said. I got God's message and I gave it to Dan. He'll go to bat for Bamboo and he'll try to hit a home run. It may help his decision, just a tad, to think that if he doesn't, he may have no arms left to swing the bat."

"This born-again bit really works," Elspeth offered.

Again they reached for their drinks.

"Hold it, I said." Fluck continued, "I really meant what I said to Haggerty. Oh, how I love Jesus Christ for showing me the way of the Lord," he shouted, thrusting his arms toward the ceiling. "He is my Saviour—our Saviour."

All eyes in the bar were fixed on Irving as he proclaimed, "Let us pray on bended knee before we partake of His drink. Thank you, Jesus for giving us success today." Reaching into his jacket, he pulled out his Bible.

The others watched and listened in astonishment at the monster they'd helped create, as Irving read a verse from the Book of John about Christ's work on their behalf, then led them in prayer.

The rest of the delegation-cum-congregation was praying for the drink that they now needed more than ever.

Later, Dwart and Elspeth sat conversing quietly in a corner of the departure lounge.

"What do you think of Fluck's sudden and miraculous conversion?" asked Elspeth. "Personal-ly, I find it offensive. And we have to travel back with him."

"I'll bet more conversions take place in prison than anywhere else. Prison's where inmates start paying for their sins and they don't like it. So they start looking for a way out, to restore their reputations and to be accepted by society again. Some of them may be sincere, but it's a happy hunting ground for Jesus freaks."

"Do you think Irving is sincere?"

"No way. I wouldn't trust him as far as he could throw me. In my experience, the more fervent a Christian a man professes to be—and that goes for other religions as well—the closer you'd better watch him. I'm still staying as far away from Irving Fluck as I can get. His new-found faith was a bonus for us, so I'm not knocking it, but he's no pal of mine."

"But you are going to help him?"

"We'll stick to our deal. We'll help him at his trial and that should cut some ice with the judge."

"Let's change the subject."

Dwart didn't think it was the quick heavy jolt of good scotch which made him do it, although that might have given him courage; it had occurred to him previously. "Elspeth, I don't know how to put this to you."

"Put what to me? Don't get randy in an airport."

"What I'd like to say to you."

"You want to say something to me, then do so."

"Well, I was wondering what it would be like, if you'd agree to be, how shall I put it, my permanent straight woman?"

"You mean we'd be an act, together?"

"Yes."

"What kind of an act did you have in mind, pray tell?"

"A double comedy act. I'll be the comic, or the straight man if you like."

"No, I prefer your jokes to mine. This sounds strangely like a marriage proposal. Why would you even consider that, silly man? We're too old to get married."

"I can't believe you said that. We're certainly old enough."

"That's just it. You get the old age pension?"

"Don't start going Jerry hat trick on me, Elspeth. Yes, I get the pension," said Dwart, with a touch of irritation.

"So do I. Why would we want to jeopardize part of that just to have a preacher say a few words over our heads?"

"Well, I thought..."

"Not long enough, darling. If you're asking me to live with you, the answer is yes. But let's not get married, it's too hard to get out of and doesn't make economic sense at our age. If the government saves money on one thing, they only waste it on another. So let's both keep our full pensions and a degree of independence."

"Well, you've certainly put me straight about this."

"That's what you wanted, wasn't it? A straight woman!"

23

DEEP THROAT INSPECTION

Two days later, Dan Haggerty called C-JOY, asking for Gaylord Grabas. The change in Haggerty's attitude amazed the Robin. Haggerty had switched from black-hearted officious ignoramus to angel of sweetness and light.

"You've got the go-ahead," Haggerty told Grabas. "We have an open date on the eighth of next month at the U.N. He could go on during the morning session, at ten. Is that suitable for your group?"

"It certainly is, Dan. We can make it."

"You and your entourage should be in New York a few days early so we can set it up without rushing. The media here would like that, and I must say I'm amazed at their enthusiasm. Fax me your accommodation requirements immediately: the number of people in your party, number of rooms required, special needs if any, type of fresh food for Bamboo. Or does the zoo in Toronto want to contact our zoo here and talk to them about that? I'm afraid it's a little out of our line. We like to provide some security for our guest speakers, so we'd prefer that you use the accommodation we recommend. After I've set it up I'll get back to you with the details."

"That's just great, Dan. Now, can I make this information public immediately?"

"Yes. Let us know as soon as you break the story and we'll release confirmation from the U.N. to all the networks and wire services. The media can take it from there. Our press release will say the United Nations have agreed to hear a speech from Bamboo, a mountain gorilla formerly from the Virunga Mountains of Africa, presently living at the Ontario Provincial Zoo in Toronto. The speech will take place August eighth at ten a.m."

Grabas did the rest. He saw to it that the news got a lot of play in Toronto. He had Bamboo return to the Pink Pussycat for the announcement that the U.N. had agreed to hear him speak. A huge crowd of fans and wellwishers milled around up and down Dundas Street, anxious to catch a glimpse of the ape who spoke English.

The mayor was in attendance and with TV cameras rolling, Ontario's finest formed an honour guard for the ceremony. Dwart hovered anxiously over the circus. Elspeth and Bamboo had joined hands to show the throng there was nothing to fear. In fact, Bamboo was holding onto her hand. Dwart had told him to wave occasionally to the crowd, and every time he did, they laughed and cheered.

Grabas also covered their return to the zoo, with some shots of Amanda and Bamboo together in their compound quarters. Dwart went back to his rooming house on Markham Street, where he found a parcel from the U.S. He carried it up to his room and placed it on the kitchen table while he opened the fridge. He needed a cold beer and some shut-eye. It had been a trying day. After taking a deep draught of Moosehead, he tore open the package. Spilling from its innards came assorted sizes and colours of Calvin Klein shorts. Everybody wanted in on the act.

Dwart contemplated how he was going to present this proposition to his cohorts in the Bamboo cause. He mentally shuddered, imagining their probable reaction.

We have plenty of chiefs, he thought, but what we need is more bucks, and there's a goodly sum to be garnered for the cause from this possible windfall. He read the accompanying letter while sipping his beer. It asked for some pictures and suggested a meeting. Next week in New York would work, Dwart mused.

IN PHIL TRAVERS' OFFICE AT THE ZOO, TRAVERS and the Robin had just finished thumbing through the first draft of Bamboo's speech, while Dwart waited anxiously, drumming his fingers on the corner of the desk.

"What do you think, as if you aren't going to tell me?" Dwart tried to hold back a smile.

Grabas, who'd been sitting by the window, rose and began to pace. "Way too complicated," he blurted.

Leaning forward in his office chair, stroking his beard and playing with his office pencils as usual, Phil remarked with a worried frown, "Did anyone ever tell you, Farquhart, that you're raunchy and uncontrollable?"

"I resent that, but I can't deny it." Dwart's smile began to fade.

Gaylord laughed. "I can just see Bamboo saying, 'I can't understand why humans want all other species to kiss their ass.'"

A wan smile from Dwart.

"Or," and Phil read from his copy, 'Why do you humans hate each other? Do you just like to fight because you're a particularly vicious type of killer ape who always wants more power and territory? Is that the truth, or are your alleged beliefs in justice, fair play and the golden rule the truth?"

"Is this a put-on, Farky?" Grabas added. "You know Bamboo's not in an adversarial debate. It's a speech at a conference. When you're asking for help, it's counter-productive to tell an audience of potential benefactors that they act," and Gaylord glanced down at the page, "'in a self-serving, irresponsible, bloodthirsty, murderous, self-destructive and primitive way, yet loudly proclaim superiority to the great apes.'"

"You're right," Dwart sighed. "Trying to tell people the truth, the whole truth and nothing but the truth often doesn't work; and I should know better than to try to write a serious speech. It's not my bag and I'm sorry. Anyway, I was just getting all that stuff off my chest. I know Bamboo can't say it that way."

The Robin stopped pacing and said, "I liked the part where the apes ask for a little of the affection humans lavish on dogs and cats."

"You guys are making me feel like the blind skunk who fell in love with a fart," Dwart noted. "Phil wanted me to do a draft and that's what I did, while you boys did what you had to do. And I told him for starters that I was just going to sit down and write whatever thoughts came to mind. We were only looking for a string of ideas. That's all we agreed on. So lay off, will you?"

"Come off it, Farky, there are some good points in here, we've got the basics of a speech, thanks to you, so don't start getting owly on us. Let's go over it and get down to the nitty-gritty—a few simple ideas that Bamboo can get across."

"Agreed," Dwart replied. "I'm best when I'm light and stick to jokes. But when I do some serious thinking, my view is that through the constant increase in our human population and the environmental pollution we produce, we're dooming ourselves and all other species to eventual disaster and possible extinction. And when I get feeling really low, I think we humans are no better than domesticated animals ourselves, in willing servitude to the machinery of science and politics, reacting without using our ability to reason or protest."

"That's quite a speech, Farky. Better calm down," said Phil.

"Just letting off steam. Now, let's just decide what points are usable, in words Bamboo can learn. That's what we set out to do, after all."

"COME OVER HERE TO THE ZOO, AND YOUR wish will be fulfilled," Travers crooned into the telephone.

"Ah, my old fairy godmother," Gil Brodeur replied, "and what wish might that be, pray?"

"The one where you get to look down Bamboo's throat while he's fully conscious and has full freedom of movement."

"You mean the examination where that crazy Farquhart has told him to grab me by the balls?! No thank you."

"He wouldn't really tell him that. He'd only tell you that he did."

"That's easy for you to say, you're not examining that big ape at a range of a few inches. Have you taken a close look at his choppers?"

"Not under those conditions. Now, come on, Gil, you said you wanted a gander at what happened in his throat. I think we need to know."

"I meant a laryngoscopic examination under anesthesia."

"And we said we aren't going to do that, Gil. Believe me, he's a pussycat, he won't hurt you. Farquhart is only kidding around, you know that."

"Do I, now? Could we use a little P.C.P.—phenylcyclazine?"

"What?"

"Angel dust."

"What does that do?"

"Puts primates into a stupor. You remember Stupor State, Phil, your old alma mater."

"I'll ignore that. No, if you want to find out, you have to do it the hard way. No drugs. Don't be such a chicken-shit and get over here."

"You're a hard man, Phil. I'm glad you found Bamboo and that he's out of that business at the Pink Pussycat—of which I hear little else from that idiot Robin Grabas on C-JOY."

"Grabas isn't so bad, Gil. He's working with us, and he's doing a bang-up job on the ape story."

"If you say so. Is Bamboo in good shape?"

"Yes."

"All right, I'll do it. Nobody calls me chicken-shit. I'll be over this afternoon about two o'clock, before I lose my nerve. Farquhart had better be kidding about the balls bit. And I want Farquhart to be there. I want him to be looking right down that ape's throat with me, and I want him holding one of Bamboo's hands and his girlfriend holding the other. I'll even put up with his jokes."

At two o'clock the staff entered the animal oper-

ating room at the zoo. Travers, Brodeur and
Paddon burst into laughter at the sight of Dwart
trying to persuade Bamboo to try on a blue and
white striped pair of Calvin Klein shorts, size sixty.

"One time," he was saying as they entered,
"one time only. Make picture. Make money. Big
deal. Just try 'em on. No stay on."

They all gathered around Bamboo, who, like
most intelligent animals, had an overpowering
sense of curiosity, which was the only reason
Dwart finally got him to try on the underwear.

Bamboo looked at the smiling circle of people
he'd learned to recognize as friends. Dwart had
told him the little white-eyes was called Doc and
was the one who'd fixed his throat that bad time,
and that he wanted to look at it again. The shorts
were another matter. He knew men wore them,
but not why they wanted him to do so. He was
having great difficulty with Dwart's attempted
explanation.

The rest also wondered about the dress-up bit.
Dwart explained, "It's just a publicity idea, an ad,
billboards, maybe a TV commercial. He'll only
wear the things for those occasions. We can talk
about it later," he added, obviously uncomfortable.

"I don't want him to appear ridiculous, but it
might work out okay, certainly money-wise, and
maybe we should go for it. The money, which I
think could be considerable, would go to the
cause, and we need it."

"Bamboo take off shorts, Doc?" Bamboo asked.

"No, leave them on," replied Brodeur. "If I've got a choice of examining any of your bodily orifices, I think I prefer the throat, thank you. Now lie down on the table, please. Dwart, you'll translate as we go along?"

Bamboo lay on his back on the operating table.

"Farquhart, I want you to stand on that side and keep talking. Now, Bamboo, this is not likely to hurt you, I want you to know that. But I can't really guarantee that. I have to get a good look and you may have to have instruments and lights down your throat. So it might hurt, just a bit, mind you. You may gag and be uncomfortable for a short while, but just remember, please remember, that I bear you no ill will and that I will be as fast and painless as possible. Boy, will I be fast. Now say 'Ahh' and open wide."

The instructions were too long and quick for Bamboo, but he got the gist after Dwart explained in simple language and signing. As Bamboo complied, he said what Dwart had asked him to say at their private rehearsal of this situation, "Grab him by balls?"

"Maudit—!" Brodeur leaped back from the table, and everybody laughed, including Bamboo.

Approaching the ape again, Brodeur said, "Open wider, please."

Brodeur peered into the gorilla's throat, he and Paddon took X-rays and the medical examination was over. The jockstrap and athletic cup Gil had borrowed from his son's hockey equipment bag hadn't proved necessary.

Back in the admin office an hour later, they watched Brodeur go over his notes.

He gazed out the window briefly, looked back at his notes, then spoke. "Based on our examination, Dr. Paddon and I think, first of all, that Bamboo's vocalis and ventricularis muscles have become tighter and thicker as a result of the remodeling of the scar tissue left after my repair job. Second, the vocal fold ended up slightly enlarged after healing occurred, and this contributed to a totally new effect on Bamboo's vocal cords.

"Finally, a minor result of the muscle fibres I used to cover the thyroid cartilage is that Bamboo's voice-box shell is a little more apt to resonate. He has only the one modified vocal cord on the left side, which is why, as you've noticed, his speech isn't quite like that of a human being, and he gets those occasional grunts. With practice he may be able to overcome that."

Brodeur looked up from his notes. "I'll do a more detailed report for the medical journals. This phenomenon is going to be carefully scrutinized by medical and veterinary scholars, both now and in the future."

"We're not going to continually examine him, Gil."

"I know that, Phil. By later I mean much later. If

he were to die, an autopsy would be performed, by the best experts in the profession, to further describe and corroborate what happened. If I'm lucky, I'll do the job, if I live longer than Bamboo does."

"You're assuming Bamboo'll be at the zoo then, or available for such an autopsy," said Dwart.

"Why wouldn't he be?"

"He might be back in Africa on his own turf, or in Hawaii as the founding member of a new gorilla protectorate or sanctuary."

"Well, somewhere. Surely he will drop us a line from time to time, keep in touch."

"I'd like to think so." They all smiled at the gorilla, who said, "Bamboo like happy there."

TRAVERS WAS GROWING INCREASINGLY FRUSTRATED with the airline clerk. "I said I want to get two first class seats on your Toronto to New York flight, return, for a Mr. Bamboo; one first class for Mr. Farquhart, right next to Mr. Bamboo; and thirteen connoisseur class return fares as close to the first class cabin as possible, for parties named Travers, Brodeur, Egan, McClintock, Grabas, Paddon, Fowler, Rowe, McDonald, Thorpe, Cherry, McCourt and Fields."

"Who will be occupying the other seat with Mr. Bamboo? Mrs. Bamboo?"

"No one. He'll be occupying them both himself."

"I take it he's a rather large person, or is he ill, perhaps?"

"Maybe he just likes his privacy. He is big, but do you really want to know? I mean, why do you ask, as long as he wants the seats?"

"Because I've been listening to C-JOY for days and I've also been reading the Toronto newspapers."

"So?"

"Is this Mr. Bamboo an ape?"

"He is an immigrant to Canada."

"But he's not a Canadian citizen or a landed immigrant, right?"

"Not yet, although he has applied. What difference does it make what his status is? He'll have proper identification to show if anyone asks him."

"You didn't answer my question."

"What question?"

"Is Mr. Bamboo an ape?"

"Technically, no."

"Let me put it another way. What is he?"

"Ah, he's a gorilla, gorilla beringei."

"That's what I thought. And where's he from?"

"He's from Toronto. He lives here. Originally he was from Volcanoes National Park. Canada brought him over to this country as an immigrant and an expert on apes, so he has a job. He's applied for landed immigrant status. The prime minister is reviewing his application as we speak."

"Look, I wouldn't care if he was an Elvis Presley look-alike, but if he is an ape, he can't travel on our airline."

"What you're saying is in violation of the

Charter of Rights." What am I saying? thought Travers, I've been associating with Farquhart and Grabas for too long and their bullshit is rubbing off.

"You're discriminating against a minority group. He's going down to New York to address the United Nations General Assembly as a guest speaker, at the invitation of the secretary-general. Does that sound like he's persona non grata in either Canada or the United States?"

"Dr. Travers, I'm trying to help you, but we just don't allow animals to fly on our planes, unless they go as freight and are properly crated or in authorized cages. You're going about this all wrong."

"Mr. Bamboo is a V.I.P—he's a world figure. You can't let him travel in a crate or a cage."

"Why do you keep calling him Mister? He's an ape."

"I want him to go first class. It's a matter of image and publicity. Also, he needs a large space, and the two seats should do nicely. He's not going to hurt anybody. It's only a short flight."

"How do we know that? Even if we could do it, who would fly with us, with a great hairy ape aboard?"

"Take out an insurance policy with Lloyds of London. They'll insure anything. We'll pay the premium. Put him down on the passenger list as a person and your problem is solved. Furthermore, we have fourteen people with him and some of them are expert ape mongers."

"As I said before, I would like to help you out, and I just had an idea. Why doesn't the Ontario Provincial Zoo book the whole flight, for a full load, Toronto to New York and return? We could make a special non-scheduled flight. Everyone on board will know the score. In effect, you charter a plane and sell the space to anyone who wants to go to New York for a few days, particularly to hear Bamboo's speech at the U.N. Call it the Bamboo Express and sell it on that basis."

"And I thought you were being difficult. That's a brilliant idea, and we've just got time to promote it. Thank you! It gets us around all the problems. The passengers can sign a release or waiver of all claims as a condition of travel. Let's book that charter right now."

GRABAS SOLD THE DEAL OVER C-JOY AND through the newspapers. With media support, he filled a 727 with people who were prepared to pay their air fare plus an extra two hundred dollars for the privilege of travelling to New York with Bamboo, while at the same time supporting his cause. The excess money from the Bamboo Express was added to the Bamboo Virunga Trust Fund. Proceeds from the Calvin Klein ad contract and other projects were earmarked for the same fund.

At the New York end, Haggerty had arranged to lay on limousine transportation to the accommodations provided by the U. N. In the case of Bamboo, Travers, Farquhart and Grabas, this was to consist of V.I.P. quarters right in the United Nations complex.

When the flight arrived in New York, Haggerty was there to greet the entourage. Introductions were made all around. Haggerty seemed confounded at actually seeing, hearing and meeting the great ape.

"Pleased to meet you, Bamboo," he said, gingerly holding out his hand. "That is, I take it, both your first and last name."

"Me please," replied Bamboo, engaging Haggerty in a far from docile handclasp. At first he'd been reticent, but Bamboo had come to like the humans' friendship gesture.

"Please call me Dan. We might as well drive the long way around so you can see a bit of the city on the way."

"Bamboo has been watching some TV documentaries about New York and the United Nations. Is there anything you'd like to see, Bamboo?" asked Dwart.

"Would you like to visit the New York Zoo?" asked Haggerty.

"Have gorillas zoo there?"

"Yes, but I'm not sure how many."

"Like to go there one time."

"I can arrange a trip, maybe on Friday."

"Why not publicize his visit there, Mr. Haggerty?" offered Gaylord. "'Bamboo visits possible relatives.' It'd be a good story. We can get some great footage and give New Yorkers a chance to see Bamboo."

"I don't see why not. The zoo officials here have expressed a desire to meet Dr. Travers, Mr. Farquhart, and of course, Bamboo. They're providing all of Bamboo's food while he's here. You and I can set up the meeting and publicity as soon as we get to the U.N., Mr. Grabas."

They arrived at the imposing facade of the United Nations building with its ranked flags fluttering in the light breeze and disembarked at the security entrance. The delegation was escorted to a suite of several rooms high above the river. A spacious sitting room with a floor-to-ceiling glass window enhanced the view. So much so, that Phil Travers felt queasy when he approached what felt like the edge of a precipice. Several divans and easy chairs in tastefully contrasting colours furnished the room, together with a large central and highly polished teak coffee table, two writing tables on opposite walls, reading lamps and a well-filled bookcase. The occupants would be able to enjoy a measure of privacy or gather collectively.

"I think we'll be comfortable here." Dwart mentally compared these digs to his own on Markham Street.

The trip and its preparations had been tiring. The group decided to settle in for a rest before the next round of activity consumed their energy.

Gorillas eat and sleep a great deal, and on this occasion, Bamboo slept longer than the others, and longer than usual. When he awoke, his throat was sore. He went through the bedroom door into the common room of the suite. Dwart was reclining on the chesterfield reading the Times, a paper thick enough to have supplied the average farm family of his yesteryears with several weeks' worth of paper for the outhouse.

"Won't be long now, Bamboo. The tough part'll be over soon. You're going to be great. How are you feeling?"

Bamboo slumped into a big chair. "Not good, friend," he said, but the words came out in a barely audible rasp.

Dwart bolted upright. "What's the matter with your voice?"

Bamboo shrugged and pointed to his throat.

"What the—what have we got here?' Dwart was at his side, looking him over with great concern. "Say something else."

Bamboo tried, with the same result.

"Look fella, let's get you back into the nest." Dwart led Bamboo by the arm into the bedroom. "Now just take it easy, I'm going to phone Doc and Paddon and get them over here right away."

"Me gorilla sick?" rasped Bamboo.

"Don't talk anymore. That's just what we're going to find out, and fast, so not to worry." He returned to the main room, grabbed the phone and dialled Brodeur's room at the Milford Plaza.

There was no answer. Dwart had him paged in the Honolulu Bar and Grill, the hotel's restaurant. Gil came on the line within a couple of minutes.

"What's up, Dwart?"

"We need you and Paddon over here right away, we've got some kind of a throat problem with Bamboo."

"Oh, no! We'll be right there." Brodeur hung up, picked up the zoo vet, paid the tab and they raced outside and grabbed a cab. Twenty minutes later they were looking down Bamboo's throat and taking his temperature.

"What do you think?"

"He's not going on any more city tours, I can tell you that much," said Dr. Paddon. "He's going to stay right here while I doctor this. Bamboo, just rest right where you are, while we figure out how to treat this."

Bamboo was only too happy to comply, while the others went out into the main room.

"He must have picked up a bug on that damn plane," said Gil. "There've been too many people around him lately. I heard one lady doing an awful lot of coughing on the plane and that recycled air isn't good for anyone. We should have thought of those risks."

"Well, we didn't. What do we do now? You're the vets," said Phil.

"Can you fix him up?" Dwart fretted.

"Ordinarily it'd be no problem, and we can probably still get him over it in a few days with antibiotics," said Paddon.

"What's wrong with him?"

"He's got an inflamed throat, probably a form of laryngitis. I hope it isn't the flu coming on, that's all. That takes longer to cure. We'll figure it out, take some smears, decide what drugs to use."

"You have to cure this fast, you know that."

"We know."

"Doc, you did say 'ordinarily' it's no problem."

"His throat is certainly not your standard army issue," replied Paddon. "What I meant was that he hasn't got much there working for him, so we have to be careful, that's all."

Gil spoke up. "Dwart, the doc here is the best at this end of the business. I'm more of a surgeon, but I'll be thinking about this also. So try not to worry too much."

24

GLOTTAL CONFABULATION

Bamboo and his entourage stepped out of the elevator on the floor leading to the assembly hall of the United Nations. As they proceeded down the corridor, they were surrounded by a horde of reporters, and microphones were thrust in front of their grinning faces. Grabas, running interference in the forefront, met a barrage of greetings and questions.

"Ladies and gentlemen, you know Bamboo has suffered a bout of laryngitis in the last few days. The good doctors here have been giving him the best attention known to medical science. They've succeeded in restoring his voice. But let me tell you, it is a dicey proposition as to whether he can complete his speech. So you'll have to pardon Bamboo if he doesn't indulge in much of a warm-up. He has to save his voice for the speech. He'll be available to you later if he's able, and he'll certainly be delighted to be interviewed once his throat has completely healed."

"What treatment was used?" asked the man from *Better Homes and Gardens*.

"Dr. Paddon had a fresh batch of his mother's chicken soup flown in twice a day from Toronto," quipped Grabas. "It contains some special antibiotics."

Dan Haggerty and other officials met them at the V.I.P and speakers' entrance to the assembly hall. The door led to the area in front of the stage, on which the speaker's podium and several microphones were situated. A couple of the officials kept their distance, wary of the gorilla, who was still regarded as one of the world's most ferocious animals. But their political instincts soon took over in the presence of TV cameras, and they responded automatically to Bamboo's outstretched hand as Haggerty handled the introductions.

The security guard swung open the doors. Bamboo again held onto Elspeth's hand as Haggerty and Farquhart headed the parade. They marched along the aisle before taking their reserved seats in the front section. Dwart noticed they were playing to a full house. Bamboo slowed to a halt as he gazed at the size of the room around him. It didn't appeal to his jungle-oriented aesthetics. It was big and awesome, and his gut reaction was to begin to thump mightily on his chest and charge, tearing up some furniture as he did so. But a squeeze from Elspeth's hand helped him keep his instincts in check. The assemblage sat in total silence. Animals, and many people, can sense fear and detect hostility in the air. Bamboo certainly sensed some fear of his presence.

The assembled members then did something that Bamboo found strange but pleasing—they rose as one and brought their hands together, making a thunderous clapping noise. Bamboo looked quizzically at Dwart.

"You're getting what's called a standing ovation, old boy. Enjoy it. It means they like you. I got a standing ovation once, but I didn't know it at the time, because I was addressing a convention of midgets." At Bamboo's even more puzzled look, Dwart said, "Never mind, I'll explain it to you later."

The members resumed their seats and the secretary-general strode onto the stage. He touched his tie in a brief, habitual gesture, then placed both hands on the lectern. His penetrating eyes surveyed the impressive scene in the great hall of nations.

"Ladies and gentlemen," his voice rang clearly through the public address system, to be immediately translated into most of the languages of the world, "this is a momentous occasion in United Nations history. Something that is without precedent, even in the old League of Nations. For the first time on any stage anywhere in the world, someone other than a human being is going to address us in one of our own languages. Not an alien from outer space, but a representative of a species we have always categorized as an animal. Now, I have not heard the speaker myself, but I am assured that he—that we—will communicate one with the other. Different levels of communication are possible, and I won't belabour the meaning of language, because we will shortly be able to judge for ourselves. If we can understand our guest, or the meaning of his remarks, regardless of the quality of his grammar and sentence structure, if we understand him by any means whatsoever, then an interesting question arises: does this ability to communicate make him one of us? There will, as usual, be great disagreement on that point, for how do we define homo sapiens? Is he only an animal with a big brain who is able to speak a language?

"Perhaps if we listen to another species for a change, we may learn something of importance about our relationship with animals, and might even come to some consensus of opinion in that regard.

"I, like you, am eager to hear from our guest speaker today. After he has finished, I would like to address the assembly again, after a short recess to give us time to digest his remarks.

"So now, my very pleasant task is to introduce to you a figure you have all been hearing about in the media: the great ape who has learned to speak the rudiments of the English language.

"Originally from the Virunga Mountains of

East Africa, and more recently from the Ontario
Provincial Zoo, ladies and gentlemen of the
United Nations, Bamboo the great ape!"

Once again a great round of applause greeted
Bamboo as he swung along the aisle. He tried to
maintain as erect a posture as possible, but the
knuckles of his long arms still occasionally
brushed the floor. As he reached the edge of the
speaker's platform, he leaped to gain it rather
than taking the stairs. As he had been coached,
Bamboo stepped behind the lectern, which was
stage centre in the massive hall.

Bamboo looked out at the conglomeration of
people sitting behind desks spreading out in semi-
circles from the stage.

He was silent, but his mind said, "Think, stupid
devil," while the tension grew in the hall. He
glanced down at the small group of friends who
had accompanied him to this strange place.
Could he do it? The audience was restless with
expectancy as he stood before them. Dwart gave
him the high sign from his seat. He'd paused long
enough. It was now or never for his fellow apes.

"Happy good you come!" His voice was still
low and husky, but the multiple microphones
picked him up clearly; so clearly it frightened him
into silence again. His voice had seemed disem-
bodied and unfamiliar to him in this outlandish
auditorium.

Bamboo tried again, his heart racing.
"Difference you, me? Head!" Bamboo beat on

his head with his open hands, harder than any person would ever do. "Hard head, more hair," and he moved his hands up and down his torso, pulling at the hair.

"What same, you, me? Eye," and Bamboo pointed to his eyes. "Hand," and he held up his hand. "Love! Bamboo love eat. You love eat. You Bamboo love. Gorilla happy hug you," and he made a hugging gesture. Several people in the front rows moved nervously.

"Head stupid, trouble word me, me learn, you patient, me visit. Life sad bad gorilla. Bamboo gorilla. Life sad, frown, sometimes bad sad. Human, big cat, bird, ape person, stink trouble world today. Me see much world, see Toronto zoo, New York, see machine, see machine call idiot box. Gorilla no have in jungle. Strange thing human make. Strange fly machine. New York sky buildings. Strange. Most strange thing: thur-mus bottle. Me cold—get hot drink. Me hot—get cold drink. Strange! How thur-mus bottle know what gorilla want? Gorilla make human joke. Old Fart friend teach." Bamboo pointed at Dwart.

The assemblage burst into laughter once the translators caught up to Bamboo. The tension was broken and Bamboo felt better.

"Bamboo gorilla. Thank you me speak you. Bamboo speak first time for animals. On idiot box, too." He gestured toward the television cameras. "What good there Tee-Vee? See picture, call fun, make hit-in-mouth, see people make dead.

Call news. See fire, see flood, see fight, see dirt, toilet-devil, bad that. Also hear talk: hear 'do others you happy do you,' human call golden rule. Dwart tell me."

A great many listeners applauded this remark and Bamboo saw them smile. He was feeling much better, less threatened. This wouldn't be too bad after all, but now he had to tell them how he felt and they might not like it. His fears stemmed from the knowledge he'd gained in the jungle, something that Dwart knew also, but had never expressed to Bamboo: the golden rule had holes in it. All humans weren't the same, and many ignored the rule.

"Gorilla have rule: 'live, let live.'

"Sorry say, gorilla call human person killer ape. In jungle, shoot, trap, cut trees, hit-in-mouth. Gorilla no place go. Too many human world. Human not use golden rule for gorilla, kill, we die, we capture, go zoo. Sorry say that gorilla not dumb. Gorilla good, have place jungle, human have place, all have place world. Gorilla jungle long time. Plants, forest, long time. All animal gone, all forest gone, what human do then? Suffer, starve, you no-eat. You dead good-bye. Great apes near same now. Me nag you stop— think—no hate, no hit-in-mouth, no insult, no make die, no make hate, make golden rule.

"Me smart ape, me see truth. Me see leopard in jungle, me quiet. Leopard strong, gorilla strong. Leopard not friend but not fight. Not kill jungle.

Not fight when lots jungle, lots eat. No need hit-in-mouth, kill.

"Bamboo love visit, save animals you. You like gorilla, like Bamboo, me speak for animals.

"Zoo bad. Bamboo no ask go zoo Canada. Canada gorilla me now. Only few gorillas Virunga now. Human kill most. You strong. United Nations save gorilla please. If destroy all, big trouble human animals. Then human not so smart, human sad down die.

"Bamboo, make life smile, clap, good for you, for human, for me, for animal. Let love us, you. You, all silverback here big chief human gorilla— you help all gorilla please. Me speak good help animal.

"Me get smart zoo, thank friends." Bamboo motioned toward Phil, Dwart, Elspeth, Gaylord, Burr and the rest. "Thank now you friends," and he swept his long arms wide around the assembly hall. "Good you listen, you chiefs, you silver-backs.

"What say next, many hard words me learn, try say good. Pass paper. Bamboo make motion. Bamboo say gorilla need home hurry. Thank you."

Again Bamboo threw up his long arms and stretched them wide, his gesture encompassing the whole room. Amid the resultant acclamation, he jumped from the platform in the same manner as he'd mounted it, returning to the seat among his friends, who clustered around, touching him in congratulation.

"It's hard to tell when you're smiling, Bamboo," said Phil Travers, overjoyed with the speech. "but you should be." The others chimed in with their plaudits.

The motion paper on the delegates' desks read: *That the United Nations immediately consider ways and means of providing a gorilla sanctuary, where it will be safe for gorillas to live under the protection of the United Nations, whether this sanctuary be in the Virunga Mountains, elsewhere in Africa, in Hawaii or in some other location.*

The room buzzed with conversation during the short interval following Bamboo's speech, the delegates demonstrating an unusual effusiveness in their discussions. Representatives of mutually hostile nations, who usually only spoke with each other when they had to, were exchanging comments, even shaking hands. Many read the detailed supporting information that Dan Haggerty's department had carefully prepared and left on the desk of each delegate.

Standing beside his old friend Dwart, Bamboo watched people milling about in excited conversation, and his dark eyes were wide with astonishment at the scene before him. "Why, Old Fart," he asked, "what talk?" and he signed a yakkety-yak motion with his hand.

"You knocked 'em dead, Bamboo. Great speech!" Dwart replied.

"No. Me no hit-in-mouth," Bamboo said, "no hurt."

"I didn't mean that. I meant they really liked it. You impressed them. They think you are a good gorilla."

Bamboo wrapped the Old Fart in his huge hairy arms. It was an unprecedented demonstration of affection on his part and he didn't quite understand it. He just knew he really liked this one human who had tried so hard to help him.

"For God's sake, Bamboo, you're breaking my ribs," yelled Dwart, but his heart filled with joy and pride for his friend.

Many of the delegates crowded over to the area reserved for the Toronto party and shook hands with Bamboo, who now appeared calm and unperturbed by the whole thing. His composure gave him an air of dignity that hid the doubt and fear he'd been continually holding at bay. But he could recognize sincerity in their eyes and it gave him hope.

The secretary-general took the stage again and brought the meeting back to order.

"Thank you, Bamboo, for a truly startling display, which certainly succeeded in communicating your views to this body. Ladies and gentlemen, we have now heard..." He paused for a moment, "Mr. Bamboo speak. I mentioned earlier the possibility of our reaching a consensus of opinion regarding our relationship to, and treatment of, animals, particularly endangered species; how humanity is treating them and how we should react to their plight, in both their interest and our own.

"Personally, I am in favour of Mr. Bamboo's motion. I support the proposition that homo sapiens should show other living beings the same respect we show ourselves, at least with regard to vertebrate animals that are most like ourselves.

"We are all God's creatures in one form or another. We must put our differences aside, and try harder to achieve peace and harmony in this world. We must try to be friends. As our founder Woodrow Wilson said, 'Friendship is the only cement that will hold the world together.'"

Bamboo easily recognized the word friends, and it warmed his heart. Maybe these people could be his friends, maybe they weren't all poachers, head-and-hand hunters.

"Can we completely disregard the welfare and rights of less developed creatures?

"It has fallen to our generation of humans, because of our dominant position on this planet, to decide, literally, who dies and who lives, which species survives so that others may live.

"I am not saying that it is a simple matter to place a limitation upon our use of other animals.

"What I am saying is that while we debate the metaphysical issue, there is a formidable argument for exercising restraint in our treatment of other species. For it is not reasonable for us to hound and hunt any species to the point of extinction. And yet that is what we are doing, sometimes by design, but more often by unthinkable neglect. If we fail to apply our collective minds and resources to the problem, it will be too late. The whales will be gone, the pandas, the dolphins, the tigers, the gorillas. And our world will be a poorer place because of it."

Bamboo could not easily grasp much of this, but he did realize that this chief silverback was urging his band to help the great apes. He looked at his friends, noting the varying degrees of hope and pleasure on their faces.

Bamboo couldn't know, however, that their outward expressions hid their doubt about the ability of the member nations to suspend hostilities long enough to accomplish a common goal. Or as Thoreau said, thought Dwart, show a little more honour than rogues.

"Today, now, we have a chance to do something constructive. We have a chance to save a species, which through man's own actions and no fault of its own, has nearly reached that point of extinction. Let us seize this chance for the great apes. For if we do not, we may never know the extent of the differences and similarities between ourselves and other species, particularly our closest relatives on earth.

"Technically, Bamboo cannot propose a motion to this house. Only a member nation can do so. However, as an officer of the United Nations, I can, and I do so now. I make the motion you see before you on your desks. We have choices, of course, about how to proceed toward the goal. Some of these have already been ably researched by U.N. staff. You have all been provided with that brief, which sets out several possible approaches to saving gorillas from extinction.

"Our speaker today, can, I hope, help us immeasurably in these endeavours. The supporting material proposes that a representative committee from seven countries be struck in order to devise specific and detailed plans on procedure and funding. The motion also calls for U.N. executive action on their recommendations. Now, having made the motion, I need a seconder. Let us give gorillas the security, the dignity, and the tranquillity to which they are entitled. Is there a seconder?"

A host of delegates rose to demand the floor, but they were beaten to it by the representative from Singapore, who came down the aisle at a clip and headed for the microphone.

"Mr. Secretary," he stated, "we in Singapore have the most beautiful zoo in the world, a fact which not many in the World Zoological Society will contest. And we have long understood and emphasized the dignity and humane treatment of animals. With all deference to the many larger nations I see standing ready to second this motion, Singapore wishes to be the first to espouse its principles and second the motion. However, Mr. Secretary, is there any reason that a motion may not have as many seconders as wish to be recorded?"

"None. Thank you, sir. The motion has been made and seconded, and is properly before the Assembly. Member nations, please record your vote, for or against, on the computer."

When the vote was tallied, the U.N. made history for a second time that day.

The secretary-general's rich baritone rang out: "Motion carried, *unanimously!*"

This time the expression on Bamboo's face was unmistakably a smile as he said, "Gorilla happy hug you!"

**For information on organizations
working to ensure the survival of the great
apes, please contact:**

The Gorilla Foundation
Box 640530
Woodside, CA 94062
Ph: (650) 851-8505
E-mail: koko@gorilla.org

The Dian Fossey Gorilla Fund
800 Cherokee Ave SE
Atlanta, GA 30315
Ph: (800) 851-0203
E-mail: 2help@gorillafund.org

Jane Goodall Institute
Box 14890
Silver Spring, MD 20911-4890
Ph: (301) 565-0086
Web site: www.janegoodall.org

By mail from ▨ SALAL PRESS

_____ **Coots, Codgers and Curmudgeons**
Hal C. Sisson and Dwayne W. Rowe. Hilarious collection of tales from small-town western Canada. Evokes a time when the funeral parlor hearse doubled as an ambulance and baseball games pitted Red Deer, Alberta against Butte, Montana.

"Puts the boots to the widely held belief that lawyers lack a sense of humour." —Vancouver Courier

"Fans of W.O. Mitchell and Greg Clark will find this book irresistible." – Stitches

1-894012-04-6.................Canada $14.95 US $9.95

Ask at your favorite bookstore or use this form to order.

Please send me .... copies of the above book. I am enclosing $............ (Please add $3.00 for shipping first copy, $0.50 for each additional copy. Send cheque or money order only, in Canadian or U.S. funds.)

Name _____

Address _____

City _____

Prov./State _____ Postal/Zip Code _____

Send order to:
Salal Press, P.O. Box 36060, Victoria, BC V9A 7J5. Allow six weeks for delivery. Price and availability subject to change without notice.